LOYAL TO OUR DEAD

ANN MCGREAHAM

Copyright © 2010 Ann McGreaham
All rights reserved.

ISBN: 1439264465
ISBN-13: 9781439264461
Library of Congress Control Number: 2009911507

CHAPTER 1

HAPPY HOUR

I bent my right leg behind me and put my foot on the tank, as though I was leaning against a wall. I leaned back and looked up, scanning the sky for aircraft. I didn't expect to see a plane. I rarely saw one in this city. My posture reminded me of all the brick walls, vehicles, and tanks I had leaned against in Iraq and stateside during my eight years in the army.

Jerry Wong came around the tank and saw me. He seemed startled at first and then he recovered. "Oh, it's you, Pam," he said, taking out a cigarette and squatting down below the vehicle's profile, so that a person at the door wouldn't see him.

"Come closer, you can't be seen from over here," I said. Smokers had to stay away from building entrances and hazard areas. This tank was just a decoration on the lawn, but I pictured it on fire. A tank might run over a mine or improvised explosive device, catching fire like the vehicles I'd seen burning in Iraq.

"What are you doing out here?" Jerry asked.

"I love the smell of metal, axle grease, and diesel fuel," I said. "I can't miss my daily dose of axle grease."

He nodded but was intent on lighting his cigarette. "Watch it," he teased. "Some people get addicted to the smell of diesel fuel." The smell of metal, fuel, and oil was faint, overpowered by the smells of hot blacktop and vegetation. Missing were the smells of gunpowder, sewage, and baking sand—the smells of Iraq.

"Are you coming tonight?" he asked. We began talking about the Friday get-together; our work group met at a nearby bar every second Friday for drinks and snacks. I liked talking to my coworkers away from work. All the former army personnel had interesting stories, and being with the group on Fridays reminded me of being in the army and going to the Officers' Club. I liked Jerry even though he was the kind of civil servant who counted off the days until retirement as though he was serving a jail term. He had fifteen years down and fifteen to go.

The rest of the day passed quickly. I watched a film that demonstrated a new vehicle's ability to climb over obstacles and its improved navigation system. I started checking over the documents for the new vehicle and was one of the last people out of the office, to my surprise.

As usual, I was the only woman at happy hour. The two other women at my workplace were married and had young children. I often hoped that some of the women working for civil service might come. Once in a while a man brought his wife. The talk at the bar was less interesting than the stories I'd heard in officers' clubs at various bases. The general consensus was that the weather was chilly, TV had been boring lately, and the theaters had no good action movies. The usual mix of civil servants, military, and defense contractors were used to disagreeing about work projects but agreed about sports, weather, and TV. I was bored, exchanging pleasantries.

Major Pete showed up with a friend he introduced as Mark, "Fresh out of the army." I was curious because Mark was too young to have retired. I looked for a West Point ring but saw none. He seemed to be about thirty, medium height, dark haired. His buzz cut was beginning to grow out, and he had tried to slick his hair down. I wondered why he left the army. He was too young to have been discharged for being ineligible for promotion to major after fourteen years of service. Maybe he had chosen not to sign up again—the choice I had made.

"What brings you to Detroit?" someone asked him. I expected to hear him give the name of a defense contractor.

"I would like to live near a real city. I've been stationed for years in places with nothing to do but go to the Officers' Club. I was tired of living in the country."

"Which country?" I chimed in. "I got tired of Iraq, too." I liked the men to know that I had been in a combat zone.

"Desert country," Mark answered. "Overseas and Sierra Vista, Arizona. I thought I would like to see a tree or take in a movie now and then, instead of watching the cacti grow. I might even go to a department store or take a book out of the library."

"Yes," someone said. "The comforts of home—sewage disposal, trees, running water, and just about everyone speaks English."

"How does it feel, being out of the army?" someone else asked.

"Nice to not have to polish my shoes," he replied.

"Are you from here?" was the next question.

"I grew up in New Mexico. I was born in Huntsville, Alabama."

Since Huntsville is a site for army air and space, I wondered if his father had been a career army officer like Michael's father.

"My friend Pete encouraged me to work here."

"You wanted to see the sights in Michigan?" I asked.

"Detroit's a sight." Listening to the questioning reminded me of being with my relatives. Only my dad was different; he always told me that if a person wants you to know something, they'll tell you.

"My favorite sight is the tank command in my rear view mirror on Friday," Jerry said.

"Where do you work?" somebody asked.

"In Sterling Heights," Mark said. "I work for a defense contractor, so now I produce paperwork instead of reviewing the paperwork from defense contractors."

"What kind of work do you do?" one of my engineering coworkers asked.

"I'm doing some work with data security right now."

"People putting classified data on unclassified Web pages was quite a problem on one program I worked on," Pete said.

"I'm glad I haven't had to confront anybody with that," Mark answered. "Sounds like the offender would lose his clearance, as well as get fired."

"Pam has something in common with you, being an army veteran," Jerry added. "She grew up here, and she knows all the fun places around town. Ask her about the local entertainment."

I was amused that Jerry was attempting to pair us up. I had a feeling that Mark was single, but sometimes I am wrong.

"You could probably get a job at the Tank Command if you wanted to," someone else said. "They and the defense contractors are always looking for people who know army equipment. Sometimes they need people willing to go to Sierra Vista."

"I can get along fine without seeing Sierra Vista again," Mark said.

"Did you work on a UAV?" I asked.

"Not directly," he said, and hesitated.

I remembered that many things about UAVs would be classified. I overstated the classification statement, saying, "I suppose that you can't confirm or deny the presence or absence of a UAV or its reported data in any given place at any given time." I laughed, and several people joined me.

"I can confirm the presence of paper UAVs on desks in my workplace," he said, and laughed. "We have very creative plane designers."

"Sounds interesting," I said. "I've been a mechanical engineer for eight years but have no paper plane experience for my résumé."

"Did you just quit or get a medical discharge?" my coworker Tom asked and then repeated his sob story. "I was discharged after almost ten years because I messed up my foot running. They said I wasn't physically fit for duty any more because I might not be fast enough to escape on foot if our position could be overrun. I was in the artillery, miles from our targets. When did the arty last get overrun—World War II?"

"What bad luck," Mark said politely.

"I knew a clerk in the motor pool who got a medical discharge for foot problems. Has a motor pool on a base ever gotten overrun?" I added.

"Let's not talk about the army," Jerry said. "We get enough of that at work. We went back to our usual conversation topics: weather, TV, movies, and sports. I hadn't told the story about the burning troop carrier yet. Perhaps I would never tell it.

I was glad when Mark joined seven of us at the Chinese buffet. I had thought that the questioning might alienate him. He had avoided providing much information. In a culture where "What do you do?" is the most common exchange between new acquaintances, a person who does not define himself by his job is rare. I wondered if he was hiding something. Maybe he had gotten a dishonorable discharge.

Pete had brought a camera to show off, but I was quiet, bored, and wondering what our guest thought of this.

"We had good star viewing in New Mexico," Mark said, turning toward me. "I haven't taken any sky pictures for years. I didn't have the right kind of camera in Iraq, where you could really see a lot of stars in areas where we had bombed the power out."

As we were leaving the restaurant, Mark walked with me to my car and then asked for my phone number. "Two ex-army—I guess we have some stories to share," he said. "Maybe some cynical stories." I was intrigued. He was ex-army with no West Point ring and no wedding ring—just like me. I hoped he would call.

As I drove to my apartment, I looked at the trees along the streets. My apartment complex was old and nondescript but surrounded by nice vegetation, unlike the windblown deserts of Iraq, where I had dreamed of walking through forests in Michigan. I had just gotten in when Mark called. I didn't hear any background music, and I was surprised that he hadn't gone back to the bar with Pete.

"What is a good tourist attraction like a museum that you would recommend to someone from out of town?" Mark asked. "Would you show me one? Pete said that you aren't married. I'm not married. This weekend, next weekend—just pick the time and place."

I was glad that he told me he wasn't married. Many of the men who asked me out were married. He could be lying, of course, and men who were getting divorced often said they were single.

"I know a science museum with a garden," I said. "I haven't been there since I was in college. We could go this weekend. I'm going to visit my parents next weekend."

"Is tomorrow too soon?" he asked. "I'll take you to lunch first. Could I pick you up at eleven?"

I said okay. I was surprised that he had called so soon. He acted quickly, as I did. In the army, I had learned that some tomorrows never came. I felt tears welling in my eyes.

"How long were you in the army?" he asked.

"Since college," I said. "Eight years—three in Iraq."

"Eight years for me, too," he said. "When did you get out?"

"About five months ago," I said. "Were you glad to get out of the army? How do you like being a civilian?"

"I really looked forward to leaving. Being a civilian takes some time to get used to, though."

"The army is more companionable," I said. "That's the main difference that I found."

"You miss the army?" he asked.

"I miss meeting friends and coworkers at the Officers' Club and gym after work, and hanging out with people on my team. Now I have more spare time than when I was in the army, and I don't know what to do with it. I was busy all the time in the army."

"ON YOUR FEET," he barked. "Miss that, too?"

I laughed. "Thanks for reminding me of the annoyances of the army. I miss being around my friends in the army—not taking orders in the army."

"I miss the social life with coworkers in the army, too," he said. "I've been out of the army for two months. Since I got a job here last month, I've been trying to find some local activities to get involved in."

"That's a good idea," I said. "This area has lots of veterans associations. I enjoy packing care packages for the troops overseas. It's too bad that the Iraq and Afghanistan Veterans of America doesn't have a local group, with meetings like the VFW. They have a few meetings around the country."

"Do you belong to the American Legion or VFW or one of the other veterans groups?" Mark asked.

"I went to the Veterans of Foreign Wars to donate snacks for packages going to the troops overseas, but I didn't join. The VFW seems to be mostly Vietnam veterans or people even older. Community of Veterans is a good Web site for recent veterans. It's got message boards, and many Iraq veterans post. Have you seen it? I belong to that."

"I've heard their ads," Mark said.

"Their radio ads are enjoyable, presenting people asking army veterans obnoxious questions that are the same kind of questions my family asks me."

"I've heard some of those questions myself. I know there are many associations for veterans around here, but I'd like to put the army behind me and not put energy into being a veteran. See you tomorrow," Mark said and rang off.

I wasn't sure that my place looked good enough to have a man over. I had slipped from my army habits, reverting to the housekeeping standards of my family but not quite as bad. No mismatched socks and doll clothes littered the floor, and the dishes weren't in the sink, but the coffee table was covered with junk mail. I would have to do some cleaning tomorrow morning. I had never bought much furniture; I slept on a futon on the floor and used a large box as a bedside table.

Deciding what to wear for the visit to the museum, now that I couldn't wear a uniform, was no easy task. My jeans were okay, but my blouses were awful. Blouses weren't tailored like army blouses with tucks at the waist and front seams leading to the breasts. I could wear a T-shirt, but that seemed too sloppy, and I would need a jacket.

I hadn't invited many people to my apartment. My only regular visitors were my friend from high school LuAnn and her little girl, Sandy. I'd had a few men over—like the nutty marathon runner I met in the park, the guy I met in Tequila Tom's bar who was a drunk and had two ex-wives who didn't understand him, and the guy I'd known in the army who thought I could help him get a job when he retired. Usually if I met a man in a bar, I would go home with him instead of coming here.

Mark and I could go to Tequila Tom's and have a tasty fish lunch, but many people knew me there. I should suggest a place where I didn't hang out. I would run in the early morning, and then clean the living room. But for now, I would sleep. I lay down and thought of drifting off to sleep in Michael's arms.

CHAPTER 2

GUN AND GARDEN

Saturday morning I was less sure that I wanted to spend the day with Mark. I didn't know much about him. He might talk about our date to my coworkers, and my workplace is a snake pit of gossip.

I went for a run before breakfast. Mark showed up promptly at eleven. He seemed to have combed his hair with his fingers, which amused me. He might have had an army haircut for so long that he didn't own a comb.

"I hope I'm not late," he said. "I overslept because I went over to Pete's late last night. His wife called me and said that Pete was drunk and playing with his Beretta in the living room. She wanted me to take the gun away from him."

"Was he threatening her?" I asked.

"No. She didn't feel threatened, but she was afraid that he would discharge the gun in the house and scare the kids. She said that he shot at the TV screen once, missed, and the bullet hit the wall."

"I wonder what was on TV," I said, and laughed. "Maybe news on the Iraq war was playing, and he wanted to shoot some

Iraqis. In the morning he probably wondered where the hole in the wall came from and denied causing it."

"Could be," Mark said. "I talked him into putting down the gun, then took it, and left when his wife distracted him into looking for a misplaced bag of potato chips."

"He might shoot himself," I said. I took a seat in my tattered armchair and gestured for him to sit on the couch.

"I don't think he would kill himself," Mark said. "He's very religious, and he thinks suicide is a dishonorable cop-out. He even criticizes the suicide prevention groups."

"Very honorable, huh?" I said. "I remember a chopper pilot who tried to shoot himself because he thought he was going to get busted in rank, and he couldn't face the dishonor."

"What did he do that they were going to bust him?"

"Took some uppers and was incoherent over the radio."

"If they busted pilots for taking uppers, how would anybody else get a medevac? Probably after his command thought it out, they decided they loved him," Mark said. "Helicopter pilots are fearless. 'A good day for flying, that's a good day for dying. A good day to live, that's a good day to die.'"

I replied, "Fine day, cloudless day, there will never be a better, more exciting day than this. Might as well fly into the hillside today because it's the peak of my life."

"You got it." Mark said. "Remember, they're good at their job, or they're dead at it."

"Or they're just fatalists," I said. "The bullet that has your name on it might happen any time, any place. Maybe in Detroit."

"Or getting hit by friendly fire," Mark added.

"Once I was getting on a troop transport chopper, and I asked the pilot if he had ever taken a lot of flak," I said. "To my surprise, he said that his worst accident was at a stateside base when he was warming up the engine, and it caught fire. He said he ran to get away, and then remembered that he had four children at home. He had started repeating 'four kids, four little kids.' Then he fell down on the tarmac and started crying. He lay there so long two medics came out with a stretcher and wanted him on it. He said that he had explained that he wasn't hurt, but he had thought of his four kids. He looked like he might cry as he was telling the story. He said, as though reciting a poem,

'And, that's when I knew Jesus saved me.

I went home, taught the kids,

They're all saved now.

Whatever comes, it's all right.'"

"Wow," Mark said. "I wish I had that kind of faith. He figured that if his kids accepted Jesus as their savior, they could deal with their father's death. I'm more of a fatalist. None of the bullets in Iraq had my name on them. I looked carefully at Pete's ammo last night, and none of his bullets had his name on them, either." We both laughed.

"Are you religious?" he asked.

"I was raised Methodist."

"The type of Methodists who do a lot of singing? He began clapping his hands. "Like, 'It's me, yes, it's me, Lord, standing in the need of prayer.'"

Why this song? I wondered. Was he thinking about praying for Pete?

"Exactly that kind of Methodist," I said, and began singing like a six-year-old, "Michael, row the boat ashore." *Michael*. I stopped.

"Well, you've got a home in Gloryland that outshines the sun."

"I'd like to lay off this," I said.

"I wasn't making fun of you," he continued. "That was a good riff. I like your singing voice. I like improvisation. Little children asking for prayer seems ironic. I had the image of that little kid growing up and being on a firing range, holding a rifle or Beretta Parabellum, and singing 'Standing in the need of prayer.'"

I wonder if he is talking about himself, I thought. "You must be religious," I said.

"I'm an amateur student of religion," he explained. "One thing I find interesting is the use of music and singing in religious services."

"Do you have kids? You seem to know all the Sunday school songs."

"No, I'm divorced, and we didn't have any children."

"Do you want a drink before lunch?" I asked.

"No."

"That's good because I don't have any liquor right now. If you don't want a drink with lunch, let's go to the Mongolian Barbecue Restaurant. If you want a drink, I know a good place further north of here."

"How about you?" he asked. "Do you want one?"

"No," I said. "I had plenty last night."

"Fine. Let's have Mongolian barbecue," he said. "This is a cute apartment."

"There are some nice apartments here in the suburbs," I replied. "Some bases have mostly dumps. I was briefly in Texas before being deployed overseas and rented off base. The complex didn't look bad when I moved there, but the maintenance man was arrested for drug dealing, and nobody was sweeping up the broken beer bottles after that.

"The MPs would beat at the door next to me at night, looking for somebody AWOL. On the other side of me, a woman was running a business, and the headboard of her bed kept hitting the wall. Men were pounding on her door at night. When I went over to have a girl-to-girl talk about the headboard, she offered me a beer and tried to make me. A woman passed out on the stairs near the laundry room, and three enlisted men who just finished a squadron basketball game were debating whether they should rape her while I was doing my laundry."

"Did you do anything about it?" Mark asked.

"I'd met her, and I told them she'd had everything up to her place but a sheep and a goat, and I'd heard that some really bad VD was going around. They left her alone that time, anyway. Maybe they just got some condoms first."

"Weren't you afraid of the men?" Mark asked.

"No. I had been drinking and playing poker with them before. They were career sergeants and were probably kidding or daring each other."

"Great story about the headboard," Mark said. "Role reversal. I've never visited a prostitute myself. I got married about the same time I went into the army. We had been living together since graduate school. She remarried after our divorce, and we very politely exchange holiday cards every year."

We went down to his car, an old Chevrolet sedan with the passenger door dented and beginning to rust. The car was nice otherwise, though. The interior was clean, and there was a towel spread on the passenger seat. Mark drove to the Mongolian Barbecue, a small restaurant in a strip mall.

"Do you come here often?" he asked.

"Yes. It's close to where I work. Many of the people I work with are Asian, and they recommend it. Sometimes after happy hour, we come here instead of going to one of the Chinese buffets."

After our chicken and vegetables were stir-fried, we returned to our table. As we took our chairs, Mark asked, "Do you work with Jerry Wong, the guy with the Buddha medal on a chain around his neck?"

"Yes, at times." I had never noticed the Buddha medal.

"His wife gave the medal to him in place of a wedding ring. He said that his family goes to an Amida Buddhist church and invited me to join them for a service sometime, since I'm interested in the religions of Asia."

Amida Buddhism? I was surprised at his striking up a friendship with Jerry.

"I don't think I ever met an Amida Buddhist before," he said. "I saw some Buddhist temples in South Korea. Once I went to Japan and visited some Zen temples in Nara. Some of them are beautiful, hundreds of years old."

"I've never been to Asia," I said. "Did you enjoy the dinner last night?"

"I enjoyed the group dinner, but people kept asking me where I work now, which is like asking how much money I make."

"They really wanted to know if you are another engineer—most of them are," I said. "Where were you stationed overseas besides Iraq?"

"Germany and Korea. I liked Korea the best," he said. "Korea changed my way of looking at things. I liked Germany, too. I speak German. My grandparents were from Germany, and my parents speak German as well as English."

Mark was dark and small, unlike Michael, who was blond, sturdy, and had strong features. I wouldn't have guessed that Mark was of German ancestry. His last name was Vonn, if I had understood it correctly. I wondered if he was Jewish. Maybe his grandparents came here because of Hitler.

"I wish I knew languages," I said. "About all I know of foreign languages is that 'parabellum' has to do with war, so our Beretta Parabellum is the Beretta for war. Engineers rarely study languages in college."

"Do you like engineering?"

"Yes. I like cars, but I like tanks, bridging vehicles, artillery vehicles, and amphibious vehicles even more," I replied. "My dad and I would tour the Tank Command, TACOM, during public open houses. I'm working on new vehicles, and that's exciting. Most of my coworkers are a lot older than me, so it's a strange atmosphere. Many of them retired from the army. It's hard to get used to former majors and colonels as coworkers. I make sure not to let them push me around."

"Most defense workers seem to be over forty," Mark said. "One person in my group is nearly seventy and retired from some other defense contractor."

"I wish there were more women where I work," I said. "I will have to find female friends somewhere else."

We ate lunch, each of us going back for a second plate. "Shall we head out for the museum and garden?" he asked after we ate. "I want to walk near trees, even barren ones. I've spent too long in the desert." We got in the car and headed to Cranbrook Museum and Gardens.

"The fruit trees may be flowering at the garden," I pointed out. "Spring is beautiful in Michigan." I remembered going to a park in Washington, when the lilacs were blooming. Michael and I had walked around the group of lilacs on a hill, and then rolled down the grassy hill like children. Michael did a somersault on the lawn and then stood on his head. I tried to stand on my head and tumbled onto the lawn. We laughed and went back up the hill, so we could roll down it again.

"Apple blossoms—how does that poem go? 'Rendezvous with Death, spring comes back so full and fair, apple blossoms fill the air, by Alan Seeger," Mark said.

"I thought Alan Seeger had his rendezvous with death in Algeria or some other part of North Africa. Isn't North Africa dry, like Iraq? Do they have apple trees there?"

"The headquarters of the French Foreign Legion were in Algeria, but he died in France at some disputed barricade between the German and French trenches," Mark answered.

"You're spoiling my mental picture. I always pictured him leading a charge down a sand dune at midnight in some flaming town in North Africa."

"He was thought of so highly because he was fighting Germans. If he had died fighting Algerian rebels, burning whitewashed little rebel towns while yelling '*Algerie Francois,*' Americans wouldn't have liked him. Algeria is French? Might as well holler 'America is British,'" Mark said.

"That poem is reprinted all over the place. Even the navy people use it."

"Can navy people identify with running away from duty, except psychologically? On a ship, you couldn't run away from your rendezvous and be untrue to your pledged word in the flowery language Seeger uses," Mark said. "If soldiers run away, there are few places to go."

Desertion? This conversation was getting weird. "African mercenary armies?" I suggested. "That would probably be going from the frying pan into the fire. Maybe you could get a private security job at Blackwater if you knew many kinds of weapons."

"I wouldn't want to be a security contract employee, as they call them," Mark said. "They all have goatees. I wouldn't look good in a goatee." He laughed. "You have to be foolhardy.

Either they think that they are invulnerable, or they want to kill themselves."

I said, "As a mercenary, you commit suicide, and your relatives still get your life insurance."

"Yes, and the life insurance is paid in U.S. dollars—good money if you're from Central or South America. If you can't go back to your own country, maybe being a foreign mercenary is the best job that you can get."

I began singing, "'Venezuela wants me, and I can't go back there. I wish I had you, to talk to. No, I wish I had you, to beat you.'" I put my hand on his right arm above the elbow, where he had a large scar, possibly from shrapnel. I would ask him about it if we got to know each other better.

"Tough, aren't you? When you parody these old pop songs the Vietnam veterans play, you could have made a romantic rhyme, like, 'I want you to be true,' he responded, adding the next line, 'If ever men deserve to die, then we do.' Where did that come from? Not 'If ever a man deserved to die, then he did.'"

I said, "It must be hard to go into a foreign army and have to learn their language. Get stressed, and you probably revert to English and can't communicate. The officers are screaming obscenities at you that you don't understand." I was curious about what he did in the war.

Mark parked his car, and we walked through a tree-lined path and crossed a bridge to the first fountain, which was set in a grove of trees. We sat down to admire it.

"I love being outdoors," I said. "I would rather walk in parks than do anything else. I don't care if we go to the museum or spend all our time in the garden."

"I like the garden. The fountains remind me of Europe," Mark said. "I liked Germany. I wouldn't be able to follow cursing, though. My brother and I speak German like seven-year-old kids."

"Were there just the two of you?" I asked. "I have two younger sisters."

"Yes, I have just one brother. Did any of your sisters follow in your footsteps?" Mark asked.

"You mean, become a mechanical engineer because I did? No. Neither went into the army, either. My youngest sister, Susie, dropped out of high school. Going into the army would probably have been good for her. She might have developed some direction instead of chasing around aimlessly. She was pregnant at fifteen. I'm ashamed of her, and I'm always concerned that some sleazy guy might try to hit on me because I'm her sister.

"Susie took a lot of attention. For example, one Saturday my mother took the three of us to the dentist. Susie is the youngest of us, and Mom wanted her to be first so that she wouldn't get nervous while waiting. Susie fussed and fussed and wouldn't cooperate with the dentist. My mom was coaxing her, alternating between being upset and being angry. Finally, the dentist said we had wasted half an hour of his time, and we should leave. No charge but don't come back.

"We went out to the car, and Susie was pleased because she'd gotten her way. I thought about the situation more and didn't get in the car. I said, 'Susie can't keep me from going to the dentist. She doesn't control my life. I'll go to the dentist myself. He didn't want Susie, but I didn't make trouble in there.'" I was getting mad as I remembered and raised my voice.

"My mother said that Susie was only frightened. I acted as obstinate as Susie did, and my mother finally told me to go back in if I wanted to, but I would have to walk home. Home was only two miles away. So I went back to the dentist, and he took me. I told him my dad would pay him. I still get mad at Susie for things like that. She was cute when she was a baby, but that only lasts a while, and kids have to grow up and be an adult."

"That conflict must have been hard on your middle sister," Mark said.

"Maybe. I didn't ask her what she thought." I got mad at Susie about many things. She was messy, and I would have to clean up. I regretted that I had displayed my temper to Mark.

"Carolyn did okay," I said. "She didn't take sides in conflicts." Carolyn always had her own way of dealing with things. She often had stomachaches after family events. Sometimes she got headaches or threw up. Maybe she didn't do okay.

I continued, "My dad said I did the right thing at the dentist because we should keep the appointments that we made."

"What happened to your youngest sister?"

"She married some worthless guy, had two more kids, and got divorced. I don't see her often. Next weekend my mom is giving a birthday party for one of Susie's children. I'll see her then."

"How far is your family home from here?" Mark asked.

"I grew up in Dearborn, just twenty miles away. My parents still live there." I was sorry I'd brought up this old story and wanted to change the subject. "Did you get along well with your brother?"

"He was four years older than me, and like another parent. He had a lot of patience with me. He teaches now."

We walked by the manor house and the nearby flower beds.

"Have you been inside the house?" Mark asked.

"That wouldn't interest me much," I said. "Do you want to tour it?"

"No. I've seen European-style rooms in Europe."

I added, "I toured some old buildings in Europe. My parents were excited when I went to Europe, especially when I told them I toured a castle. I guess they always wanted to go to Europe."

"You can help them plan a trip."

"I don't think they will ever go to Europe. They're busy with Susie's kids. My mother is excited about the boys, probably because she had all girls. My dad probably wants the boys to grow up fast and learn the family automobile body repair business."

We walked across the lawn toward the ponds. *If ever men deserve to die, then we do*, I kept repeating to myself. What did Mark and Pete do in Iraq?

"To be in a family business, a person has to have the interest and the talent," Mark said. "My grandfather was a physicist, so were my father and uncle. My brother teaches physics at the University of Nevada, and I majored in physics myself. Physics is interesting, but I didn't want to do the kind of work my dad did or teach like my brother. When I was young, I thought that I would like working in an observatory. I used to love photographing the night sky.

"When I went in the army, I wanted to see the world. Maybe I should have just saved money and taken a trip around the world instead of traveling as a soldier and seeing military bases."

"Ah, the army, and its life of adventure, where you have no time to enjoy life after you spend the day at work, run four miles, go to the gym, take care of your clothes, and clean the place you live," I said, laughing.

"And drink with your co-workers on weekends," Mark added.

"I really liked the jobs I had in the army and the social life," I said. "I could overlook some of the formalities. What I didn't want any more is war and war and war. Three years in Iraq. I would go into the National Guard if the war was over, but not if I risk being sent to Afghanistan. I've been lucky, but some day my luck might run out."

We had reached the ponds, bordered with weeds and full of water lily pads, and I looked into the dark water for frogs and turtles. "I think I saw a frog," I said. "Something hopped." Mark pointed to a ripple in the water, near a small bridge.

"No, that was a turtle sliding off a fallen log," I said. "See the turtle's head rising above the surface."

"You sure notice everything going on around you," Mark said. We stood silently, scanning the pond, and saw two small turtles swimming.

After walking around the ponds, we walked near the big house again. Concrete turtles were on the top of one fountain, looking as out of place as turtles on a fencepost. We sat on a bench beside it to watch the falling water.

"I liked Korea better than Europe," Mark said. "Some of my Korean friends said I must have been Korean in a previous life."

"Reincarnation," I said. "Do you believe in reincarnation?"

"Reincarnation isn't a matter of belief," he said. "You're reincarnated or you aren't. Reincarnation explains a westerner liking Korea by saying that he was Korean in a former life."

"Do you believe you were reincarnated?"

"I'm too much of a scientist to speculate on psychological or sociological theories. But why did we join the army? My father and grandfathers weren't in the army. Were yours?"

"My father was in the army for a while, just out of high school."

"Old-school Asian thought would be that we were in the army in a previous life and had some karma to finish," Mark added. "Is that an illogical reason? With all the possibilities, why choose the army?"

"You mean, maybe we were army officers in a previous life?"

"Maybe. Maybe I was an army ant in a previous life. Maybe you were a turtle in a previous life. You like tanks, and you watch turtles on logs. Maybe you have turtle-consciousness from a previous life." He laughed and then put his arm around me, stiffly.

"Maybe I came here looking for my turtle relatives, so that we can swim through a pond and eat bugs together. I like swimming and maybe I like the taste of bugs, but I've never tried one. Maybe I like it here because I lived here in a turtle shell."

"Gee, most women think they were Cleopatra or somebody else glamorous in a previous life," he said, laughing. I liked the sound of his laugh.

We walked in silence past the lake to the Japanese garden. A turtle? Turtles have hard shells and seemed nearsighted.

The sound of rushing water filled the Japanese garden. One Japanese maple was a perfect red, and some of the flowers were budding. I asked, "If I like Japanese gardens, does that mean I was Japanese in a previous life?"

"No, it means you have good taste." We sat on a bench to look at the pond and the reflections of bushes and trees in the water.

"How would a belief in reincarnation affect a person's life?" I asked.

"That you have to try to be good, or you end up living as a cockroach and getting squashed," Mark said. "Reincarnation is just an unproven theory."

"Sometimes I used to think that there was another me, different from the person I usually am," I said. "Somebody I don't approve of and sometimes dislike. That person used to hide behind my uniform." *I thought about Iraq, the troop transport in front of us burning, when I reached for the rifle.*

"Maybe there is a part of myself in uniform that did things I don't like or approve of when I look back at them. But it's still me," Mark said.

He has probably killed people, I thought. Carrying a weapon, firing at a human cutout on the range, and we still don't expect that one day we will kill someone. We sat quietly in the garden. I tried to impress each lantern, each tree, and each plant in my mind. After a while, we walked back past the manor house. Mark stopped at each budding or blooming plant as though it were an object of scientific inquiry, touching and smelling it.

"Would you like to go someplace next weekend?" he asked. "I'd like to go to a park or a garden again—if the weather is nice."

"I'm going to see my family Saturday. Susie's daughter has a birthday party. I don't look forward to it, but afterward I'm going to see a school friend of mine, LuAnn, who lives on my way back from there."

We were silent for a while. I kept puzzling over those words, *If ever men deserve to die, then we do.*

"We could go somewhere next Sunday," Mark suggested. "Do you go to church?"

"No," I said. "I run in the morning and loaf the rest of the day."

"I could come by about one. I'll take you to an art show, if that is something you would like."

"I'd like to go to the art show. Do you go to church on Sunday?" I asked.

"More or less," he said. "I've tried a few local services."

Back home, I invited Mark in for a soda and some snacks, but he said he had to go and see Pete. He seemed agitated.

"Do I get some affection?" he asked, pulling me toward him and kissing me.

I put my hand on his scar and rubbed his arm. Then I ran my hand up to his shoulder and kissed him on his cheek. I began nibbling at his earlobe, but I resisted putting my hand down his slacks, where I was sure he was getting hard. I whispered in his ear, "All is well, safely rest, God is nigh."

How had that gone? I wasn't sure. He had been quiet much of the time, maybe because he was worried about Pete. I was disappointed because I thought that we would watch TV or see a movie. Suddenly I remembered that Taps is played at funerals, as well as at nightfall. We had been talking about possible suicide, and I had sent him off with the funeral bugle call, "Day is done, gone the sun, from the hills, from the lakes, from the sky, all is well, safely rest, God is nigh." I hoped that I hadn't hurt his feelings.

The TV guide listed all-day reruns of "Ice Road Truckers." I could imagine driving a big truck in the cold and dark, the headlights barely illuminating the road at night. At least the danger was predictable and consistent. No one would be firing rockets or planting improvised explosive devices on the road.

Mark had mentioned that when he was young, he had wanted to work in an observatory. Working in an observatory at night would be like driving the ice road—cold, dark, quiet, isolated. Michael had never liked being alone. He liked team sports and parties. He was big, blond, and talkative. We would run together, back in Washington.

I decided to go running again. Afterwards I would go to Tequila Tom's and have a burger; then I'd come home and watch TV.

CHAPTER 3

VISIT HOME

My workplace was agitated Thursday because we had a meeting with managers from our company's headquarters in Washington. The management gave us a press release about our company getting a major government contract in California. Three of my coworkers began a conversation about the announcement, in an aisle between our cubicles.

"At least they didn't lose business this year," Wade said.

"They may have," Tom explained. "They announced that they got six million dollars worth of business on some contract, but maybe they were expecting twelve million."

I joined the conversation. "Does this affect us?"

"Who knows?" Tom said. "The government gets dissatisfied and then passes the work to some other defense contractor, who usually hires new staff from the company that lost the contract. I wouldn't be concerned, since the press release is about California. This industry isn't like the army. People move from one company to another."

The upper management met with each of us separately. I was asked if I had problems being one of two women on the project and one of the youngest people.

"No," I said. "I was usually the only woman working on the equipment in the army, and army men talk and act worse than the men here."

We all went out to lunch at a nice restaurant with a bar where several civil servants were drinking their lunch. We talked about sports and the stock market. I noticed how reticent my coworkers were. I thought they must mistrust the upper management.

I looked forward to visiting my parents Saturday, which was unusual for me. The atmosphere at work was strained since my coworkers kept speculating that the management meeting would have some negative repercussions for employees. I thought that the purpose of the meetings had been for upper management to assess our local management.

Since I was a guest now, I knocked at the door of my childhood home, noticing the peeling paint on the door and on the porch. One of the steps was reinforced by a cement block. I clutched a bag with the latest Bratz doll in it. I wondered if the doll was right for a girl my niece's age, and then I realized I wasn't sure how old she was.

Mom answered the door, saying, "You're early. I haven't gotten things ready yet."

I volunteered to help. "I came a little early because I have to leave early. I'm going to the reservation to see LuAnn. You remember her."

"Did you have to go today? You haven't been here for months," she said. "Have you seen your sisters lately?"

"No. I've been busy working. LuAnn and I are going to a powwow," I lied. "I haven't been to a powwow in a long time."

"Powwows are held all summer. Susie's daughter has a birthday party only once a year."

"But Susie has three children, so there are birthday parties for her and the children every few months. Carolyn and her baby have birthdays, too." I sat down at the kitchen table. The vinyl tablecloth seemed to be the same one we had when I was a child.

"Are you going to get a job teaching, instead of just working for a company?" my mom asked. "Think of the stories you could tell the children about the countries you've been to."

"You have Carolyn, and she is a teacher," I said. "Is dad in the garage?"

"He's in the back yard setting up chairs."

I set my package down and went outside. Dad was learning against the garage, having a smoke. I noticed that he was developing a paunch. "How are you doing, Dad? Busy escaping the gossip and nagging?"

"Well, look who's here," he said. "I'm surprised that you came. Not that we don't want you here. I would like it if you came more. Visit me at the auto body shop sometimes, so we can swap some army stories where nobody else can hear."

"Yeah, the language is too bad," I said. "I'll tell you about this motherfucking convoy, and we took fire from some ragheads, and—"

"We used to say gooks." He laughed.

I laughed, too. *I remembered picking up the rifle...* "I'll help you put some fucking paint on some fucking truck, and we'll toss down some cool ones and swap some war stories."

"How's work?"

VISIT HOME

"Like the army but with civil servants and defense contractors wearing jeans, looking sloppy, and wisecracking. What surprises me about my workplace is how few women there are and how much older people are than in the army."

"I suppose they want people experienced with army equipment. If you don't like it, come help me in the shop. After all, you're an engineer. Maybe we could expand into fixing engines."

"I nearly flunked a class in engines. My main project is a reduction of weight on the armor of a troop carrier. Also, how heavy a load can the new vehicle take before we have to redesign the axle?"

"Redesigning axles is pretty deep for me," dad said. He pulled a flask out of his pocket and offered me a drink. The cheap whiskey burned going down.

"I've got to leave early, so I came early," I said.

"Don't start squabbling with your sisters. I get tired of you girls bickering and tattling on each other. Susie has a hard life. I try to be a father to her kids, since their own father split, but I can't handle the boys. I'm too old to be a substitute dad. I don't see why the law can't get some money from the deadbeat she married. Apparently he's too worthless to hold a job, so he doesn't have steady income and can't pay child support."

"I guess he wouldn't be reliable enough to paint cars. Doesn't he pay Susie anything at all?" I asked. I wondered if her ex-husband was the father of the child she had in high school as well as the younger two.

"They'll serve the bum some papers and get fifty dollars sometimes. Carolyn has a good man, Tim. I liked Michael, that big blond guy you brought over once. Solid, I could tell. Do you have another boyfriend now?"

"Maybe," I said. I took another slug of the rotgut and passed it back. My throat burned less than it had before. "I need to drive today. I can't drink much."

"Remember, Pam, life goes on," dad said and tilted the flask to his lips. "We lose some things in our lives, but then we gain others." He paused and offered me the flask again. "This'll cool you down. Maybe you girls wouldn't be bickering if you had enough happy juice. Your Aunt Marcia and Uncle Matt were asking about you. Visit with them for a while before your other aunts arrive and the women gossip all afternoon."

"Are we going to go west and visit grandma and your brothers sometime? I asked. "I got their Christmas presents, and I was glad to hear that everything is all right, but I haven't seen them for a long time now. I'll miss the farm. Did they manage to sell it?"

"Yes, finally. I last visited my brothers and mom just before you came home. I took Carolyn and her baby Bobby. I'm glad your grandmother lives with your Uncle Ron. She is too old to live in the farmhouse alone, but she misses it very much. We can make a trip again when I can take the time."

"I could drive two hundred miles easily. I would especially like to see Cousin Jimmy."

"You still have a crush on your cousin Jimmy? Or you want to swap engineer stories? He's working in Chicago, as far as I know."

"I always liked him," I said. "I liked walking around the farm with him or going to parks. It was fun to overhear people guess whether he was my older brother or my father."

"Actually, they were seeing your first dates." Dad laughed. "Where is Canada, Jimmy? What is the moon made of? Show me a hubcap. Where do mosquitoes come from? No wonder

VISIT HOME

Jimmy is such a know-it-all. We'll go see your grandmother. I promise."

Uncle Matt and Aunt Marcia were in the back yard, sitting on lawn chairs. I walked over to them.

"Look who's here," Uncle Matt said. "Pam, out of the army, for good, at last."

"It's nice to be home."

"I'm surprised you're not married yet," Aunt Marcia said. "You worked with so many men."

"No, I didn't get married." I'm not a widow. I wasn't a wife.

"I thought that you would become a teacher," Aunt Marcia said. "You were so good with the little kids. You liked to show them things, and you had so much patience."

I remembered playing on the lawn, naming the plants and insects for the smaller children. "Life didn't take me that way."

"You could still teach."

"Why would I want to teach? What would I teach—drill practice?" I said, feeling angry. "I have a job with a defense contractor. I work on new military vehicles, and this country is at war. I served my country stateside and in a war zone."

"I don't see why we send women to Iraq, where they get shot at," Uncle Matt said. "We've got women getting killed. I bet the Arabs don't like women soldiers walking around in pants."

"Yes, we walked around in pants."

"I don't think women should be shooting guns," he said. "In Vietnam, we kept women at home."

I was growing increasingly angry. "That was then, this is now."

"Women shouldn't be in war zones," my uncle said. "Think of all the men it takes to protect them. It's just a waste."

"Women carry weapons, too. I carried a pistol. I shot a rifle."

"Think about getting captured. They treat the women worse, so much worse."

"Do they tell you that on TV?" I asked. "Captured men get raped, too, you know. That's the culture over there."

My uncle was sputtering. "They treat the women worse," he insisted.

My aunt abruptly changed the subject. "You were such an example to your sisters," she said. "They used to worship you. They missed you all these years. You can be such a help to your nieces and nephews."

I remembered sitting in my aunt's lap, showing her a bug I found. Her lap was warm and ample. Now our conversations were conflicts. I should do what they want. I should be a teacher. I should visit my sisters. My family didn't care about my job or about my life.

I walked over to Carolyn, who was sitting with her husband Tim, and the baby. I hardly knew Tim.

Tim smiled. "Ah, here's the Terminator, out of the army," he said. "Carolyn tells me so much about you. How was Iraq? Were you near the front lines?"

I was growing increasingly angry. "Actually, I was in Maryland before I came here," I answered.

"You were overseas for so long," Carolyn said.

"Yes, I was. Are you teaching?" I asked.

"I substitute a little now that I have the baby," she answered. "Sometimes I work at a day-care center, which is better because I can bring Bobby along."

VISIT HOME

"Mom and dad must be happy with you," I said. "They always wanted me to teach."

"Mom did. Dad didn't care what we studied or did for a living. He probably thought we should all go into the army like you."

That surprised me. However, dad favored me, and mom favored Susie, and Carolyn was ignored. "The army isn't for everyone. Neither is teaching."

"Susie's having a bad time."

"She always seemed to," I said. "Susie had the same opportunities as you and I did. It's too bad she didn't use them."

"I don't think it's that simple," Carolyn said. "She made some bad choices and couldn't reverse them."

"Do you see her often?"

"No. I'm very busy, with the baby." I knew that Carolyn and Susie had some spats when they were in high school together.

"Come by for dinner sometime," Tim said. He didn't volunteer their phone number or current address, but I probably had written them down someplace.

I replied, "That would be nice."

Susie and her children had arrived, and I walked over to them. "Remember your Aunt Pam?" she asked her boys. "She used to be in the army."

"Girls can't be in the army," the larger boy said.

The younger boy made a fist and pointed his finger. "Bang, bang," he said.

"Girls can't shoot," the older one howled.

"I carried a revolver all the time." *I remembered the troop carrier on fire and the shooting from the windows. A rifle was on the floor beside me.*

The older boy pulled a toy gun out of his pocket—a cap pistol, I assumed. "Girls can't fire guns," he said.

"Girls aren't good for anything," the younger boy agreed.

The older boy pointed his toy gun at me. "Bang, bang," he said.

"Don't ever point a gun at someone, even a toy one. A policeman might shoot you for that," I said. "Drop it." I moved toward him, and he fled.

Susie walked toward us. "They're just playing," she said.

"In my neighborhood in Washington, an eleven-year-old boy decided to rob a woman in a shopping mall parking lot with his toy gun. She began screaming, and an employee of one of the stores pulled a real gun from his glove compartment and shot the boy. A mob killed the boy in the parking lot. Your sons are just setting themselves up for trouble when they have realistic toy guns and point them at people."

"Nothing like that happens here," Susie said,

"Juveniles don't get shot in Detroit?"

"The kids are just playing," she answered.

I went inside. Aunt Bev had joined my mother, and they were putting potato chips and dip on trays. "I wish you would see more of your sisters," mom said. "Your aunts and uncles used to be part of your life. We had birthday parties and holiday parties. Don't you remember? I thought that when you came back you would see us more often, but we don't see you any more than when you were in Washington or Fort What's-Its-Name."

"Or Iraq," I said.

"You have time for your friends but not for your family."

"None of you visits me either. I'm not far away."

"Well, people are busy with the kids. Susie brings the children here when she needs to do shopping or get things done at home. It's hard to go visiting."

I was silent.

Mom continued, "My sisters are my best friends. They help me when I need it and are available to me to talk whenever I want to talk. You avoid your sisters. You have been here for months and never visited them. You act as though you don't like them."

"I don't dislike them," I said. "I'm just busy."

You didn't plan your life with us in it," my mother continued. She was right.

"Why did you even come back?"

"Detroit is my home, too," I said.

"You're so hard on people, Pamela. Susie's kids need to know somebody like you. Carolyn needs a friend." She paused. "You think you're always right, and everybody else is always wrong. You even had to go to a different dentist than your sisters did. That just made more work for me."

"What!" I exclaimed. "I walked to the dentist—don't you remember?"

"You're so cold, Pamela. Susie needed a friend. She needs one now."

"Why is everything about Susie and what she wants and needs, and whether she is willing to go to the dentist?"

Susie's older boy came into the kitchen, with his toy gun. He pointed the gun at me, saying "Bang, bang," looking to my mother and aunt for approval.

"What did I tell you about pointing guns at people?" I said. "Drop that right now."

"My mother said it's okay."

"Then go point it at her."

He walked behind me and put the gun to my head. I felt a surge of adrenaline and reached for the Beretta that was no longer there. I turned and backhanded him across the face. "What did I say about pointing guns, you brat?"

He fled.

"Don't be so hard on the children," my mother said.

"If he tries that on the wrong person, he'll be shot," I said.

Susie ran in. "You can't discipline my child," she said.

"Then you should, sometimes."

"Why did you come here? I didn't invite you, and it's my daughter's birthday. Nobody wants you here, you know-it-all."

I had enough. I got up to leave. Susie, my white-trash sister, and her nasty illegitimate brat could have the territory. I went out to the garage, where dad was watching TV on a small set. "I'm going up to the reservation now," I told him.

"Don't let the civilians drive you away," dad said. "They probably asked you how many people you killed. People used to ask me that when I got back from Vietnam. I hated hearing that question. The worst thing in my life was seeing other men die. In the infantry, I saw many men die. A friend of mine was killed while standing very close to me."

"What difference would it make whether I killed anyone?" I asked. "So that my relatives would have something to gossip about? So that they could say that I used to be a nice girl before I shot people in Iraq?"

"They just wanted to know if you were safe. They worried about you when you were in the war."

"I was lucky. I never saw anyone near me die, although I may have seen people killed at the distance of a rifle shot. I would usually be working in a motor pool or at a desk." I reached for the flask. "I'll have a slug for the road right now."

Dad handed me the flask and said, "I wish that you wouldn't leave so early. How do you like being a civilian again?"

"Leaving the army is as hard as going in—harder, in fact. I miss the army every day. I was ready to leave the army, but in some way, I wasn't ready to be somewhere else, if that makes sense."

"You have a job, and you will make new friends, just like when you went to college and into the army. After I got out of the Army, it took me about a year before I adjusted to being a civilian. Coming back from Vietnam, I was nervous, and watchful of the things around me, looking for danger all the time. At home, I had to catch up with what my friends and family members had been doing, and connect with them again. Your mother grew up a lot while I was gone, becoming a woman more than a schoolgirl. I couldn't find a good job for a while, either. At least you have a job that fits right in with your education and your work in the Army."

"I like my job, but I'm not used to having so much spare time. Army life is very structured, and you always have things to do. There's flag raising, group run, and team exercises. It's strange to have a lot of personal time, without much to fill it. Making friends is harder, too. In the Army, I could always meet people like myself at the Officer's Club or the gym. In civilian life meeting people is harder, and usually I don't have much in common with the people I meet."

"Eventually you'll find new activities, places you like to visit, and people you want to be with. You will feel like you belong here again. I've always been sorry you lost Michael. He seemed like a nice person. I thought you'd be married by now and busy with your kids."

I had thought I would be married, too. I'm not a widow. I wasn't a wife. My eyes filled with tears. "I have a new male friend," I said. A slight exaggeration. After all, Mark might stand me up tomorrow, and I might never see him again.

"Bring him over sometime. Don't be ashamed of your family. Let him meet us. We will like him. I like everything you do. You're my boy. I missed you when you were away."

"I've never been ashamed of you." I wasn't ashamed of my dad, just Susie and our tacky house. "I'm just busy with work and getting settled."

"Is he an army guy like Michael—West Point and career army?"

"No, he left the army. My coworker introduced us."

"Is he good with cars?" dad asked. "These new cars run so complicated, with all these computers, you need an education to figure then out." I had a vision of Mark fixing cars with dad at the body shop. I must have smiled.

"No good with cars, huh? I have three daughters and no sons-in-law who like cars? He must know something about cars, working at the tank plant." Dad was teasing now. I couldn't picture Mark working on cars, but I hadn't asked. Maybe he fixed cars when he was young. I hardly knew Mark. Why had I mentioned him?

"I don't know if he works on cars. I'll bring him over, and you can figure out how much he knows."

"Typical engineer, huh? Don't like getting their hands dirty. I want to meet him anyway."

I walked back through the yard, where Susie's kids were throwing mud from the flower bed at each other.

Driving toward Detroit, I felt relief. Many times when I was in high school, I had slept over at LuAnn's house. She and her father and younger brother lived two blocks from us then. We would go to her house after school, because she needed to watch her brother. Her mother was dead. Often I would stay to help her cook dinner, then eat at her place, and later call my parents for permission to sleep over.

The "reservation" I was going to wasn't an Indian reservation, as I had implied to my parents, it was a cheap apartment building between Dearborn and Detroit. A few Indian families lived there, and they called it the reservation as a joke. I had lied about the powwow too. Lu Ann and I weren't going to a powwow soon, but I wanted to make plans with her to attend one.

LuAnn and her daughter, Sandy, were watching a police TV program when I got there. I wondered if people in bad neighborhoods like to watch television police make arrests because they know people in real life who should be arrested.

"Welfare says I should go back to school," she said, after we said hello. "Job training, or else I should get a job as soon as possible. What do you think?"

"Take cooking school at the junior college. You already know how to cook, so the training program will be easy."

A man entered the apartment and introduced himself as Bob, the manager of the apartment complex. He was tall and florid, with reddish brown hair.

"I'm Pam, LuAnn's friend from high school," I said.

He carried a whiskey bottle, and poured us each a shot. "Coke?" he asked. "Water," I said. I hoped the booze wasn't as cheap and raw as my dad's.

"Bob's a good friend of mine," LuAnn said. "He's a good manager. He keeps the dopers out, and the halls are pretty clean here."

"Lots of drugs in this neighborhood. I don't care if they use, but I throw them out of this place if I know they deal," Bob said. "I toss the hookers, too. I don't want their customers around, standing in the hall, waiting their turn." He poured a Coke for Sandy and sat down. Sandy climbed onto his lap.

"Isn't it hard to evict people?" I asked.

"If you do it legally, it is. They think I'm crazy and violent, so it usually isn't hard for me. I put on some acts to give me a reputation."

"He even took a gun away from a guy," LuAnn said.

"I beat him up in the hallway, afterward. The other tenants called the cops."

"Then what happened?" I asked.

"The cops laughed and called an ambulance. They beat up anybody who pulls a gun on them, too. I bet that guy had a long rap sheet. The police probably knew him better than I did."

LuAnn started making chili to put on fry bread for Navajo tacos.

Bob told other stories about the apartment building. He said that he might have another vacancy soon because one of the tenants threatened another with a knife in the parking lot and the police arrested him.

"Do they complain to you about each other?" I asked.

"They bitch about everything all the time. Scumbags and nutcases. Most of the tenants have been in the funny farm or the slammer. LuAnn told me you were in the army. So was I. Airborne."

"You like jumping?" I asked.

"Well, the first time I did it, I was so scared I hardly even remember it. People usually like to jump, until they have a hard landing, get stuck in a tree, or fall in a river. After you have a bad experience, you may not like it. I didn't."

"You jump?" Sandy asked. "Like this?" She jumped on the floor.

"He jumped out of airplanes with a parachute," I said.

"Parachute?"

"He's a brave man," I said.

Bob said, "I'll find a video about parachute jumping and show you, Sandy. I have some videos at my place, and you and your mother and I can watch them tomorrow."

"Airborne must be exciting," I said.

"I didn't like the army," he said. "I remember how the master sergeant kept nagging me and telling me I was stupid. I said that I don't think that smart people would jump out of planes. Then he started calling me a stupid smartass."

"I think airborne people are like pilots. They think that a good day to live is a good day to die," I replied.

"That's what our warriors say, Sandy," LuAnn said. "A good day to live is a good day to die. Indians are always good warriors. That's why movies call Indian men braves."

Sandy was quiet and looked puzzled.

"Tomorrow, a movie and popcorn," Bob told her.

We sat down to eat. I loved the Indian food that LuAnn cooked. We settled into an evening of snacks, TV, stories, and jokes. I drank too much to drive home and spent the night on LuAnn's couch.

I dreamed about the army. I was in an unfamiliar place that looked a little like Fort Lee. The colors were being raised, and I stopped on the sidewalk and raised my hand to my heart, touching the jacket of my uniform. The trees were in full leaf, and the sun rising orange behind a bank of clouds. Some civilians rushed by me, on their way to work. When the flag was up, I looked down at the sidewalk, and saw that my shoes were loafers, and I was wearing brown slacks. I wasn't in uniform any more.

CHAPTER 4

KOREAN ZEN

When I woke up Sunday morning, I was hung over and confused. I looked for LuAnn, but she wasn't in the apartment. Sandy came in from the bedroom. "My mother went to Bob's. She said you would watch me."

"Should we go buy some eggs?" LuAnn was so poor that I felt guilty eating her food. Sandy went with me to the grocery store, and then we ate eggs and sweet rolls while watching TV cartoons.

LuAnn came in and asked me if I liked Bob. "He seems very nice," I said.

"I wouldn't say nice, I'd say fun. I haven't had so much fun since we were in high school. If you like, we could share." I wasn't sure if she meant sharing an apartment, sharing Bob, or both.

"I have a job and a boyfriend near where I work," I said to dissuade her from whatever she was proposing.

"A boyfriend you are serious about or just for fun?"

"I'm not sure yet."

"Make sure that he is a fun-loving guy. Bob is the most fun of anybody I ever met. He drinks, and he's crazy, but that's what I like about him. Bring your boyfriend over some evening. We can all get to know each other."

"I'll ask him, and let you know," I said. I hoped Mark wanted to come and visit my friends. I wouldn't want LuAnn to think that I was ashamed of her.

I hurried home to get ready for the art show. Mark arrived right on time. "Did you enjoy your picnic yesterday?" he asked as he sat down on the couch. I was ashamed of having such tacky furniture.

"Not much," I said. "People say the same things over and over. I like seeing my dad, though." I didn't want to tell him about Susie, her kids, and the toy gun. He might think that I quarreled with my family all the time. I did quarrel with them whenever I saw them, but he didn't have to know. "Did you enjoy the nice weather?"

"No, I worked," he said. "I traded shifts with someone who needed Saturday off."

"Do you want to come over some evening this week?" I asked. "I'll cook some chicken."

He said that he would check his schedule, and we went out to his car. As Mark drove, he said that the show would feature some oriental art and a model of a proposed statue. I was surprised when we arrived at an old house in a very old neighborhood that had a sign proclaiming it the Zen Center. Instead of using the front door, we walked through a small garden that was partially open to the sidewalk and partially screened off from the street.

"I guess you're surprised by this," Mark said. "It's Asian sacred art, with a Korean influence. I told you I liked Korea."

In a small lounge beyond the garden, we took seats before a TV screen. I was disappointed to find that the first part of the show was an appeal for money for a gigantic statue of Buddha. The statue would be placed outdoors in an Asian city and be taller than most of the commercial buildings, so that people could be inspired by the statue when they looked at the skyline. Seeing a statue would certainly be more inspiring than looking at the abandoned buildings with broken windows that are common in Detroit. Mark watched the film quietly and politely, in the manner he had assumed at the Friday happy hour when people talked about television shows.

A man led the six of us who had been in the lounge into a large room lined with panels hung with Asian artwork. In the center of the room was a group of tables, and the middle table bore a statue of the Buddha sitting in a chair like a westerner, surrounded by other statues, vases, fabrics, and bowls with crystals in them.

In silence, people walked slowly around the tables, admiring the artifacts. We had walked around the room twice when Mark led me into a small adjoining room. A woman sat on a platform in the pose of the Buddha. She looked like a statue of the Buddha, wearing thick black robes. Mark bent over, and she touched his head with a bell. Although I have reservations about participating in ceremonies I don't understand, I did the same. She nodded at us. She seemed serene.

Some people were sitting on cushions in the back of the room, meditating. "Do you mind if we join them for a few minutes?" Mark whispered. I agreed, and he selected two sets of cushions from a storage trunk and put them on the floor where the other people were sitting. "Just sit as best you can," he said in a low voice. He made a smooth movement of crossing his legs and lowering himself onto a round cushion that sat on a large, flat one. I could tell that he was familiar with the routine here. I scrambled awkwardly to an uncomfortable cross-legged position.

I tried to sit upright like Mark and the others but felt fidgety. This sitting took discipline, evidently. We sat a while, and my legs started getting sore. Mark knew that I was uncomfortable, so we left after ten minutes, headed to his car, and Mark began driving north. "I came here this morning for the service and to help make lunch," Mark said. "I take a class here on Wednesday evenings. I hope you don't mind my springing this on you. The show was a good opportunity to bring you because the public is invited this afternoon, so people come and go as they please."

"I'd never seen anything like it before. I'm curious about the woman who blessed us with a bell. Does she work here?"

"Elizabeth teaches some of the classes. She works in a fruit and vegetable market near here," he answered.

"Does she teach a class you take?" I felt jealous that Mark spent some evenings here but didn't agree to come over to my place on a weeknight when I had invited him for a chicken dinner. I wondered if Elizabeth taught his Wednesday class and felt a pang of jealousy when I imagined that he hadn't immediately accepted my invitation for dinner because he'd rather be with her.

"Yes, she teaches a class for four weeks, and then someone else will teach another. I wanted to show you this place because it is an important part of my life. I went to school, and I joined the army, but I didn't learn how to live or how to understand my own life."

"Do you like the people here?" I asked. "Most of the people are about our own age." I wondered if this would be a good place to make friends.

"They seem to be nice people. Most of them are pretty quiet, and I don't know anyone here very well. If I get more involved in the group, I probably will meet people I like."

"Do you go to churches, too? Do you ever go to Jewish and Christian services?" I asked. "I'm asking because you seemed to know the kids' songs from Protestant churches."

"I go to a church once in a while out of curiosity. Catholics have all kinds of interesting rituals, like confessing your sins. Confessing sins and being absolved of them would be a nice personal ritual to participate in," he said. "Confession would be more meaningful than going to mega-churches where they sell tapes about Jesus wanting you to be rich. New Age religions tell you to align your energy with your wishes, and the world will fulfill your wishes. What if you wish that events in the past hadn't occurred? Buddhism is more practical. Align yourself with the world and be satisfied."

Confessing your sins? "We all wish that some past events hadn't happened," I said. "I could make a long list of past events that I wish hadn't occurred."

"Sometimes I wish that the war hadn't occurred," Mark said. "But that's probably shortsighted."

"Sitting takes discipline, just like the army," I said to fill a long pause.

"We were meditating like the Buddha," he explained. "Meditating does take discipline. The energy is different when more people are meditating, too—more intense, like losing yourself in a crowd."

After another long pause, Mark said. "I joined the army so I could be one in a crowd of other men."

KOREAN ZEN

One in a crowd? I thought for a while before speaking. "Did you often feel lost in a crowd?" I asked. "We were in a crowd when we stood in formation or marched in a parade but not when we did our own job."

"I thought that by becoming a soldier, I would lose myself in terms of my birth identity and find myself in another sense."

"That's too philosophical for me," I said. "You mean, we devote ourselves to a cause much bigger than ourselves, and that's how we learn who we are?"

"Something like that. I thought that I could take 'duty, loyalty, honor' as a motto and somehow transcend my personal problems."

"I bet you were disillusioned," I said. "The army causes more personal problems than it solves. By joining the army, we find ourselves in an alien culture that has different values than the ones of high school, college, or general society. I miss the army, though. It's hard to get used to being a civilian."

I told Mark that LuAnn was my friend from high school, and that she had invited us for dinner next Saturday night. "Would you like going to a powwow?" I asked. "She is Indian, and we go to powwows sometimes."

"A powwow sounds interesting," he said. "It's nice that you still have friends from high school. Will your friend tell tales on you?" He laughed. "I did things in high school that I don't want to admit."

"I have a funny story from grade school," I said. "My father tells it frequently. My dad drove home an old jeep, which he had taken on a mechanic's lien because the owner couldn't pay the repair bill and abandoned it. My mother criticized his taste and said she would never ride in an open vehicle, breathing auto exhaust. We kids wanted to ride in it, though, and we piled in, Carolyn beside me, and Susie on my lap. I liked riding high above the road. I asked dad if jeeps are built in Detroit and said I wanted to build them when I grew up. He told me that the jeep factories were far away.

"Where do they drive jeeps, Daddy?" I had asked. He told me that the army uses them. I asked him where the army was and said that when I grew up, I would go there. Dad tells people that when I was seven years old, I told him that I wanted to be in the army. It was a family joke after I went in the army."

"I don't know any humorous jeep stories," Mark said. "Jeeps are unsafe. I was in a jeep that overturned when a wheel went onto the shoulder of the road."

We pulled into the gravel lot, parked, and began walking slowly on a gravel road that followed the curving river. I wanted to find out more about what he'd said before—"If ever men deserve to die, then we do." I asked, "Were you and Pete in the same unit in Iraq?"

"No, I wasn't in the infantry like Pete. Sometimes I supplied the infantry with information about enemy locations."

"I suppose that analyzing signals and signal noise used your education in physics. I suppose you can't say much about your job either."

"No, except that it is interesting work to do. I liked the work and was glad that I didn't have to spend much of my service close to the front lines. If I had been doing work other than intelligence, I might not have been in the army for eight years."

"I am just surprised that you work in security now, when you used to do technical work."

"I got pretty burned out with signal analysis. I was working constantly—more than sixty hours a week, sometimes. I wanted a job that wasn't as demanding."

"Painting cars is like that—it's not hard and doesn't require your full attention," I said. "I used to listen to music while painting cars. I knew when the job was complete. Nobody died from my mistakes. So, you did some work with the unit Pete was in, when you were in Iraq?"

"I supplied information to a lot of people, and Pete was one. Pete is a good leader. He goes out of his way for people he knows. He tries to help younger officers. He has a few quirks, but he offers a lot to the army. Do you work much with him now?"

"I hardly know him," I said. "I go to his workplace for meetings. Sometimes we attend the same meeting. I was just curious how you got to be such good friends." What had he and Pete done? Maybe Mark just rhymed some phrase, to the old song—if ever men deserved to die, then we did, the words themselves not referring to anything.

"Pete gave me good advice in the army," Mark said. "He told me to get out because I wasn't likely to have a career there. I knew that myself. After four years, I stayed in another four years because I had just gotten a divorce, and I wanted some stability in my life. I owe Pete for advising me not to stay in the army. Also, I have a soft spot for anybody who visits me when I'm in the hospital."

"Did you get a Purple Heart?" I asked, remembering the scar on his arm.

"Yes, I did. I had an encounter with a couple of bullets. I was lucky I didn't get killed."

"How did that happen?"

"My unit got ambushed. It's a long story. Let's just enjoy the outdoors right now."

"I'm sorry that you got hurt at all," I said. "The war is hard to talk about. A lot of things happen that are very hard to assimilate, much less explain to someone else." I put my arm around his waist as we began walking along the wooded road. "Sometimes I get very emotional about my war experiences." Mostly, I wanted to hide them.

I thought of one of the men I had dated in Maryland, who had been injured in a brawl outside a remote guard post in Iraq. He had told me several incomplete versions of the story—first it sounded as though his injury had occurred when a chopper he was in took fire and then it sounded as though his unit's position was attacked. One evening when he had been drinking a lot, he told me that his injury was from a broken liquor bottle he fell on during a drunken free-for-all at the remote post, after the chopper had been damaged. No wonder that he wanted people to think that it was a battle injury.

I felt myself smiling, and to cover it said, "I hear frogs croaking. We're coming up to a pond. Maybe some of my turtle relatives are here." I heard a rustle in the grass; a small snake moved into view. I scanned the ground for toads. Young toads would be venturing out into the open at this time of year. Birds were singing in the trees. "I'm looking for great blue herons," I said. "There's a rookery nearby. Have you ever seen one? They stand three feet tall or more. I got very close to one once. I could have touched him, but he saw me and jumped up on his long legs and took off. His wingspan may have been four feet."

Mark was lost in his reverie. "No, I haven't seen a heron that large," he said. "I would like to see one." We continued down the road to the river, where some men were fishing from the banks.

"When you get quiet like this, what are you thinking of?" I asked.

"Right now I was thinking of the cranes in Korea and how large they are," he said. "They do a mating dance that is indescribable."

"You could share your thoughts about birds with me. I like to see birds, and I have never seen any cranes." I said. "I love seeing the river at different seasons. It gets very full with the snowmelt and sometimes floods the roads, including main roads. I wouldn't eat fish from it, though. They might taste like gasoline or diesel fuel. We're pretty close to the automobile factories." We walked along the river in silence. The river was high this time of year, and the water rushed by so fast that it foamed at the bends.

We walked until it got dark, and then went back to the Mongolian Barbecue to eat. I remembered being with Michael in Washington and celebrating the anniversary of meeting each other. We went to a restaurant that had a group of small dining rooms. The darkly paneled walls of our dining room displayed large paintings in ornate frames, and there were antiques on some shelves. The windows were shrouded in heavy curtains and room was dimly lit, so the waiter put a candle in a jar on our table. We ate steak and lobster tail, with champagne. After Mark and I ate our barbecue dinner, I asked him if he wanted to go somewhere and have a drink.

He replied, "I think I had enough liquor in the army to last me for the rest of my life." I was used to drinking at Tequila Tom's in the evening, but if he didn't want to go out for a drink, that was all right with me. He drove to my apartment.

"Let's watch television," I said. "My favorite show is 'Ice Road Truckers,' but it's not on tonight. What's yours?"

"What's 'Ice Road Truckers' about?" he asked. "I've never seen it."

"It's a male soap opera. Truckers drive heavy trucks loaded with equipment and supplies on a Canadian road made from ice, in the winter. They haul generators, diamond-mining equipment, oil rigs, and other machinery too heavy for a plane. They complain about the cold, and sometimes the road cracks. They make comments about each other like, 'Is Joe man enough to drive the ice road?'"

Mark said, "They create the road by watering the roadway and having it turn into ice? That sounds tricky to drive on. The dialog sounds like the army, but with cold weather instead of hot. You can watch it while you're ironing."

"I'm a civilian now," I said. "I don't iron. When I'm by myself, I do my e-mail on my laptop while watching television. As you said, reality television doesn't take your full attention. What do you like to watch?"

"I don't have a television," he said.

"Your religion doesn't approve of TV?"

"Or any entertainment. Why distract yourself from reality? My reality now is that we are alone. Come over and sit in my lap."

I sat on his lap, and he put his arms around me, pulled me tightly toward him, and began kissing my neck. I let myself relax against him. "You can stop biting your nails, Pam," he said, taking my finger out of my mouth. "You're safe here—you're inside your home."

He shouldn't have to ask for affection again. I kissed him and stroked his hair. Then I licked the scar on his arm. "I like battle scars," I said. I kissed his scar. "This turns me on. I'd like to help you relax," I said. I put my hand in his crotch.

"You're the one who needs to relax," he said. "The muscles are tight on your shoulders." He kissed me.

We went into the bedroom and lay down on my narrow bed.

I was glad we were both home from Iraq. I pictured a bombing attack lighting up the sky. People will die tonight, I thought, but I won't. I'm safe. I would like to be in love again. I would like to love the nice man I'm with.

In the morning, Mark got up early to go home and get ready for work. "What do you dream about at night?" he asked. "You run in your sleep."

"Armored vehicles. The army. Iraq. I dreamed I heard weapons fire. I dreamed I was running."

"Do you still run four miles a day? I guess you can take the woman out of the army, but you can't take the army out of the woman." We started laughing, and he left. I went running before breakfast.

CHAPTER 5

FAMILY AND MICHAEL

Mark called me Monday night. He said he would like to talk about Sunday. He said, "I don't regard sex as just a way to relax after going on a date. Sexual relationships imply a certain commitment. We aren't college students who talk over our dates with our friends and ask their opinion. They may even say, 'I screwed that person, too.'" I was surprised to hear Mark use that kind of language because I'd never heard him swear.

"I don't think this is true-confession time," he said. He probably didn't like me being so forward. Army men pick up whores all over the world, but they feel free to disapprove of a woman's sex life. He continued, "I just want you to know that I respect you. I want to know more about your life."

"That's a gentlemanly thing to say," I said.

Mark asked, "What is your relationship with your family? I find it strange that you are twenty miles from your home but rarely see your sisters." I was sorry that I had told him the story about going to the dentist and got so angry about it.

I said, "I don't feel we have much in common any more. I thought of living somewhere else when I got out of the army. But I had been working with armor in the army, and the work is here." I realized just then that I had wanted to come home and show my family that I was successful.

"I don't enjoy my family a lot, except for dad's relatives. They live on the other side of Michigan, so they don't come to my mother's parties. I get so stressed at the parties that I just want to leave."

"What bothers you when you get together with your relatives?" Mark asked. "I wish I had a big extended family nearby."

"The issue goes way back to my childhood. My mother and her sisters were so glad to see each other that they ignored other people, including us kids. When I was grown up enough to be included, I was painting cars sometimes and was proud of it. My mother's relatives were disappointed. Then I was angry because I thought that painting cars was an accomplishment."

"Did you like painting cars?"

"I liked working in the shop more than doing housework. I've had a chip on my shoulder at family parties ever since. Then I grew up and was an army officer, and my family doesn't like that either."

"You just need to get reacquainted."

"I never feel like making the effort. My relatives ask me questions about the army, to try to show interest in my life, and I don't know what to say. Describe the sound of mortars outside the Green Zone? Talk about watching a bombing raid? Complain about the food in the chow halls?"

"Why not?" Mark asked. "If you talked about the food, the living quarters, and what you did during the day, they would get a picture of your life in Iraq."

"I didn't keep up with what my relatives were doing when I was in college or the army. I don't know what to say to them. When I was in Iraq, I would e-mail my dad at the shop every day that I could, just to tell him I was all right, and he would usually e-mail me back briefly about home, but I didn't always assimilate what he said. I'm not really sure what I owe my family, either. If I understood what my duty to my family is, maybe I could fulfill it."

"Do you tell your parents that you find visiting them stressful? It sounds as though you can't talk to your family about things that are important to you or how you feel about anything. Maybe you can alleviate the stress by going running or by lying down for a while. Your former home isn't really a home if you are just concerned about your duty, whatever that is, and you can't confide in anyone or be tired or unhappy there."

"I didn't think about lying down. It just didn't occur to me. When I go over to LuAnn's place, sometimes I lie down when I'm tired, but I don't do that at home."

"It's strange that you can relax more with your friends than with your family."

"I spent a lot of time with LuAnn's family when I was in school. LuAnn welcomed help with the family chores, and her dad was very accepting of me. The Indian culture usually molds their children by setting an example, not by telling children who they are and what they should do for a living."

"My family was very opinionated about what children should do," Mark said. "My father would take my brother and me to the Army Air and Space Museum in Huntsville. We always had to pay homage to great scientists. My father would tell us that contemporary physicists walk in the steps of scientists like Wernher von Braun, whose desk and personal effects are enshrined in the museum."

"Your family really pushed you boys to be physicists, didn't they?" I asked.

"My father told us that physicists were heroes," Mark answered.

"That's a heavy trip to put on your children," I said. "Do your parents still feel that way?"

"No, I don't think so. We haven't seen each other much in the last few years. I went to see my parents when I got out of the army, but I didn't go to Nevada to visit my brother." I thought, his family doesn't visit him, and mine doesn't visit me.

"I share many good childhood memories with my brother, like going along with his friends to camp out and explore Indian ruins. When I went into the army, he was surprised and didn't approve. My brother made a remark that he knew I liked camping, but that going into the army seemed extreme. My parents were disappointed. So we both disappointed our families."

Mark paused, and then asked, "Who is Michael? You talked about him in your sleep."

I was shocked. "I'm sorry, Mark. He was my fiancé. He was killed in Iraq."

"Pam, I'm sorry. Was that when you were in Iraq, too?"

"No, we had met in Iraq, but he went back before I did. I never quite got over it. I didn't want to get involved with other men in the army because I was afraid that they would get killed, too."

"Feel free to talk about him." Mark said. "Mention him when you're thinking of him. Say that he liked this kind of coffee, or we used to go to that park. Don't avoid talking about him to spare my feelings. After all, I was married, and I talk about Darlene. We never forget our dead, Pam. We just find a way to go on without them."

"He was career army, West Point. Getting married wouldn't change the fact that he died. I'd have the flag from his burial at Arlington, which his parents have." My voice was cracking.

"Pam, I'm coming over, all right? Get out any pictures of you and of him that you would like to show me."

"I'll find my pictures sometime. They're at the bottom of a chest in the closet. I haven't taken them out in a while, and I don't want to now."

"I'll be there in ten minutes," he said.

Mark showed up, looking disheveled. I was amused by the way his hair was growing out and ruffled it. "It's nice of you to come over," I said.

He put his arms around me and held me. We went into the living room.

"Michael died years ago. We met in Iraq, and both of us were stationed in Washington afterward. During that time with him, I was so happy. I didn't know that the life we led together was slipping away. We spent about a year together in Washington, but he wanted to go to Iraq again. As his deployment neared, I held onto every moment we had together. I counted the days until he would get back—until I knew he was never coming back. I used to dream that I would see him again. I would see soldiers who were his size and think they were Michael.

"But when he came back home, he seemed like a different person. He was distant and quieter than he used to be. He was in a hurry to get back to Iraq. We had planned to get married, but now he didn't want to marry until he had taken another tour. It was like he didn't plan for the future any longer. I think he had a premonition that he would die in Iraq and had accepted that he would be killed. I begged him not to go. I'm not a widow. I had never been a wife." I began crying.

I remembered going with Michael to pick up his parents, who had come from Kansas to see him off. Overseas departure was a routine to his mother. She had seen her dad go overseas, her husband, and now her son. "Being an army wife is the hardest job in the world," she said to me after Michael's plane left. She acted as if she was interviewing me for her job, army wife. "We'll help you, of course. Call us whenever you want to."

"Mike," she said to her husband. "Do you want to get a drink while we have some girl talk?" He obligingly went away.

She continued, "I never trouble the men with my problems when they're overseas without me. I don't want them to think that I don't miss them, either. I say that things are okay at home even if they're not. You shouldn't distract them." I could picture her twenty years ago, seeing her husband off and keeping tears from falling, as I was trying to do now. I pictured her younger and thinner, being brave for her kids.

Then she said, "Desert Storm didn't take a long time. The troops have been overseas for years now, so the war will probably be over soon." She spoke as though I had not been in Iraq myself.

I sat dumfounded, as she assessed my qualifications for a military wife, and Michael's wife in particular. Then Mike rejoined us and assessed my education, the kind of living my dad made in the auto body business, and whether a crossed-sword type of military wedding was appropriate when we were—well, living improperly. (He avoided saying "in sin.") Apparently, I could wear white since I hadn't been married before—but people would know, wouldn't they?

I resolved to find a justice of the peace. I'm not sure what Michael would think of being married informally. Our parents could witness. Then we could all have dinner, and the men could talk about baseball or fishing. I took his parents' phone number but never used it. They called me when he was killed in Iraq.

I cried, and Mark held me. "The coffin was closed at his funeral. I never saw his face again after he went back to Iraq. If you know how to deal with death, tell me. I would like to believe that we go to heaven, but I can't seem to. I think we just join the long parade of soldiers buried in the earth, and our bodies fertilize the grass that grows on our graves."

Mark and I lay down on my bed, and he put his arms around me. "I'm sorry, Pam," he said again. After a while, I heard his breathing deepen, and then he fell asleep.

I was glad we were both home from Iraq. I pictured a bombing attack lighting up the sky. People will die tonight, I thought, but I won't. I'm safe. I would like to be in love again. I would like to love the nice man I'm with.

CHAPTER 6

PARTY AT LUANN'S

On our way to LuAnn's apartment on Saturday, Mark and I stopped at the liquor store. I explained that LuAnn liked fortified wine, and I had no idea what Bob drank. I bought some no-name vodka along with the cheap wine. Mark was astonished when I explained that LuAnn would add whatever we brought to the liquor LuAnn already had on hand, probably street wine and cheap whiskey. "Indian style," I said. "Bring your bottle, and we'll pour it in the punch bowl with the rest and see how it comes out. If it tastes bad, add Coke." I bought two big bottles of Coke as well, and some pretzels as a treat for Sandy.

"That seems like a lot of liquor," Mark said. "I won't drink much, and you don't seem to drink much either."

"LuAnn isn't working and gets welfare right now. She doesn't get money, just food stamps and a housing voucher. Either she is spending her food stamps for our dinner, or Bob is paying for the food. If his only job is managing the dumpy apartment building that they live in, he probably doesn't have much money either. We should buy some extra liquor for them, for some other time," I said.

"Do they drink a lot?" he asked.

"LuAnn does. I don't know Bob well," I said. "Sandy is LuAnn's daughter from her former marriage. She's divorced."

Mark and I arrived at LuAnn's to find that she and Bob had been drinking for quite a while. Sandy was in her bedroom reading a book.

"This is Bob," LuAnn said by way of introducing him to Mark. "He's the manager of this apartment complex."

"This is Mark," I said. "He and I both used to be in the army, but we didn't know each other then."

"Hey, I was in the army. Airborne," Bob said.

"Pleased to meet you," Mark said politely. He seemed to be undecided whether to shake hands. He carefully sat down on one of the dilapidated living room chairs.

"Don't spoil your dinner with drinks and snacks," LuAnn said. "We're having chicken and potatoes, with coleslaw, green beans, biscuits, and pie."

"You really went all out," I said, and brought out the liquor. As I expected, there was a punch bowl on the table. LuAnn served us each a drink from it, and then poured in some of the vodka I had brought.

"What's this?" I asked, tasting it.

"Vodka with some blackberry brandy left from last night," she said.

I gave Mark his drink, walked to one of the sagging living room chairs, and sat down.

Bob was sitting on the couch. I noticed he had a tattoo on his forearm. "Is that a turtle?" I asked.

"Yes, part of it is a turtle. The turtle is for Turtle Island, the name that some of the Indian tribes called North America.

So the tattoo is about us. The top part is the Great Spirit. See how the turtle looks up at the Great Spirit? Notice that the colors of directions are wrong on the turtle." Bob pointed out that the turtle's back was divided into four parts, each a different color. "The turtle is looking up at the Great Spirit because the directions are wrong. How can you know which direction to go, if you don't look to God to find out?" Bob said.

"That's really nice," Mark said, going over to admire the tattoo. "Did you design it yourself?"

"Yes. I designed this one, too," Bob said, pointing to a tattoo on his forearm with a design of a frog parachuting. His tattoo story was good, but I wasn't interested in airborne stories, which usually were about heroically jumping into a difficult situation and being rescued.

"Did you like airborne?" Mark asked. "They're pretty gung ho. They don't say 'yes sir,' they say 'airborne.'"

"Jumping was all right until I hit the silk pretty low and broke my leg. Then I didn't want to jump any more. I knew how to weld, and they found a vehicle maintenance job for me until my leg was okay. I managed to talk them into letting me stay in maintenance, until I got out of the army."

"I broke my leg in a jeep accident," Mark said. "I always disliked riding in jeeps afterward. Every time I had to ride in a jeep, I'd try to talk my way out of it."

"You got thrown out of the jeep?" Bob said.

"Yep, that's how jeeps mess up. If one wheel gets onto a different surface than another, they can flip."

"Breaking a leg is quite an experience—you hear somebody screaming and then realize that it's you," Bob said.

"I only heard it for a moment. I hit my head on something on the ground, and I was knocked out or I passed out," Mark said.

"Then you got the morphine shot before you woke up. Lucky you," Bob replied.

They continued with Bob's story of a medical evacuation. Mark said he couldn't remember anything between hearing himself scream and waking up in the hospital. Then they began telling each other military hospital stories. I went to help LuAnn in the kitchen.

I was curious to find out what LuAnn thought of Mark. Not that she was a good judge of male character. Her boyfriends and her ex-husband were evidence of her poor taste in men. Her ex-husband, a cook, changed jobs from one hotel to another, never seeming to improve his position. He also drank a lot. LuAnn claimed he ran around with the waitresses.

"What do you think?" I asked her.

"He seems pretty serious. Can you have fun with him?" she asked. "He doesn't get mean, does he?"

"He hasn't been mean. He's very quiet, though."

"That could be a good thing. Some men talk about themselves all the time, and that gets boring. Does he criticize you?"

"He hasn't yet. I can't stand criticism. I get so much of it when I go home to visit. I would go home more otherwise. That reminds me, how are your dad and brother?"

"My brother is hanging out on the reservation now. I'm surprised because I think it's kind of depressing up there. The reservation is so small, and there wasn't much to do until they built the casino. The weather is very cold in the winter, too. I'm glad my father decided we should leave. I like walking around the neighborhood here and taking the buses to different places. Sandy gets more variety, like visiting the zoo and museums on school trips."

"Does your brother have a love interest on the rez?" I pictured the little boy who was always reading a book.

"Yes, but she wants to move to town."

"I'd like to visit the reservation sometime," I said.

"For what?" LuAnn asked. "You can gamble in Detroit or go to Ontario."

Sandy joined us for dinner. The food was so good that the men kept getting up to serve themselves more from the array set out on the kitchen counters.

"What was a day in the army like?" LuAnn asked.

I answered, "On a base, in the morning, they raise the flag while we pledge allegiance, if we are nearby, and many people run in the morning. We can gather in a group and run for three or four miles. Then we clean up for work."

Mark added, "Then we have regular jobs like office work or maintaining vehicles or police work. People do all kinds of work to keep the base going, just like in a small town. Only we wear uniforms while we work."

"In airborne, we spend a certain amount of time practicing our specialty—parachute jumping, as well as first aid, map reading, and escape techniques," Bob said. "The rest of the time we do miscellaneous work like making inventories of equipment, painting stripes on parking lots, and whatever else needs to be done. Overseas, many soldiers in the airborne spend most of their time guarding buildings."

"An army job is much like a civilian job," I said. "For me, what is different is that now I work on the design of new vehicles that exist only on engineering drawings, but in the army, we had the vehicles, and I was responsible for determining whether they needed repairs or the addition of new equipment. Overseas, we kept adding armor."

"So you walked around the motor pools and bothered people like me," Bob said, and laughed.

"More likely, I examined armor to see if it needed refitting." We both laughed.

"Once in a while we dress up and have a parade," Mark said. "Unless we can beg off, usually by saying our jobs are too important to parade around. Overseas, we rarely have to bother with that kind of thing. Where I last worked in the army, it was so hot much of the year that we might wear T-shirts to work."

The men both got up and helped themselves to a slice of pie.

"Did you go into the army right out of high school?" Mark asked Bob.

"Before I finished," Bob said. "As soon as I was old enough that my mother could sign the papers."

"That must have been planned for a while," Mark said.

"Yes. See, I had this stepsister who was two years older than me. There were five of us kids all together—I mean three of my mom's kids and two of my stepfather's. Well, my stepsister and I liked each other too much. Things happened. So she got sent away to live with her aunt, and I stayed home until I was old enough to go in the army."

"How did you get together in your home?" I asked.

"Our parents both worked. The first time, I was home from school with a sore throat and cough. Julie cut school that afternoon. She surprised me. I mean, I didn't expect things to go so far. Then we found time alone later."

"But you got caught," I said.

"Probably that was a good thing because she could have gotten pregnant."

"So she ended up being banished, and you went into the army. Did you see her when you were on leave from the army?" Mark asked.

"Just a few times, when she visited her dad. See, she was a senior in high school when we got together, so when I went into the Army, Julie had already finished high school, and had a job. Then she got married, so she never came back to live with her dad.

"Julie wanted to get married, more than anything else. We would talk about having an apartment together. She used to tell me about the furniture she liked. We talked about the kitchen table, the curtains. We would have a tablecloth in white and green, and flowers on the dishes."

"That's a sad story," Mark said. "Teenagers in love, but too young."

"Did you get along with your stepfather?" I asked.

"He tried to treat us all equally. He wasn't mean, and he didn't hit me. He and my mom drank a lot, and there was a lot of yelling. Us kids usually did the housework while they were drinking."

"The army must have been hard when you were that young," Mark said.

"I got through. I was real scared at first, but the sergeants seem to be easier on the youngest soldiers." Bob paused for a moment. "I finished school later, though. I got a G.E.D. while I was in the army."

After we ate, Bob invited Mark to join him on his motorcycle for a trip to a couple of strip malls that had pizza parlors. He said that after dinnertime, the pizza parlors threw out pizzas they couldn't deliver, and it was a good time to stock up on food for the next couple of days. "The pizzas are still fresh, and it helps with the grocery bill," Bob said. "I don't make much on this job, and the liquid refreshment gets more expensive all the time."

Mark joined him without reluctance. He said he liked motorcycles and would like to ride around a little. I hadn't expected Mark to participate in a venture that was sleazy, if not sordid.

"I think that Mark's pretty nice," LuAnn said after they left. "Is he fun, too?"

"They're certainly doing some male bonding," I said. "Maybe breaking a leg gives you something in common with other people who have broken a leg."

"I'm glad I never broke my leg, though," LuAnn said. "You should marry him if he asks you. Have a kid, like Sandy. The happiest I've ever been was when Sandy was a baby."

Sandy, hearing her name, came out of the bedroom, where she had retreated after eating. LuAnn said to her, "Don't you think Pam should have a little girl for company?" Sandy sat on LuAnn's lap while LuAnn and I reminisced about high school. LuAnn and I used to snitch beer and cigarettes, and hide behind her dad's garage to indulge ourselves. We thought her father didn't notice. I realize now that he knew about our drinking but was glad that we were drinking where he could watch us, instead of being with other teens in cars.

LuAnn turned on the television for me while she washed the dishes. I volunteered to help, but she said the kitchen was too small. "Some remote military bases have military television," I told her. "It runs infomercials on how to brush your teeth and iron your clothes instead of commercials, along with idiotic statements about turning the water off before you leave home and getting license plates. Usually some old sergeant is demonstrating how to shine your shoes or something. The infomercials are so dumb that they're funnier than the TV shows." I turned the television to the reality show about police chases and arrests that she liked.

The guys came back from dumpster diving with two cold pizzas, a sack of rotting apples, mushrooms, canned vegetables, and some steak that had just passed it sell-by date. Bob rushed to put the steak in LuAnn's refrigerator.

"Hey, Mark, you're not a stuffed shirt, for an officer. I've got some stash under the sofa pillows. Do you want a smoke?" Bob asked. He reached under a sofa cushion, pulled out a baggie of marijuana and began rolling a joint.

LuAnn and I declined the joint, but to my surprise, Mark toked the joint with Bob. "This is pretty good," he said. "I used to smoke some weed like this with a doctor in Iraq."

"You got a friend that's a doctor, and you're smoking instead of using something heavier like painkillers and anesthetic?"

"I'd never admit to shooting up, would I?"

"Mark, I like you. I'll come visit you if you go to jail," Bob offered.

Mark looked surprised. Bob added, "Lots of people will visit you if you're in the hospital but only your best friends will visit you in jail."

"Thank you," Mark said uncertainly. "If you go to jail, I'll visit you, too." I thought that he might be visiting Bob sometime soon.

Mark seemed uneasy, obviously trying to think of something to say. Then he said, slowly, "Most people figure that if you're sick it isn't your fault, but if you go to jail they blame you and forget the good things about you."

Bob said, "And maybe it isn't even your fault you're in jail. Some guy down at the pool hall insulted the girl I was seeing before LuAnn. So he started it. Now, what's a man going to do—defend his woman or let somebody bad-mouth her? The charge I got was assault and battery, but they reduced it to making a public disturbance."

PARTY AT LUANN'S

"That's tough luck, anyway," Mark said. "A man should stand up for his woman." The conversation gave me a bad feeling, and I wondered if Mark hung out in tough bars on weeknights. I hoped that he was just being friendly to Bob.

Bob then explained that he was divorced, and his wife left him because he went to jail for driving under the influence. He said that his wife had been the sexiest woman he had ever met and that the way she moved was enchanting. He repeated the word *enchanting*. He added that his wife was nice, too, like LuAnn.

"Tell them how much your wife weighed," LuAnn said.

"She weighed a little over three hundred pounds, and she was soft like a pillow. She always wore stretch slacks, and she looked so nice." I suppressed a laugh. I was picturing her rolls of fat encased in stretch slacks and wobbling as she waddled around.

"She had to be respectable since she worked as a clerk for the motor vehicle department, and they don't like their employees married to somebody who's done time."

"I got arrested on a DUI once," Mark said. "I told the police that I had to get back to the base. The police officers had all been in the service, and after I sobered up in the jail, they decided not to charge me. I was lucky." I was appalled that Mark had spent a night in jail. He could have gotten in trouble from the army for being arrested on a DUI. A sergeant I knew got a big fine from the army for getting arrested for drunk driving. I'd also heard that civil offenses can appear on your annual fitness report.

"I'm divorced, too," Mark said. "She cheated on me."

"That's tough. I say, when they cheat, give them a good whipping on the ass, so when they sit down they remember who it belongs to," Bob said. The rest of us laughed.

"I was in the hospital when she split," Mark said.

"Bitch. You're better off without her."

I thought that I might never have known these things about Mark if liquor hadn't penetrated his reserve.

Bob said that civilian time was easier to do than military time and told us that the brig at Fort Campbell "smelled like a troop carrier that guys were puking in." Mark looked like he was enjoying himself immensely, letting go of the polite and reserved behavior I had seen until now.

"You got any kids, Mark?" Bob asked. "I got two stepdaughters, but no kids of my own."

"No, I don't. Do you still see the kids now that you and their mother got a divorce?"

"Yes, once in a while. Mostly I take them for fast food because their mother doesn't have any use for me. Kids are fun. Have some kids or marry somebody who has some. You get some kids, and you wonder what you did before you had them."

The two men continued drinking and talking; LuAnn put Sandy to bed and got ready for bed herself. "Got a couple of blankets?" I asked. "I'll curl up on the floor. There's no use breaking up the good time the boys are having—unless you want them to go home now."

"Stay here for a while," she said. "It's late, and you would have to drive home at night after drinking." I often drove after drinking when coming home from Tequila Tom's Tavern, but I didn't want to tell her.

"I'm a soldier, and I can sleep anywhere and with my boots on," I said. "I mean, I used to be a soldier." I lay down on the floor on my back and fell asleep right away, although I slept lightly and woke often to change my position on the hard floor.

Later, I heard the sound of vomiting. LuAnn got up and went into the bathroom; Sandy joined her until LuAnn sent her back to bed. I went to the bathroom and saw Bob retching near the toilet and Mark lying on the bathroom floor in a pool of vomit, soaked with sweat. I hadn't drunk until I vomited since I was at the university. LuAnn coolly pulled a mop out of the bathroom closet and began cleaning up the floor. She got a bucket, filled it with water, doused both of the guys, and mopped again. "Here's an example of male bonding," I said. "Puke on the floor and lie in the other's vomit. This is fraternization, too." I started laughing.

"What's fraternization?' LuAnn asked.

"Fraternization is when officers and enlisted men socialize in the army."

"Pretty close socializing—vomiting on each other," she said, and began laughing while rinsing out the floor mop. "The men can stay in the bathroom," she added. "I don't want them going back into the living room and getting puke on the furniture."

"You seem pretty experienced at cleaning up vomit," I commented.

"It happens a lot here," she said. "Mostly, it's my friends. I don't drink as bad as I used to. My kid throws up sometimes, too. She will eat too much or eat food that doesn't agree with her. With kids, though, they often don't make it to the bathroom and puke on their clothes. That's worse, but there is less of it."

A little later, Bob got up. LuAnn woke me up, and we walked him down to his apartment, which was exceptionally filthy. Old pizza boxes and tins of beans littered the counters and table, and there were empty beer bottles everywhere. Sacks of garbage stood by the sink, which was full of dirty dishes and drinking glasses. I was sure LuAnn and Bob spent their time in her apartment because she was too fastidious to deal with this mess and wouldn't want to clean it up.

LuAnn poured another bucket of water on Mark and said "Rise and shine. It's morning." The sun was coming up behind the clouds, outlining the skyscrapers downtown.

Mark's face was pale as snow, and he kept saying that he was sorry while holding his head. His legs were wobbly. We walked with him down to the car and put him in the passenger seat.

Mark put his head against the window of the passenger seat as I drove. He repeated that he was sorry. I told him that LuAnn and Bob were used to people drinking too much and that it didn't bother them. Finally, he quieted down. I didn't know if he had fallen asleep or passed out.

I realized that I didn't know Mark's address, just the cross streets he lived near, so I had to wake him up to find out. I was surprised at the shabby old brick apartment building that he lived in. His apartment was a basement-like place, with the windows looking out on the parking lot. It was very small, an efficiency apartment with a partition making a bedroom in one corner.

"Do you want to take a shower?" I asked. "Where do you keep your pajamas?"

"I feel pretty sick," he said. I helped him into the shower stall, and told him to throw his clothes onto the bathroom floor. Then I turned the cold water on.

"Nice cold water," I said. "Should sober you up."

I looked in the bedroom, which contained a mattress on the floor, a dresser, and pictures on the wall and partitions. One unusual picture was a painting mounted on a scroll made of fabric scraps. Ornamental bowls, bells, pictures, and odd objects were on the dresser top.

I opened the top drawer of the dresser, and found pajamas right beneath his underwear. After putting the clothing in the bathroom, I took the opportunity to snoop in his apartment. The room contained a futon on a frame, two bookcases, a small kitchen table with two chairs, an end table, and two floor lamps. I was surprised that a bowl of fresh flowers was on top of the shorter bookcase. The kitchenette was spotless.

Mark finished showering and dived into bed. I came and sat beside him.

"I need to apologize to your friends," he said. "I made such a fool of myself last night."

"LuAnn won't dislike you for that," I said.

"How can I tell her I'm sorry?" he asked.

"Send her flowers," I suggested.

"I think you should go home," he said. "I just want to sleep it off." He pressed his face into the pillowcase.

I caressed the scar on his arm. Then I pulled his T-shirt up and began rubbing his back. I felt a scar on his shoulder blade. "I love war scars," I said.

"Those scars aren't from the war. They are from the jeep accident I talked about with Bob," he said. "I had a broken leg, but my arm was broken, too. That scar on my upper arm is from the bone pushing through the skin. I'm glad I was unconscious when it happened."

"That must have hurt. I guess you were laid up for a while." How did he get the Purple Heart? I had assumed that the scar on his arm was from a wound he received in the war.

"I've got a headache, and I don't feel like talking more now," Mark said. "I sound like a female begging off sex. Not now, I have a headache."

"I don't use that one," I said, and laughed. "They don't care if you have a headache, since they aren't fucking your head. I tell them that I have a stomachache and I feel like I'm going to vomit."

"I think I might vomit, too," Mark said. "I have a headache and a stomachache, and I think I'm going to vomit."

"I hate to leave you when you are so sick," I said. He was shivering, so I pulled the blanket from the foot of the mattress around him. Then I went into the living room area. I didn't want to abandon him when he was sick like his ex-wife did.

CHAPTER 7

MARK'S STORY

I examined Mark's bookcases. The smaller bookcase, with the flowers and mementos on its top, held books about religions. The taller bookcase held books on physics and astronomy, a few reference books, military history books, and photography books. I looked for some military memoirs but didn't find any. I used to like books about military operations in remote parts of the world.

I found an album of photographs Mark had from the army, mostly pictures of groups of soldiers standing against buildings. In one picture, Mark was in a group of men in formation on tarmac. They were wearing olive T-shirts, so it must have been taken in the heat. I was surprised at how tough he looked, with his square jaw accented by the chinstrap on his helmet. He looked strong and resolute. I looked at the picture for a while and put the album back. If I got a picture of him, I would like that one.

I found an astronomy book with many pictures. I made some tea and sat on the couch with the book. I was reading when Mark got out of bed. He came into the living room and said, "You're still here. I thought that you would have left." He poured himself a glass of water and drank it.

"I wanted to be here to help you if you needed something," I said. "Also, you were talking about things last night that I am curious about. You said your wife walked out on you when you were in the hospital."

He sat beside me. "Here's how you could really help. I need to sleep some more, but why don't you go home and start your day—go running or whatever. Come back with some Asian takeout for dinner, so I won't have to cook."

I walked with him back to bed. He buried his face in the pillow, and I covered him up again.

My apartment was about two miles away, a short run, but I didn't have my running shoes with me. The day was beautiful, sunny, and not too hot. Many houses had flowers in their yards, and I stopped by a yard with a huge, fragrant lilac bush in bloom. Another house had a honeysuckle hedge.

The street was echoing with birdsong. I had often run on this street before, but I had never seen so many birds. I saw a robin with three chicks. She gave a worm to one, but its sibling grabbed the worm out of its mouth. The mom grabbed the worm back and gave it to the first. Then she took a small item, like a seed, and stuffed it into the mouth of the thief. She began sounding the ground for more worms. The robin is like my mom, I thought. She had three chicks, and when she had only one worm, so she tried to feed the chick who needed the food the most. One chick wasn't fed, just as Carolyn, my middle sister, was ignored.

When I went back at dinnertime, Mark greeted me at the door with a hug and a kiss on my cheek. With the Chinese takeout in one hand, I put my other arm around him. He seemed vulnerable in his T-shirt and old jeans. I had brought steamed chicken and vegetables, with the containers of sauce on the side. I shouldn't have chosen garlic sauce when I was anticipating romance.

"I never asked you how you feel today, Pam," he said. "I was too caught up in my hangover, and I apologize."

"I feel all right," I said, removing the cartons from the bag. "I'm just hungry."

"I liked your friends very much. Write down LuAnn's address so I can send flowers and an apology for making a fool of myself."

We sat down to eat. "I looked at some of your books and noticed your album this morning. I hope you don't mind. I was struck by a picture of you in formation in a T-shirt. I could tell the person was you, but in the picture, you didn't look like you do now."

"Sounds like Fort Huachuca, down in Sierra Vista. I have some early morning pictures—camouflage in the morning chill, and T-shirts later in the day because of the heat."

"You looked very firm and decisive. The helmet and T-shirt are an odd, striking combination."

"I was hot and frustrated during that picture shoot. First they took some pictures without film in the camera, and we had to stand around sweating in the heat while someone got the film. Typical army hurry up-and-wait scenario. I was glad the helmet partly shaded my face. I was trying to distract myself by remembering music and playing it in my mind."

"The picture is interesting, though. Like you but not quite like you."

"I doubt if people I worked with remember me looking that way—bored and frustrated and angry. Most people just look spaced out in that picture, but some of them halfway smiled."

MARK'S STORY

"What kind of music do you imagine hearing?"

"German classical music composers—the music I grew up with."

"I used to think of how cameras worked so I'd look serious and not distracted," I said.

We continued eating. "I was surprised when you told Bob you would visit him in jail. I thought that I would burst out laughing, but he was serious," I said.

"I was at a loss for words, and I gave him such a stupid answer. With the story he told me about fighting in a bar, I think he might really end up in jail. I wonder what he did to end up in the brig at a Special Forces base."

"His analogy about the brig smelling like vomit in a troop carrier nearly set me off. I haven't heard anything so funny in a long time."

"Bob is a good-hearted person," Mark said. "He's had a rough life and has plenty he could complain about, but instead he talks mostly about his good times with his former wife, stepchildren, and first girlfriend. Are LuAnn and Bob your best friends here? Their life is so different from yours that I wonder what you find to talk about."

"I feel comfortable with LuAnn. We talk about everyday things like food. We watch reality television programs, like the one with police chases. I think her life is boring, but she has enthusiasm for it."

I hesitated and then said, "I don't know many women since I work mostly with men. Being a civilian isn't like being in the army, where you belong to a group of people and can go to the Officers' Club in the evening and strike up a conversation with anyone."

"For a while, I used to go to the Officers' Club most evenings," Mark said. "I would always see people I knew. As civilians, we have to find other things to do in our spare time."

After eating, he steered me to the couch and pulled me onto his lap. "I appreciate your sympathy about my accident, but you don't need to keep caressing my scar," he said. "It's a little disconcerting. I don't think about the jeep accident much any more. The accident happened five years ago, and many other things have occurred in my life since then. For example, getting divorced, leaving Korea, and being deployed to Iraq."

I had never thought to ask him if the scar still hurt. It might be tender like a bruise.

Mark continued, "If I hadn't been in the jeep accident, my life would have been so different that I can't imagine what I would be doing now or what I would be like. Darlene and I would have been divorced anyway, but I probably wouldn't have stayed in the army as long. My relationship with my parents would be different. I might not be involved in my church now. The Zen Center I attend is Korean, and my accident happened in Korea. Since I don't know what my life would be like without the accident, I can't even say that I wish it hadn't happened.

"Recovering from the accident was the first time in my adult life when I didn't have to accomplish anything. I didn't even have to make decisions about everyday things like what to eat or when to go to the gym. I had time to think about my life and decide what I really wanted. I was afraid that the injury to my arm was so serious that I wouldn't be able to stay in the army. Facing the possibility of being discharged from the Army was worse than losing Darlene had been. I was afraid that I would lose everything. Darlene had just had a miscarriage. I might be losing my health, my marriage, parenthood, and the army, and the only thing I had a chance to keep was the army. I had never wanted anything as much as I wanted to stay in the army. I think they only kept me because I was in intelligence. If I had been in the infantry, I probably would have been discharged because my shooting is impaired.

"I had a lot of time to meditate. I had been going to a Korean Zen Center sometimes. A Korean working at the base had told me that another American, Gary, was studying at the Zen Center. He introduced me to Gary, who said he would like to eat with me at the base sometimes because he had developed stomach problems from eating Korean food. Gary had been in the army, too. When I was in the hospital, he used to come and visit me often. We'd chat and he'd read Zen books to me. He said that he had turned visiting me into part of his own religious practice. We would talk about what he read, and sometimes I would ask him to read the same chapter several times because the painkillers I was taking made it hard to concentrate.

"He showed me more about meditation. Sometimes he would do his own meditation practice, especially if I didn't feel well enough to talk. After an operation, I would be out of it for a couple of days, and sometimes he fed me. The world seemed to compress when I was ill, and I spent hours looking at the ceiling."

"I don't understand the chronology," I said.

Mark said, "After the accident, I woke up in intensive care. My arm and shoulder were immobilized for about two months. Since the bone pushed through the skin in my arm, the bone had to be set surgically with metal pins. My shoulder was too badly injured to allow arm movement. My right leg had been broken, too, but the fracture wasn't complex.

"I had six operations on my arm and two on my shoulder. After I was out of the hospital, I still needed more surgery on my arm. My recovery took a long time. I was in the hospital about four months, had some rehabilitation so that I could walk again, and then had more rehab as an outpatient. I didn't work again for about seven months.

"The world seems to narrow down when you are ill or wounded. Looking from the outside, having a serious injury seems all negative, painful, frustrating, and boring. However, when I was ill, I was so absorbed in myself that my life seemed filled with occurrences. Instead of going to work and relating to my coworkers, I waited for people to do things for me, talk to me, or try to entertain me. Instead of thinking about eating steak, I would wonder if lunch would include applesauce. Instead of planning to go to the gym, I would think about being moved in bed. The horizon was narrower, but the subject of thought was similar—me. It was all what I felt, what I wanted, and what I didn't want.

"Bad things like operations happen, and good things like making friends happen. Life went on, and I slept, ate, and related to people. Sleeping became time-consuming, like having a job. Normal life is on a double cycle—how do I feel physically and how do I feel emotionally. Being hospitalized adds a third cycle because the drugs divide the day into periods of sleeping time, pain time, alert time.

"When I was taking the painkillers, I didn't feel like myself. When I tried to get in touch with myself, I couldn't find myself—the play of emotion and sensing that I call my personality. I lost contact with the normal pattern of my thoughts and feelings.

"My personality must be like a musical chord that I play, which I recognize as myself. The keys are for anger, happiness, sadness, attraction, aggression, guilt, jealousy, elation, indifference, or anything else that I normally feel. Taking drugs such as painkillers moved the balance between emotional tones, so that I felt so unlike myself that I couldn't recognize myself as me."

"I know what you mean," I said. "There is a set of feelings that I know myself by—excitement, sometimes anxiety, and flashes of anger. I am used to the notes. I don't like to change the chord, and that's the reason I rarely drink alcohol or smoke dope. Drinking and drugs change my emotional picture, and then I don't think clearly and feel vulnerable."

Mark continued, "I didn't feel unhappy all the time that I was ill, but I didn't feel like myself. After I left the hospital, I went home to Darlene. She had already said that she wanted a divorce. Everybody who gets married figures their marriage will last. Getting a divorce is putting aside a shared dream. Her wanting to leave me wasn't a shock. The fact that she was seeing another man wasn't even a shock, but I thought her timing was tasteless.

"She didn't want to touch me. She didn't want to help me, cook for me, do my laundry, or help me dress. My arm was still in a cast that included my shoulder and went down over my ribs, and I couldn't use my right arm and could barely use my hand. All I could do was get out of bed by leaning on something with my left arm. I could limp over to the table and eat something, and I could get back in bed for a nap.

"When I went back to work, with my arm not completely healed, my coworkers would help me with my jacket or cut up food for me and never made a big deal of it. Darlene had not been able to bring herself to do simple things for me without distaste. A medic friend of mine said that many military marriages sour fast if the man gets injured. Some army wives want a strong man to protect them. She might not be able to deal with her husband needing help. So I'm not alone on being deserted when disabled. Darlene and I weren't getting along before that, either. She didn't like army bases, particularly the housing."

"You said that she had wanted a divorce before."

"Yes, but I think she was just threatening me to try to change our life together. My accident was the last straw. The accident could have brought us closer, but she acted as though being near me would give her a disfiguring disease or bring her bad luck. She never anticipated anything I needed, and if I asked her to do anything for me, she resented it. When Darlene left, I went back to my parents' for the rest of the rehab and physical therapy. My mother would take me to the Veterans Administration hospital. Being back in New Mexico was much better for me physically, but I was uncomfortable with it psychologically. I didn't like being dependent on my parents."

"Maybe your parents liked having you at home because you had been away at college and then in the army, and you were married, and they hadn't gotten to know what you were like as an adult."

"I think they regarded me almost as a stranger," Mark said. "I felt embarrassed about going back to my parents' because I was injured. I wasn't used to being around civilians, either. I remember my father getting me on a plane to Albuquerque. I was in a wheelchair and wearing camouflage. I was tired from riding in the car and just wanted to sleep.

"We had first-class seats, and I put my head against the window to rest. My dad explained to anyone who asked, 'He has a broken arm and leg, and he took some pain medication. He wants to sleep a little while.' I felt almost embarrassed by having my injuries.

"My parents went out of their way to help me. I remember how my father would buy magazines that he thought I might like and bring home books and movies. I don't think he enjoyed watching movies, but he wanted to keep me company. I had more rehab in New Mexico. Rehab is very painful, and I wasn't allowed to take a lot of pain medication during it, either.

"My parents didn't want me to stay in the army. They had an attitude like 'Okay, you were in the army and look what happened. Now that you've learned your lesson, you can get a real job.' I told them that if I signed up again, I would have convenient medical treatment for my arm. I didn't want my parents controlling my life. I got my wish and was able to stay in the army. After I got better, I was reassigned to Washington, DC, to work and had some follow-up surgery on my arm."

"Your arm wasn't healed yet when you started work?" I asked.

"I could write and type by resting my elbow on my desk, but the muscles in my shoulder and upper arm weren't strong—they still aren't normal. I don't want to sound like I'm whining about being injured. The accident had to happen for me to be myself. So, I was injured and seriously ill for nearly a year, five years ago, but now I am a healthy, strong former soldier who was running miles in combat boots every day until recently. Perhaps you keep touching my scar because you have some bad experiences you want to tell me about, Pam. Do you have an injury story?"

I said, "My only injury was trivial. I got a three-stitch cut on my leg from debris kicked up on a testing range. The only thing bad was the horrible doctor who said women shouldn't be there anyway and I was lucky it didn't hurt my face. I think your wife had poor timing. There was something mean about leaving you when you were sick. She should have known that being in the army has some risks attached."

"Unfortunately, my right arm lacks muscle tone, which prevents me from picking you up and carrying you into the next room. I assume that you don't want to go home tonight. It's dark out, and you're better off here. It's cold out, and I'll keep you warm."

His bed had clean sheets that were surprisingly printed with flowers. I lay down on my back, and Mark lay down next to me. I moved on top of him and kissed the scar on his right arm, forgetting that he had told me not to touch the scar.

"That must be unpleasant, since I have been sweating," he said.

"You smell like you've just started a morning run," I said, moving my head to smell his body odor.

"You smell like saltwater—like the sea," he said and licked my armpit. "You taste like it too."

I was on my back, spreading my legs, holding him, and pulling him tightly on top of me. He backed off for a moment and put on a condom.

His bed was slightly lumpy. I remembered the star-filled night sky of Iraq lit up by a bombing raid. I sat in a ditch by the vehicle compound to watch it, and a sergeant joined me. I was excited, exhilarated. I felt like the world was ending, and I wanted one more moment of pleasure at the end of the world—the last day I would live. I was sweating from the desert heat. As the fireworks continued, I lay in the ditch and pulled the pants of my uniform down. We made love in the ditch with the bombs whistling through the night sky and blossoming into fireworks in the distance.

CHAPTER 8

LAKE AND CANOEING

Mark came to my apartment Friday evening after dinnertime. We decided to go to a park Saturday, and go hiking and canoeing. I wanted to begin Saturday morning with a run, as usual. Mark had decided to join me and was wearing new running shoes. He said that he hadn't run distances since he left the army.

We kept in pace for the first mile, and then he slowed down, so I did, too. Michael had always been faster than me. He would pull ahead and then jog in place until I caught up, laughing and beckoning to me. Mark was not as tall as Michael had been, and had a shorter stride. "What do you miss about the army?" I asked, as we slowed to a pace at which we could talk.

"I don't miss running in the morning or shining my brass. I miss the camaraderie. The people I work with don't even eat lunch together. Most of them get cafeteria food and eat at their desks."

I added, "I like the people I work with, but we aren't really friends either. Some of the people obviously don't like each other. The other day, my boss had a visitor from a division of our company located in another city. He invited one of my coworkers to join them for lunch, and he refused with the excuse that his wife had packed his favorite sandwich for him! They must have quite a history of disagreements and resentment.

"Most of my coworkers are much older than I am, and many are retired from the army. There are a few civil servants at the Tank Command my age or younger, but I only go over there once or twice a week and haven't gotten to know people well."

"The people where I work have been together for years, so it's different from the army, where people get moved around a lot," Mark said. "The long-term employees are less interested in assimilating new people."

"Yes, and that's a big difference," I agreed. "The people I work with sometimes act like a new person is not there to help get the work done, but to take something away from them."

After running, we drove to the large metropark to the north. Mark had said that he wanted to visit a lake, and the metropark had a large one. We started out by driving around the lake, which was bigger than I remembered. I didn't want to walk six miles around it on a pathway shared with bicycles since we had already run two miles and the day was getting hot. I suggested walking on a shorter trail near the nature center.

"I would have liked the army better if the bases were in nice settings like this," Mark said, as we began our walk. "I like being out in nature with the plants and little animals all around."

"I was fascinated by the desert when I first went to Iraq because of the vistas and the starry sky. Soon I missed the trees and lakes, and wanted to live somewhere green again, like here or Maryland," I said.

"Step off the path here, and you're probably disturbing some creature's home," Mark said. "Imagine what life here would be like for an insect—or an earthworm." We were watching a bird pull an earthworm out of the ground. "Desert life is sparse, and it's more evident at night, when it's cool." We walked quietly, stopping to admire toads and flowers, listening to the birds calling around us. I showed Mark deer tracks, and we looked for deer but didn't see any.

Mark had never been in a canoe before we rented one that day. I told him that getting into the canoe was the time it was most likely to tip. Mark walked down the center acrobatically, holding his arms out for balance and barely rocking the canoe. I pushed the canoe off and hopped in the back, in the steering position. A typical novice, Mark tried to paddle too hard. Watching him paddle absorbed me because the difference in strength between his right arm and his left was noticeable as he paddled; it was almost like a limp.

"We're required to wear life jackets, but I take mine off as soon as possible," I said. "It's too hot today, and I'm a good swimmer. You swim, don't you?"

"Yes—in swimming pools," Mark said. "I've never swum in water this dark." I was curious about his preferred swimming style because his swimming strokes would be uneven.

We watched the shore birds. The ducklings and goslings were out of their shells now. "Little ducklings are cute, but the mortality rate is so high," I said. "Ducks hatch tremendous broods, eight or even twelve ducklings, and most of them don't survive. See how the mothers have only three to six ducklings with them? One mother duck seems to have only a single hatchling left."

We got close to shore to watch a group of ducks. I wasn't watching the water closely, and the canoe hit a partly submerged tree. Mark dropped his paddle in the water and we watched for a moment as it drifted away from the boat. "I feel so stupid," he said, as I dropped my paddle on the canoe bottom and stood up. I dove into the water from the side of the canoe away from the shore, and the force of my dive pushed the canoe further into the tree. The cold water took my breath away, and I felt myself gasping for air for a moment—the danger time when even experienced swimmers can drown. Without current, the paddle hadn't drifted far. I grabbed the paddle and held it with both hands in front of me, kicking my feet to swim back toward the canoe.

"I can't get into the canoe from the water," I said. "I'll tow the canoe." I swam about fifteen feet toward an open space on the shore and then walked the canoe to the muddy bank.

"I don't know what to say," Mark said, as he got out of the canoe. "I feel so inept."

"Don't be so serious. That was fun. I was concerned for a moment because I thought that the canoe might overturn when I dove in, but swimming was exciting. Towing the canoe was harder than I expected because the bottom of the lake was so rough on my feet."

"I felt stupid for dropping the paddle. You were in the water so quickly that we didn't have time to discuss what to do."

"I wasn't in danger. I wouldn't be swept away by the current because there isn't any current."

"You could have gotten caught on the tree," he said. "Do you want to go home and get dry? We're not in the army, where we wore wet clothes after it rained."

"I hated running in the rain," I said. "But it's sunny today, and my clothes will dry. Let's paddle farther but watch more closely for obstructions and snags. Once I was with a friend on a river, and we overturned. We had to go five miles to the pickup point, against a headwind. I was cold then, and I'm not cold now."

He pulled off his shirt. "At least, put on a dry shirt. Only, it's a little used."

I sniffed it. "It just smells like you," I said.

"You must have a strange olfactory sense," Mark said. "You don't seem to object to male sweat."

"Women who do shouldn't be in vehicles in Iraq with men or running in the morning with them, either. Sometimes I thought I should bring some air freshener into a vehicle, though." I laughed. "Especially in the heat of Iraq."

Mark stood silently as I took my blouse off, wrung it out, and put his shirt on. I realized that I had hurt his pride. Men like to think that they take action quickly and protect women. "I'm just impulsive," I explained. "Decisive. I've been in canoes more than you have, that's all."

"Pam," he said, and pulled me toward him. "If there had been danger, you would have confronted it." He kissed me. I was excited from the dive and swim and the exertion, and I felt my excitement become exhilaration and then sexual desire. I looked for a secluded spot where we would have some cover and not be visible from either the lake or the bike path to have sex outside. "We could lie down in the grass behind those bushes for a while and celebrate our good fortune in not overturning."

"I don't have a taste for public sex," he said. "This is a crowded park, and we're a dozen yards from the bike path. A family with kids could walk by here and see us."

"I've only seen a few people on the shore, so the probability that somebody walks by is low."

"My gosh," Mark said. "Probability. You sound like an engineer." We launched the canoe again and paddled farther along the shoreline, looking for birds and animals. Little fish sometimes swam near us. I looked for turtles whenever there were fallen logs.

After leaving the park, we went to my apartment, so I could change clothes. Mark put a bath towel in the oven while I was showering and then joined me in the shower. I was amused. "I've heard that some people have sex standing up," I said. "Should we try?" Having sex in the shower would be exciting.

Mark said, "That sounds like something done in an alley for cash."

"After drinking fortified wine out of the bottle," I said.

"I've never tasted fortified wine," he said. He sounded critical.

"We may have had some at Bob and LuAnn's."

He brought me the hot towel from the oven, "So you won't get chilled." Mark dried off with a different towel. "Keep the warm one and wrap it around you," he said. "That water must have been cold."

"How did you think of warming up this big beach towel?" I asked, putting the towel around me.

"When I've had anesthetic, I would wake up cold and was given heated blankets so I got warm faster. You'd know if you had ever had general anesthesia."

"Mark, you take everything so seriously, like you have to fix everything as soon as it breaks. Then, if you don't fix it, you probably beat yourself up for being derelict in your duty."

"Actually, I'm quite the opposite. I used to catch myself begging off on things that needed to be done, with whatever excuse I could find."

"That's a frequent behavioral pattern in the army," I said. "When trips to other bases need to be made, the person picked to go says he's coming down with flu."

"Especially if the trip is to Fort Huachuca in Sierra Vista," Mark said.

We went into the bedroom. I was still excited about diving into the water. I relived the feeling of anxiety, combined with the excitement of the dive and the exhilaration of the cold water, and the satisfied feeling as I grasped the paddle. I had been full of myself, pleased. I kept running the vision in my mind, diving, the water, the way I felt—the fear, resolve, excitement, and exhilaration. We had sex that was like a bomb explosion inside me.

"We should either swim in cold water more often or go canoeing more often," Mark said. "This was really special."

I wanted pizza for dinner, and he phoned for a pizza delivery. "Would you like dinner in bed?" Mark asked. "I'll serve pizza and water."

"Let's get fancy," I said. "Iced tea." I was going to let Mark indulge me tonight.

Mark ate very little pizza. He didn't seem to like it. "What's your favorite food?" I asked.

"Steak, spatzle, and sauerkraut," he answered. "I can make spatzle sometime, if you would like."

"I don't know what that is," I said. "I didn't know that you cooked exotic food."

"Spatzle is homemade noodles that are served with dinner in Germany," he answered. "You can get them in restaurants over there."

"Did you eat off the base often?" I asked.

"No, but my mother cooked central European food at home. I used to cook often when Darlene was pregnant. Were you homesick when you first went to college? I missed the food at home more than anything else."

"Not really," I said. "When I went to college, I was busy with my new surroundings and didn't think about home much. I guess that I was lucky. Some of my roommates and friends in college and the officers' quarters called their parents every day and told me that they dreamed of their home at night. Sometimes now I dream that I am still in the army. I dream that I am lying on my bunk, still dressed after work, and somebody in the hall calls out, 'anyone for chow?' I always had people to eat with in the army. Even if I went to the Officers' Club myself, I usually would see someone I know to eat with."

"Do you often eat alone now?" Mark asked.

"Almost always."

"You could find somebody to eat lunch with. If I see people I've met eating in the cafeteria, I join them. It's one way of getting acquainted."

"We don't have a cafeteria. There is a vending area but no tables."

"Maybe you would like a bigger company better. Where I work has a cafeteria, and some group activities like bowling teams," Mark said.

"I would like to join company sports teams. I wish the company I work for had organized activities for employees. However, I tell myself that any job provides some things and not others. I like the work. I don't have much to complain about. Being disappointed about lunch companions isn't as bad as disliking the work. As an engineer, the main part of our job is between us and the equipment, and the mind puzzles that engineering presents."

"Not socializing at work is a good reason to connect more with your extended family," Mark said.

"How to find a way to like being with my relatives is the question. When I was a little kid, I mostly played with my cousins when our family was together. We played games, went to parks, or colored in coloring books. Then I was away so much and came back as an adult. How do I find a way to like family parties as an adult instead of regarding them as a social obligation? That's my challenge. My family doesn't seem to accept me as an adult who has a different set of experiences than they have. When I am with them, I mostly want to get away. Anyway, connecting more with my family would probably mean helping more—like babysitting for my sisters."

"You might enjoy the children, if you knew them better," Mark said.

"I might, or I might be resentful. I might be giving up time I could use to do something I enjoy like going hiking or canoeing. Let's canoe on a river sometime. Dealing with current is harder but more fun. After we get more experience canoeing together, we can run a river with rapids."

"I liked canoeing," he said. "Next time I'm sure I'll do better."

"I'm not assessing your canoeing ability," I said. "Canoeing is just a way to see the water and the shoreline. In the army, we were all too competitive. Now, no one does the same job that I do, usually no one runs with me, and there is no one to compete with."

"Its strange you felt competitive in the army, with its constant teamwork exercises. The army is about building teams to make order out of chaos."

"Order from chaos—I like that," I said. "Sounds like the army. Let's get some order here. Take some orders. ON YOUR FEET."

We both started laughing. "Do you want to watch television this evening?"

"Yes, I'd like to," he said. "This has been an eventful day, and I enjoyed it very much. I'm making a resolution to run more. I rarely watch TV, but I would like to watch it tonight. Are there any programs tonight that are funny?"

I didn't know any funny shows or have any comedy DVDs. I found some TV reruns of a reality show about men catching crabs in the Bering Sea, and I wrapped the towel tighter and climbed onto Mark's lap to watch.

"You're biting your nails again," he said. "Is it the TV show or what happened today?"

I took my fingers out of my mouth. "I bite my nails without being aware that I am biting them."

"You're pretty nervous sometimes. I think you ought to try to relax a little more, at least when you are at home. Relaxing may take an effort. You're fanatic about running, as though you have to keep it up because you may have to run away from something dangerous."

"Iraq made me jumpy—all the listening for anomalous sounds and always being aware of my surroundings. Sometimes I liked the feeling. I felt intensely alive, more alive than I ever had before. I could *feel* myself living. Whenever there was firing nearby, I felt an intense excitement. I get high on adrenaline."

"I really liked the army," I continued. "But it didn't equip me to deal with life as a civilian. I think that if I had started working in the defense industry right out of college, I'd probably have the same kind of job I have now, but I would be involved in some local activities I liked and know more people. I know you found things in the army that are important to you in civilian life, like your interest in religion. I liked the army while I was there, but I think that I might have a better life now if I had never been in the army. I wouldn't have the good memories and the excitement that I look back on, that's all."

"Being a civilian just takes a while to get used to, like when we first went to college or joined the army," Mark said. "We learned things in the army that apply outside the army."

"Well, I learned to shoot, but now I don't go to shooting ranges, for example. I guess the main thing that I learned in the army is to evaluate a situation for danger."

"You still run," Mark said. "We worked with a variety of people in the army, and that's valuable. Officers are trained for leadership, too."

"I can't help missing the companionship and teamwork of the army."

"Why not write down the things you miss, and then try to think how you could have them outside the army?"

"I should do that," I said. "Write down the things I had in the army that I would like to have now, and try to figure out how to get them again."

Mark said, "Maybe write down all the bad things about the army, too, like mortar fire in Iraq. You keep comparing your present life to being in the army, and concluding that the army was better. If you write down the bad things, you may appreciate being out of the army more. You could develop a saying, like 'I don't have to go to Iraq again' and repeat it when you reminisce about the army. Suppose you just try to relax now. No mortar fire. No convoy tomorrow. Lie down, wiggle your toes, then your ankles, slowly, move up your body, one part at a time."

He moved me from his lap and sat on the floor. "There's nothing you have to do now. You don't have to be ready for anything. You're home. You're protected. Don't be startled at noises you hear outside. The sounds are just from cars or people putting trash in the dumpster."

I lay down and tried to relax.

He put his hand on my abdomen. "Feel yourself breathe," he said. "Relax your feet."

"Keep me warm tonight," I said. "It's cold in a boat on the Bering Sea."

"Just relax. Don't talk. Move your ankles in circles and try to relax." Mark turned the television off.

CHAPTER 9

PETE'S WARNING

I got to work early Monday morning. Having flextime was nice; when I was ready, I went to work. Sometimes I started at five or six o'clock in the morning. Today no one was at the security desk, although the cup of coffee sitting on it was still steaming, so the gate guard must have been in the nearby office. I put my badge in the automated entry slot and heard the door latch click for me to enter. I passed the break room and walked down the row of cubicles to my own. My coworker Brian was busy working already; he was usually the first person in the office because he liked to play golf in the afternoon after work. When I went back for coffee, even the break room was deserted.

I settled back in my cube and booted up the computer, going to the document I was analyzing against a checklist of requirements. I had a notepad beside me that I used to jot tentative comments and suggestions for additions. I thought about the previous weekend, as the workday began.

Early in the day, I had a meeting with my manager, and the manager of the other woman working on the project with me. She had apparently complained that I was using the wrong account number to perform my tasks, which was not the case. The program manager had given me those account numbers to use. I had thought that the managers would check the account numbers with the program manager, but they didn't, so we had a pointless meeting. My female coworker didn't even come. This situation was very puzzling. She must have staked out a territory for herself and decided that I was encroaching on it.

Later, I went to the Tank Command site to attend a meeting. I stopped by Jerry's desk to say hello. Jerry was reading a magazine and pulled some work documents over it as I stood by his desk. My feelings toward Jerry varied from liking him to being astonished by his attitude toward work. "Do you have a romance going?" he asked. "I thought this was the most unromantic place in the world."

"I'm not sure," I said.

"Mark is a nice person and very interesting," he continued. "He went to Sunday services with my family. He has been to Buddhist temples in Korea and Japan, which I would like my family to see." Jerry had pinned up pictures of his children, a boy and a girl, on the bulletin board above his desk.

"I think you and Mark are really suited for each other," he continued. "You and Mark can share stories of being in the army, and you're about the same age. My wife and I are the same age and have the same background. Because of that, we get along with our in-laws. You ought to get married soon, if you want to have children."

"I'm glad you get along with your in-laws," I said politely.

"We have to get along with our in-laws. Otherwise, our own family wouldn't get along either. Our culture says that we owe our parents infinitely because they raised us and without them we wouldn't have been born."

"That's a good way of looking at things," I said. "But I'm not sure of the idea that I have a huge debt to my parents for being born."

"I hope you and Mark come to like each other very well," Jerry said.

One of the program managers had called the meeting, which would feature a presentation by a reserve major who worked at one of the defense contractors on equipment for the test laboratories. The presenter wasn't a popular person, having once loudly chewed out everyone within earshot for coming to work late. He had been a colonel in the army and acted like we should salute when he spoke.

Pete came into the room before the meeting and asked me to stop by his desk when the meeting was over. During the meeting, I wondered what he wanted to see me about. "Let's get some coffee and step outside," he said when I got to his office.

Pete led me across the parking lot to an area near the chain-link fence that was bald of grass and not shaded, giving us a place to talk where no one could overhear us.

"I heard you've been seeing Mark Vonn," he said. "I don't like to see a woman get mixed up with him. I've known Mark for a long time. He can be a nice person and generous. But Mark is also a man who has failed in everything he has ever done. Look at his career. He either quit graduate school or flunked out before he joined the army. In the army, he gets assigned to one crappy post after another.

"Alcoholic. Quite the life of the party when he's drinking, isn't he?"

"In Iraq, I saw him looking stoned. People joked about him, saying that if you see somebody vacant looking, it's probably our intelligence officer.

"The army is my second home, Pam. It's not a parking place for misfits, screw-ups, and losers while they straighten out their addictions and personal problems."

Pete's opinion of Mark shocked me. Some things were true. Mark had admitted that he had been in jail and done some drugs with a doctor. How credible was Pete, who was known to make many technical errors and played with his gun at home? "I like Mark because he's interesting," I said. "We go to parks and enjoy the outdoors."

"You should know what you're getting into. Women sometimes think they can reform these bad-boy types. Notice I say boy, not man. Trying to reform them doesn't work—it just gets you snared in their problems and inadequacies."

"Thank you for your information," I replied. "I'll evaluate things in the light of what you just told me. I don't intend to try to reform somebody. I didn't know he had issues with drinking and drugs."

"You're seeing this guy, and you didn't notice?" Pete asked. "Don't you go to nightclubs and drink together?"

"No. I've only seen Mark drink at our Friday get-togethers, and once when I took him to the home of one of my friends."

Pete continued, "If Mark isn't drinking, he must have gotten some help. Does he go to AA meetings or a similar program?"

"I don't know," I said. "I don't know what he does every evening. Sometimes he goes to church."

"Well, his sobering up is something I wouldn't have guessed," Pete said. "I should add that he doesn't drink when we get together on Fridays. He and I go to the bar together, and he buys a ginger ale and offers me one. He told me that he won't drink at these events, that abstaining isn't hard, and that I should try it.

"Alcoholics are usually manipulative and like playing on your sympathy. They will say that they have bruises from an accident. Check and you find out the accident consisted of falling down the stairs drunk. People with drinking and drug problems like to blame their addiction on everyone else. They will claim that they drink because you don't understand them or watch the wrong TV programs or don't take care of them well enough. Beware of that, Pam. Don't accept being blamed."

We began walking back to the office building. "Thank you for telling me what to watch out for," I said.

"Feel free to talk to me anytime," Pete said. "And ask Mark about his Purple Heart. Not just about Iraq but specifically about his Purple Heart."

"What you said comes as a surprise to me," I replied. "I thought that Mark was depressed. He goes along with things I suggest but often doesn't seem to enjoy them."

Pete remarked, "Depression and alcoholism can go together, Pam. Maybe the only time Mark is happy is when he is drinking."

"Happiness isn't something that you chase. It comes out of the blue," I said. "Sometimes I feel happy when I'm standing beside a damaged military vehicle."

"You must have loved the war," Pete said. We walked back into the building.

I wondered how long Pete and Mark had known each other. In order to know Mark this well, Pete must have known him before they were in Iraq or through gossip. In the army, you need to know your coworkers because you trust them with your life.

I called Mark that evening and left him a message. I wasn't sure what I would say to him. I couldn't confront him with what Pete said since they were friends. Maybe I could find what kind of meetings Mark attended, to see if he went to Alcoholics Anonymous.

When Mark returned my call later, I told him about my problem at work. "I got sand-bagged at work today," I said. "My female coworker had complained to management that I was performing the wrong task, instead of talking to me about it. Then, two managers, she, and I were supposed to have a meeting about it, but she didn't show up for the meeting. I showed the managers the work description that I was following. To my surprise, one showed me an example of some unrelated work and said that I should familiarize myself with it. I don't understand my workplace at all."

"If the managers didn't tell you that you did something wrong, I wouldn't be too concerned. She lacks some credibility because she didn't come to the meeting. Could you discuss this with her?"

"I thought about it. The alternative is to ignore it. I was disappointed because I thought that we might become friends."

"Obviously you can't trust her."

"Maybe she just likes to stir things up. Some people like to cause drama so they have something to gossip about. I guess I should act like nothing happened and see if anything similar happens. I'll see if anything changes at work."

"Besides mistrusting the people you work with," Mark said. "I'm not sure that avoiding a problem helps, though."

"In the army, we needed to trust our teammates, know if they were likely to discharge their guns accidentally, and see whether they lose their heads in a crisis. Once I saw a vehicle driver follow another vehicle stuck in the sand and be surprised when he got stuck, too. Nothing in civilian life is quite as serious. My coworkers now are smart enough to know what they are doing."

"Tasks and objectives may be more clearly defined in the army," Mark said.

"That's possible. Do you miss the army? Meeting people and making friends is so much easier in the army. So many social and recreational opportunities are easily available in the army, the Officers' Club, the gym, swimming pool, and events on base."

"I missed the army for about a week after I left," he said. "I haven't since. As a civilian, you can find ways to meet people without Officers' Club functions. Haven't you been able to make new friends? I meet more varied people now than I did in the army."

I wasn't going to tell him about meeting people at Tequila Tom's. I asked him about classes and meetings at the Zen Center, and if he went to other meetings as well. He was evasive again, so I said that I would like to learn more about meditating. He told me that I should come with him on Sunday morning and that he would check on the schedule for classes. "I haven't taken a class since I left college," I said, "Except for the training classes in the army. "Does a class have books and homework?"

"There will be a book to read, and the homework is to meditate," he said. "I'll take the class again with you. That will be fun since we will be able to talk about it afterwards."

We said goodnight. To understand Pete's comments, I would have to understand the relationship between Pete and Mark better. Mark had come to the Friday happy hour with Pete, and he went to Pete's home, but Pete had a bad impression of Mark. The issue between them might go back to whatever Mark and Pete had done in Iraq. I would have to try harder to find out what they did in Iraq.

At night, I dreamed that it was hot and sunny outside. I looked across the expanse of desert at Fort Irwin and shaded my eyes from the sun to see the tanks moving in the sand. A canteen was in my hand. Then I realized that my camouflage clothing was woodland pattern, not desert. I woke up suddenly, with a sense of loss, feeling the space where the army used to be.

CHAPTER 10

CAT AND BHAGAVAD-GITA

That evening, Mark insisted that I come to his apartment. He said that he had a surprise to show me, and that he was cooking some German food. I drove over to his place right after work.

The surprise met me at his door. It was a small gray cat.

"I hope you aren't allergic to cats," Mark said.

"Not that I'm aware of. I've never owned a cat."

"Nobody really owns cats. They will live with you if they like you and the food is okay. I don't know what to name her." He was smiling.

I asked if she was a kitten since she was small. "She's kind of a cute little thing," I said. Mark said that she was supposed to be a couple of years old. I tried to pick her up, but she was skittish and ran under the kitchen table.

"She's so small," I said. "My family named pets after their characteristics. We would give the dogs names like Blackie and Patches. I don't see naming her Tiny, though. She needs a beautiful, very dignified name since she is plain—maybe Audrey or Cecily."

"Cecily sounds good. It sounds like a name in an eighteenth-century English novel. Lady Cecily. Baroness Pamela, meet Lady Cecily."

"How long were you thinking of getting a pet?"

"I didn't ask the management about it until I saw her in a pet shop. I was told that the no-pets policy didn't apply to cats because the building has mice sometimes."

"So when mice come in, people can unleash their cats and get rid of the mice?" I teased.

"I hope she can catch mice if any show up." Mark looked pleased. "I thought that she might cheer me up, and if she didn't, at least, I'd offer her a better life than she might have had. She was in the free-pet section of a pet shop in a strip mall over on Twelve Mile Road. I saw her in the window and went in to look at the pets. I saw how much nicer looking the other cats were, and I felt sorry for her. She seemed like a wallflower at a dance. I didn't think that anyone else would pick her out of all the competition of long-haired, Siamese, and tabby cats, and that they might euthanize her if no one wanted her."

I sat on the couch, and Cecily came over to check me out. Maybe Mark had selected a plain, unwanted cat because he felt plain and unwanted. "Do I meet with your approval, Cecily?" I asked. "I think we have to share a man. Mark, I hope that she isn't the jealous, possessive type. I wouldn't like her threatening to claw me if I got too close to you."

"Cats are supposed to be relaxing," Mark said.

"Purring is a nice sound compared to some of the conversations I hear at work," I said, trying to be funny.

"I read someplace that a pet helps with depression, and I've been somewhat depressed," Mark said.

"I notice that you don't seem to enjoy life very much," I commented.

"I wish I did," he said. "I keep wondering what your secret is. When we go to parks, you are so effervescent that being with you is like watching bubbles in champagne. I wish I could find a way to tap into your feelings and get a taste of them. I've heard that some specific incidence of disappointment or loss usually starts an episode of depression, but my life has been free of trouble since I got here."

I pointed out, "You're omitting that moving, starting a new job, and meeting new people is hard. Plus you left the army, which had been your home and second family for years."

Mark said, "I moved so much in the army, I must be used to being in new places and performing new tasks by now."

"I never got used to starting work in new settings and staying in bachelor officers' quarters until I got a semi permanent place to live," I said. "Could the Veterans Administration help you with depression?"

"They could probably prescribe some drugs. Anyone depressed enough to cry, they would probably dump in a psych ward. I would be afraid of losing my clearance. Are you depressed, too?" Mark continued. "You don't seem to have much contact with people. You spend most of your free time watching reality shows on television or running. Social withdrawal can be a symptom of depression. I think it can also be a symptom of post-traumatic stress disorder."

"I don't think I'm depressed. I like being outdoors, going to the parks, and we have a good time doing that. I like the work on my desk. I work nine hours most days and that doesn't leave a lot of time for going to events in the evening. I've heard that people with PTSD are usually very withdrawn, but that their withdrawal comes from being anxious about going places. They may get nervous in a group and want to run away. I don't feel anxious going places. Television is relaxing. I exchange

CAT AND BHAGAVAD-GITA

e-mails with my friends, like Lily, my former roommate in Iraq, while watching reality shows, where missing part of the show doesn't make a difference. Sometimes I fall asleep watching television."

"You engineers have so many societies," Mark said. "Suppose you joined some of them? You would meet some people—mostly men but some women."

"I didn't think of that," I said. "There is a Society of Women Engineers. I used to belong to it in college."

"That's one idea," Mark said. "Maybe we could join a club for hiking or canoeing or a nature club. You shouldn't just watch television in the evenings. If you want to meet other women, you have to go somewhere that they are."

"I just got an idea. You like taking pictures, and maybe we could join a camera club or photography club."

"I'll look up local camera clubs. Taking pictures again might be fun," Mark said.

"I'll look up the engineering societies on the Internet," I said. "I'll do it right now." I logged on to his computer, which he kept on a tiny table in the corner. There were two meetings within a month in the Detroit section, one for dinner and one at an auto plant, which featured a speaker. The one closest to me was in two weeks, about six miles from where I worked. "I found some engineering society meetings."

"I hope you will go," Mark said.

I asked, "Don't you miss the army? I used to miss it a lot. In the morning when I wake up, sometimes I think that I am still in the army."

Mark said, "What I miss is being twenty-three or twenty-four. I had an eager attitude my first few years in the army. I was seeing new places, and my whole life seemed to be going very well. I haven't been so enthusiastic since."

"Is there anything you miss now, though?"

"What I miss most about the army is having more people around me. I often lived in crowded quarters, and I got used to people nearby. I get a little nervous when I don't know the people around me, too. My neighbors could be criminals, and I wouldn't know. When I lived off the base, there were many army people living in the same apartment building. I feel nervous being alone sometimes and double-check door locks and window latches. Pets are supposed to be able to warn you if something is wrong."

"Would Cecily be able to scare a burglar away?"

"She might wake me up, at least."

Cecily climbed beside me on the couch and purred like a tank motor warming up. She climbed into my lap and began kneading my right breast. "Cecily, I'm not your mommy cat, and I don't have any milk. Are you sure she isn't a kitten?"

"They said her teeth are mature. I was told that the people who owned her had several cats, and were moving and had to leave some of them."

I agreed. "They probably moved to another state, like so many people around here. Notice how many stores in the strip malls have closed. I lost grocery and drug stores, restaurants, and bookstores. Even some gas stations that I used to go to are closed."

"I've read that 15 to 20 percent of the people here have left, and that with the auto companies cutting back, even more will leave," Mark said. "Even a doctor I went to said that his patient load was decreasing because so many people moved."

"It's sad," I said. "At least it gives us more privacy in the parks and open spaces. Maybe you feel depressed because of the recession."

"I don't find being in Detroit particularly depressing," he continued and put his arm around me. "The company is good here." I should try to be more affectionate to Mark. I didn't kiss him when I came in, for example. He probably would have liked that.

"Do you really like going to the parks or are you just humoring me?" I asked. "You often seem unhappy. You're distant. When we go to a happy hour, you don't talk about your war experiences like the other people. Did something happen in the war that bothers you?"

"Besides being in a war? I don't have good war stories like some of the other people. What kind of war stories do intelligence officers have? I sat in an office, I saw many maps of Iraq, I interpreted signal traffic, and I decided where to place sensors."

"You got a Purple Heart, though."

"I had a couple of cuts during a short engagement with some insurgents," he said. "I have a tiny scar on my hand that I can hardly find." I waited for him to say more, but he didn't. He apparently didn't want to talk about the war right now. Some people never want to talk about the war. I hadn't told him my war stories, either.

Cecily had decided to try my left breast. "Persistent, isn't she"? I asked.

"She is also equal-opportunity. She did that to me a couple of times and found it very unrewarding. I did, too," Mark said. "She managed to find a sensitive spot which I didn't know would be tender when nipped."

"So she bit your tit?" I asked, laughing. "I can do that if you like it."

"Please. No. I learned my lesson. I'll wear a T-shirt at home and not expose her to temptation."

I pictured Mark walking around without a shirt. He often wore T-shirts that were too big or plaid shirts with elbow-length sleeves that covered the scar on his upper arm. "Settle down, Cecily," I said. "Your milk comes out of a dish." She pressed against my chest and purred. I felt the vibrations through my body.

"Maybe she wants to play," he said. He went into the kitchenette and brought back a piece of crumpled paper attached to a string. He began trailing the paper across the floor. Cecily jumped off my lap to attack it. He would pull it along in front of her and jerk it when she pounced. Then he held it in the air and made her jump for it.

"She's quite an acrobat, isn't she? Is teasing her like that mean of you?"

"No, when cats get tired of playing, they walk away," he said. "The most difficult part of sharing a home with a cat is the litter box. They keep themselves clean, but the litter box smells like rotting tuna fish."

He began putting the food on the table. "No rotting tuna fish, I guarantee," He said. His cooking was unusual—breaded steak, fat noodles and shredded cabbage, with cooked vegetables.

We sat down in the living area, and Mark handed me a book from the bookcase. "Have you ever read the Bhagavad-Gita?" he asked.

I shook my head.

"The Bhagavad-Gita is the only scripture in the world about a soldier, Arjuna, an army officer in a civil war, and the issues he faces. A civil war can be one of the most difficult situations military people experience. Some of his friends, relatives, and teachers are on the other side of the conflict. God in the form of a human, Krishna, tells him that since every step of his life took him to the battlefield, he should take the next step forward. In a hundred years, everyone on the battlefield would be dead whether he killed anyone in the battle or not.

"Krishna said not to fight in a war to obtain the results of your actions. Don't fight to kill your cousin but fight because war is your duty as a soldier. Your birth in this time and place and society determined your personal duty. If you run away from the battle, you will regret doing so. People will die no matter what you do." Mark paused. "What do you think of that?"

I said, "You can't run away because there is nowhere to run. In our society, people choose to be in the army, but we can't foresee what we will encounter or how being in the army will affect us. You can run away, but you can't escape from yourself and your society and your choices."

"Suppose he did run away?" Mark asked.

"I think he might have to run pretty far. Changing your life significantly would be hard. He had a background, an education, and relatives. He would have to give up so much of himself that he would need to remake himself into a different person."

"Did you ever run away?" Mark asked. "I did—to college and then to the army."

"I'm not sure that making a career choice is running away. Running away is more like turning your back on the enemy and bugging out or deserting. Then the people who depended on you would hate you, and you couldn't go back."

"I'd like to lend you this book," he said. "Read the commentary as much as the poem. I am fascinated by the idea that we participate in whatever is happening at the time and the place we are born into, and that our society determines our duties and position in life. You could read it now or read anything else you would like," he said, taking a book from of the shelf.

"I'd like to meditate now."

"Does meditation make you happy?" I asked.

"Sometimes it does. At least, I don't feel depressed when I meditate."

Mark lit a candle on the bookcase, put meditation cushions on the floor and sat down, looking at the candle. His eyes were half closed. I began to read the book he had given me. I wished he had a TV set.

After an hour, Mark got up from meditating and read some passages from the book to me.

"I don't quite get the point of the story, though," I said. "His choice is whether to do his job or not. Soldiers don't know how they will act until they are fired on." *I remembered reaching for the rifle.*

"In war, you do your job. It's not just about killing people on the other side. People do get killed, but that's just the nature of war."

"That's pretty abstract for me," I said. "When a convoy I was in was attacked, I wanted to kill Iraqis." I turned back to the book and read some more.

"Let's go for a walk," I said after a while. "It's nice out, and we need to get some exercise after exercising our forks on that big meal."

Mark agreed, and we walked through the apartment complex and down a residential street. "Do you have to be careful around here at night?" I asked.

"Not really. Cars get stolen often, but it is probably in the middle of the night. Some guy hangs around here who is probably a dope dealer. I often see him on a corner in the evenings."

"It is very quiet in the evening where I live, too." The trees were beautiful at night. I was glad that I was back in Michigan.

Mark had some CDs of symphonies and asked me what I would like to hear. I said, "Your favorite. Did your family play a lot of classical music when you were growing up?"

"Yes. My parents play music, too. My mother plays the piano, and my father plays the violin. They made sure that we had music lessons as we were growing up, in case we had talent. I didn't. My brother plays the piano very well, but he uses a keyboard instrument now, which allows him to use special effects and have fun playing alone."

Mark leafed through a newspaper as I examined the book, and we listened to music.

When we went to bed, Cecily jumped on the bed and walked on us for a few minutes. I lay down to sleep on my left side, with Mark's right arm across me. Cecily lay down next to my stomach, and the sound of her purring put me to sleep.

"Would you like to borrow Cecily sometimes?" Mark asked in the morning, while we were eating hard-boiled eggs and toast. "You weren't running in your sleep last night. You slept quietly compared to the way you usually sleep—kicking your feet and talking."

"I dream about running sometimes," I said. "I think I have to get ready for the morning run. Sometimes I go back to sleep and wake up later, cold after kicking the blankets off."

Cecily was eating an egg. Mark watched her, enamored. I was amused. "What do I say in my sleep?" I asked.

"Various things. You mumble about rifles, convoys, and ammunition. Once in a while you say, 'Michael, I thought you were dead.'"

I got up and hugged him. "I'm sorry," I said. "Talking about Michael in my sleep isn't complimentary to you. I dream a lot about the army. Sometimes my dreams are very mundane, like walking to the chow hall for lunch, when it was a hundred degrees out in Iraq. I dream about holding a rifle. I think I hear distant mortar fire. I think I need to go somewhere in a convoy and feel scared. Then I wake up and feel relieved. No more convoys."

Mark said, "I dream about Iraq sometimes, too. Did you work at night? That's when the sky was stunning."

"We used lights and couldn't see the stars. You must have been in the country to see the stars."

Mark added, "Sometimes I was in the countryside. You've also said that a bombing raid is beautiful."

"I've got a little secret. I love bombing raids because watching is tremendously exciting. I'm not proud of some of the things I did in Iraq. I'm more or less ashamed of them."

Mark said, "People do things during a war that they wouldn't do otherwise. Fear is exciting and is close to exhilaration. And exhilaration can be close to sexual arousal. People experience that and usually don't talk about it. Don't be ashamed of the things you did in a war zone. We can't anticipate what our reactions will be when we are under stress."

"Bombing makes me think that my life may end any minute, so I should enjoy myself in my last moments," I said.

"I'm guessing that you had sexual relations with somebody during a bombing raid. A lot of people probably think of sex during stressful experiences but lack opportunity to do anything about it. Being female, I'm sure that you had many propositions, even during bombing raids. And why not accept some? You were single, Michael was gone, and you didn't have other commitments. There's nothing to be ashamed of."

"Once I had sex in a ditch behind a troop carrier during a bombing raid. I felt like the world was ending and I was going to die—him too and everything I knew."

"You also wanted to have sexual relations in the bushes after the canoe tipped over," Mark said. "Personally, I don't like to see people having sexual relations in public. I saw that when I was in college, and it seemed very inappropriate."

I took the book with me when I went to work. I hadn't run that morning, so I left for work a little early and walked for twenty minutes. The birds were singing in the trees, and the sun had risen behind a band of pink clouds.

The office was always quiet in the morning because the first meetings were later. I turned to the stack of document packages on my desk. I looked at a test plan, one of the most interesting documents. I would like to see the tests run in the lab, after they were developed. I hope that the meeting at work didn't change anything.

I decided to read the book, even if it was difficult. One phrase that had caught my attention was about finding peace when forgetting desire. I wondered what Mark made of forgetting desire. Why would you fire your weapon if you didn't desire a result?

CHAPTER 11

ZEN TEACHER

I was curious about Elizabeth, the Zen teacher who seemed to play a significant role in Mark's life. I had asked him about her, but he said that he didn't know much about her personal life, just that she lived nearby and worked at a market. I was curious about where she lived and worked, so I decided to visit vegetable markets near the Zen Center. Tuesday I started work early and left early, to drive near the Zen Center. On a nearby street, I found a small business district that had an old set of buildings with false fronts, and the little stores were more varied than those in my neighborhood, where stores were in strip malls.

I walked down the street, looking in windows. Although several stores carried groceries, only two showed vegetables in the windows. I went into both, buying some fruit and vegetables in each. I didn't see the Zen teacher, but I didn't really expect to. She might work miles away from here. I remembered that Mark took a class from her on Wednesday, so I thought I should skip a day and look at the markets again Thursday.

On Thursday, I went to one of the same markets and picked up some apples. Elizabeth, the Zen teacher materialized from the back of the store and said, "Hello. I remember you from the art show. I was hoping to see you at the Zen Center again. My name is Elizabeth."

"My name is Pam," I said.

"Please come to the Zen Center again and meditate with us. Have you had instruction in meditation?" Elizabeth asked.

I shook my head.

"Join me for dinner tonight at my home, and I will show you. I will cook a simple meal of beans, rice, and vegetables. I get off work soon—at six o'clock."

Surprised by her invitation, I agreed and noted her address. I bought the apples and walked around the business district until a little after six. I passed her walking home and waited for her in my car. "I'm sorry I didn't think to give you a ride home," I said. "I'm so used to people having cars."

"I like the walk," Elizabeth said. "I'm near where I work and the Zen Center. I don't need a car." We walked up a narrow flight of scuffed stairs that had an elaborately wooden carved banister to her second-story apartment. Judging by the antique light fixtures and polished wooden baseboards, the house had probably been beautiful a hundred years ago. In her living room was a sideboard with pictures, bells, a candle, and other decorative objects. Cushions were on the floor. There was a bookcase and a low coffee table with placemats.

"Are you from the Detroit area?" I asked. "I am."

"Yes, originally. I lived in Chicago and in California for a while. Living here is as good as living anywhere else."

"I notice that you don't have a car. Is there somewhere you would like to visit in a car sometime? I could drive."

"I have the things I need in the neighborhood," she said. "However, sometimes I think of going to the zoo. I used to go the zoo every year when I was a child. Seeing the polar bears would be fun. I'm not sure when we could get together though, since I work Saturday at my job, and Sunday I always go to the Zen Center."

"We could meet on a Friday," I said. "I have every other Friday off, since we work nine hours a day on the other work days."

I sat on a cushion in the living room, positioned so that I could see her cooking in the kitchen. She began a conversation about the vegetables she was using, the rice cooker, and the difficulty of cooking dried beans. Then she brewed tea and served it in small bowls. "Excuse me for not being more talkative," she said. "I love to have guests, but I don't entertain often. Frequently I eat at the Zen Center, which serves lunch on weekdays. Some of the people who come to eat there are from the streets. Some families are very poor and lack food. I bring unsold vegetables and fruit from the store to give people. Perhaps you would like to come and eat with us sometime or come to meditate."

"I liked the art show," I said. "Mark brought me because the Zen Center is important to him. I don't know how to meditate."

Elizabeth said that the process of sitting on the cushion, watching your breath, and letting thoughts come and go is meditation. "Don't expect that a particular state of mind occurs. Watch as you try to distract yourself," she said.

"Just sit while I finish cooking. Let the thoughts and pictures come, then let them go, and come back to your breath."

I sat on the cushion with my legs crossed like we did in the Zen Center. *I thought of the troop carrier on fire and the rifle.*

ZEN TEACHER

She served two heaping platters of food. "How did that go?" she asked.

I answered, "I thought of vehicles on fire, and other things that I remember from Iraq. I often think of Iraq."

"We get attached to the emotions our thoughts create, whether the emotion is attraction, aversion, or indifference. When you think about the past or future, you feel a corresponding emotion. Eventually the thought patterns become tedious and lose their hold on us. Keep meditating."

"'Attraction, aversion, indifference'—that sounds like an army saying. Excuse the language, but 'fight it, fuck it, or forget it' seems like the same concept."

Elizabeth laughed. "It is. Human minds work the same, no matter what words we use. We tend to react to anything we encounter with either 'I like it,' 'I don't like it,' or 'I don't care about it.' The habit of classifying things by our preferences immerses us in our own thoughts and blocks us from appreciating the world. If we can see freshly and not impose our value judgments, the world seems brighter and sacred.

"Our thoughts usually move between the past and the future, like 'I need to buy toothpaste,' or 'I'm mad about something that happened yesterday.' We don't have to invest emotional energy in each thought. We can throw the thought away, and come back to our breath. Humans like to create a soap opera out of our life and replay each episode in our mind. Eventually an event loses its emotional hold on us and we don't watch the rerun again. Living in reality becomes preferable to living in our soap opera."

"I was an army officer in a war," I said. "It's hard to forget about being in a war."

"You don't need to forget it, just don't focus on the past or on the future. War is part of the nature of the world, which is like the nature of our mind. Zen is a peaceful religion, yet Japanese kamikaze pilots were often Zen Buddhists."

"I don't understand the belief in reincarnation," I said.

"Westerners misunderstand reincarnation. To live and die, and live as an insect and be stepped on, and live as a mouse and be eaten by a cat, and live every kind of life and suffer every kind of death is not appealing. Reincarnation is like being caught in a wave which sweeps you, terrified, out to sea and then throws you back on the beach, where you lie in the sand until you are picked up by the next wave and swept out to sea again, in an endless cycle of hope and fear."

I listened to her, fascinated. I wondered what her life had been like to have a view of life so strange and pessimistic—or was it a pessimistic view? I wouldn't like to be an ant and be stepped on.

"People often move toward a spiritual life because they've been burned," she said, as though reading my mind. "I feel happy doing what I am doing. Sometimes I can hardly believe how good the world is to me and how beautiful it is. It doesn't matter what a person's problems are or what their soap opera is. The medicine for life's problems is the same."

"I am going to meditate now," she said, clearing our plates and putting them in the sink. "Thank you for coming and come to the Zen Center sometime. We have classes for beginners. Join me in sitting now, until you feel like leaving. I will meditate for more than an hour, and I don't expect you to stay, so just slip out when you are tired of meditating."

She lit a candle on the sideboard and arranged the cushions. She put a small bowl beside her and struck it with a stick; it rang like a bell. I sat down in the meditation posture, and she began chanting. I sat with her for about fifteen minutes and then left.

I sat in my car for a few minutes, trying to digest what Elizabeth had told me. The gist of it seemed to be that the stories of our past don't matter because our present is more important; if we lead a bad life in our present life, we pay for it in a future one. I didn't see why this religion would appeal to a person like Mark, who seemed to feel guilty about killing people in Iraq.

Later I called Mark, ostensibly to ask if he planned to go to the happy hour on Friday night.

"Yes, I am. I enjoy the people. The only thing I don't like about that bar is the country music. Typical country music lyrics are like, 'I'm here doing time in the jail, but it's all your fault cause you looked at some other male.'"

"You saw that guy, you said goodbye, you made me cry," I said.

"So I got drunk, and I hit that punk."

"But it's all, all, all your fault."

"You should become a country songwriter," Mark said. "Your lyrics are better than the real ones."

"Did you ever talk to Charlie, the guy who's kind of off base mentally?" I asked. "A tall, thin, gray-haired guy?"

"No, I don't think so."

"He's a civil servant with Tank and Automotive. He will say the weirdest, unresponsive things. Once I went into the break room, and he was looking at a magazine and mumbling something about helicopter engines being too loud. I thought he was talking to me, and I went and stood by him. I thought that the magazine article he was reading would be about helicopters, but it was a page of ads for camping equipment. There weren't any engine sounds from outside.

"Then I knew that the engines were in his mind. Presumably, in Vietnam, since he is about that age. I always talk to him, but his responses rarely relate to whatever I've said. I can tell that he is very nice, though. He cleans up after people."

Mark replied, "Maybe he has post-traumatic stress disorder—PTSD. I'll chat with him."

"Is talking to yourself a symptom of post-traumatic stress disorder?" I asked.

"Reliving old experiences is a symptom of PTSD," Mark said. "Maybe I have PTSD from the war myself. Some of my experiences in the army were very stressful, and I still feel threatened when I remember them. Do you have PTSD? You startle when you hear loud sounds, and then look around as though you want find a place to take cover. You are wary, too."

"The wariness could be from living near Detroit," I said, trying to make a joke.

"You talk in your sleep about rifles and burning vehicles."

I remembered picking up the rifle. I said, "I not only dream about burning vehicles, but I work on armor for vehicles. We see films on vehicle strikes and explosions to understand the vulnerability of the vehicles. I know I have a startle reflex from loud noises. I noticed that you do, too."

Mark paused, and then said, "You're right, I do. I'll see you tomorrow, after work."

"Sounds good. I look forward to seeing you tomorrow." Mark was a hard person to get to know. Michael was more predictable. Michael had modeled himself for the army. I knew how he would pet a dog, walk in the park, talk with his friends, and laugh his hearty laugh. I thought of us running in a city park, and a golden retriever breaking away from its owner and joining us. Michael was laughing as we reversed course and led the dog back to its owner. Mark was so somber that he rarely laughed.

I watched a reality show about a former paratrooper practicing his survival skills in Alaska. Then I went to bed and dreamed that I was waiting in the sunrise for the morning run to begin, amid the summer greenery at the proving grounds at Aberdeen.

CHAPTER 12

HOME AGAIN REDUX

My parents were hosting a family picnic on Sunday afternoon. On Sunday morning, Mark and I went to the Zen Center first, where I made a sincere attempt to meditate, and not to just sit on the cushion and let my mind wander. Meditation is supposed to make people feel calmer, and I needed to be less angry before going home.

I didn't think that Mark would like my family gathering, since I didn't enjoy them, but we could leave early and see LuAnn on the way home or walk in a park. "You may have to listen to a lot of female bickering," I warned him as we approached the house. I yelled through the screen door that we had arrived. I was ashamed of the peeling house paint. The screen was patched with duct tape.

Mom answered the door and said, "You're early. I haven't gotten things ready yet."

"I brought my friend Mark with me," I said. They greeted each other politely.

"Are you in the army?" Mom asked Mark.

"Not any more. I used to be."

"Do you work together?" was the next question.

"No, we work for different companies. We met through mutual friends." Mark said.

"I'll come and help, but first I'd like dad to meet Mark," I said.

Dad was learning against the garage having a smoke, and I introduced him to Mark. He wanted to know if we worked together. "Do you do any work on cars?" was his second question.

"I know enough to keep an old car running," Mark said. "I owned a couple of old cars when I was in high school. I really wanted a motorcycle, but my parents thought a car was safer."

"I'm in the auto body business," dad said. "Did you ever paint cars?" I had told Mark that dad would ask him if he painted cars.

"No, but I'd like to see how a modern auto shop works," Mark said. "Is business good or bad these days?"

"People are keeping their cars longer, so we get to fix them." Dad pulled a flask out of his pocket and offered me a swig. "I'm waiting until later to have some booze in case I need to drive out for supplies soon," he added.

"I rarely drink, but I need to fortify myself today," I said. "Before the questioning starts." The cheap whiskey burned my throat. I passed the flask to Mark to see what he would do.

"I stopped drinking liquor," he said to dad. "I decided not to drink, smoke, or swear."

"I guess you're a church-going boy. Not drinking is a good thing," dad said. "But listening to my daughters bickering will probably drive you to drink."

Dad began talking about the army and Vietnam. "I'll leave you guys for a moment, and see if mom needs anything," I said.

My mother was ready with her questions. "Are you serious about this man? What kind of work does he do?" she asked. "I think you'd be much happier if you settled down like your sisters."

I was astonished at her description of Susie's confused life as 'settled.' "I didn't know Susie was settled," I said. "Having three kids and no husband doesn't seem settled to me. How can she support them?" I knew that my parents were giving her money. I helped Mom get out some bowls of chips and dip, and took them outside. Some of my aunts and uncles and cousins had arrived by now.

I put the food on a table and went back to Mark and dad. "Why don't we go and see the body shop? No one will miss us," I suggested. I dreaded Susie and her kids arriving, because I knew we would start quarreling again and make a bad impression on Mark.

Dad drove to the body shop, which was in a long industrial building along with a machine shop, a sign painter's shop, and some other businesses. The body shop had expanded since I had been there last. Customers now entered a waiting room instead of walking along the side of the automobile bay. The service counter was larger, too, with three desks behind it.

Dad said he had bought new equipment in the body shop. He showed us his new car-painting setup and some of the other equipment. Mark took more interest in it than I thought he would.

"It's hard to get good workers in this business," dad said. "We expanded because one of the big car dealers cut back on its body work. We always have work because I buy cars other shops put on mechanics liens, and fix and resell them."

We walked out to the back lot, which was full of old cars, some of them in very bad shape. "It looks like you have a lot of work stacked up," I said. I thought I saw the old jeep. "Is that the jeep we rode in as children, dad?' I asked. "It looks like that jeep."

"Yep, that's it," dad said. "You can take it for a spin around the building if you want. It isn't licensed, so don't take it on the street."

"I would, but Mark doesn't like jeeps. He had an accident in one."

"That right?" dad asked.

"I was injured in a jeep accident in Korea," Mark said. "I liked jeeps before then but not after. Breaking your right arm is a nuisance when you're right-handed."

"I hope your arm healed well," dad replied.

"Well, these things happen, and you get over them," Mark said. I was sure that Mark had never gotten over the accident. I was glad he didn't go into details.

"I guess if I'd had boys, I would have had to deal with more accidents," dad said. "Girls don't climb trees and garages as much, and fall from them. We used to climb around in the barn loft when I was a kid. I remember falling from a rafter.

"Let me tell you about the jeep. Pam was seven when she said she wanted to into the army. I drove the jeep home, thinking we could have some fun with it. I took the girls out for a spin." I had already told Mark about this, but he could hear it from dad. I wondered now about dad's irresponsibility. He had packed three kids in an open jeep on crowded city streets, with a two-year-old on the lap of a seven-year-old, and no seat belts. I also wondered why he kept this decrepit thirty-year-old vehicle that no one had ever wanted to buy and never would.

"First Pam asked me where people drive jeeps, and I said in the army. Then she said that she wanted to be in the army."

Dad began laughing. I got a big kick out of it when she did go in the army."

"I think I'd rather have girls than boys," Mark said. "Boys get in trouble, and disgrace you." Mark didn't know yet about Susie.

"So can girls," dad said. "You got any humorous war stories?"

"No." I answered. "Not any real funny ones. A Humvee drove into a recon vehicle one day in the motor pool. The driver claimed he didn't see it. I told him to wait until whatever drugs he had been using wore off, and get his vision checked before he came back to work because he must be going blind. Not see an eighteen-foot parked vehicle in front of him? That's like saying you didn't see a wall you walked into."

Mark said, "Once I was so tired, I fell asleep at my desk and fell out of the chair." Seeing my father's puzzlement, Mark added, "My section collected data from aerial observation."

"Ah," dad said. "Intel. No wonder you seem so intelligent." They both laughed. "Any stories with real bad language, tell them before we go back to the ladies. Pam isn't a fussy lady. I used to tell her that she was my boy." I laughed too. "How do you like being a civilian? A big change?"

"I like it," Mark said, "I don't run in the morning, I don't polish my shoes, I don't say 'yes sir.' I just kick back and lead my life out of uniform."

"I was glad to get out of the army," dad said. "I never understood why Pam liked it so well, except that the motor vehicles are more formidable, and she finds that exciting."

"You had a girlfriend waiting at home," I said. "My social life was in the army."

Back home, Uncle Matt, Aunt Marcia, and Aunt Bev were in the back yard, sitting on lawn chairs. I took Mark over and introduced him to them.

"Are you in the army?" Uncle Matt asked.

"Not any more," Mark said.

"If you were in for a while, why not make a career of it?"

"I got tired of it and wanted to do something else."

"There isn't much work here any more. The auto companies aren't hiring. I've got over thirty years with Ford."

"Is your job secure?" I asked.

"I wish," he said. "They cut down on assembly-line supervision, and I have to keep more things running for them. I'll be glad when I retire."

"How long have you two known each other?" Aunt Marcia said.

"Not long," I answered. "We met at a get-together that my coworkers had. Mark had been in the army with one of them."

"Do you live near here?" Mark asked.

My aunt answered, "We moved eight years ago, after Matt got transferred to Ford at Allen Park. We got into a nicer neighborhood."

"Now they talk about sending me to the north side of town," Uncle Matt said. "I'll be glad to retire if I have to commute twenty miles to work."

Uncle Matt asked Mark, "Are you from Detroit originally?"

"No, I'm from Alabama and New Mexico," Mark said. "When I got out of the army, I found a job in the defense industry here."

"It gets pretty cold here compared to Alabama or New Mexico."

"I came here from Arizona, so it will be quite a change. I need to buy some winter boots and clothes," Mark said.

Susie and her brats had arrived, and the boys were chasing each other in the yard. I introduced Mark to Susie and the boys, and one of the boys asked Mark, "Gee, did you kill anybody?"

"That's between me and the army," Mark said. "Things that happen in the army stay in the army. We say, 'what you do here, what you say here, what you hear here, let it stay here.'" That saying didn't sound to me like army talk; it sounded more like the slogans defense contractors use.

"I bet you killed a lot of people," the younger boy said.

"Shooting people isn't a good thing to talk about," Susie interrupted. "Tell him about playing tee ball."

"I'm going to be in the army when I get big," the older boy said. "I'm going to have a gun like this." He pulled a Beretta-like toy gun out of his pocket.

"That toy gun is an officer's handgun," Mark said. "To use that kind of gun in the army, you would have to finish high school and go to college, or be in the army a long time. Otherwise, you will use a rifle. Can you sing the army song, Pam?"

"The army goes rolling along," I sang. I remembered the caisson song better. "Over hill, over dale, we will hit the dusty trail, and the caissons go rolling along." I kept singing. "In and out, hear them shout, countermarch and turn about, and the caissons go rolling along."

"Pam's job keeps the army rolling along," Mark said. "She makes military vehicles, like troop carriers and artillery vehicles—really, really big vehicles." The boys didn't seem impressed.

"You should meet my sister Carolyn, too," I said. I took Mark over to where Carolyn and Tim were sitting. Carolyn held the baby, Bobby.

"Are you in the army?" Carolyn asked. Mark must be tired of hearing that question.

"Not any more. I used to be."

"Finding a job here is hard right now," Tim said. "Companies are all cutting back."

"I have a job in the defense industry," Mark replied.

"It's nice to see people back from the war, safe and sound," Carolyn said. "Are you from Detroit?"

"No, but I used to come here when I was in the army. I was stationed at a base in Arizona and worked on a project run by the Tank Command. I was in Iraq a few years ago."

"Well, being in the army is a lot more secure than working here," Tim said.

"Making a career in the army is difficult, too," Mark said. "There will certainly be a reduction of forces when the United States leaves Iraq. Times are tough all over."

"Even in the insurance business," Tim said and launched into a boring discourse about people skimping on their home insurance. Mark listened as if he were interested.

"I'd like to have you two come over and have dinner," Carolyn said. "We don't go out much, with the baby, but we would like to have you over. I'll cook some Italian food. Do you have our phone number, Pam?" Tim wrote their address and phone number on one of his business cards.

We went over to a table to get some snack food. "Do you notice how dull my relatives are?" I said. "When you mention Alabama and Arizona, no one shows any interest. When they get together, they will reminisce about holding a picnic in a local park or speculate about the weather. Otherwise, they just talk about each other or their children. Because I'm here, they make some clichéd remarks about the army and the war. I could probably say I enjoyed shooting people in Iraq, and they wouldn't bat an eye when I said it but would talk about me with each other afterwards."

My Aunt Bev and Uncle Rudy were enjoying some refreshments. They had both gotten very fat. I introduced Mark to Uncle Rudy. Aunt Bev said, "I haven't seen you in a few months. Where do you live now? It's about time you settled down." I felt like screaming.

"I live near the Tank Command, where I work," I said.

"You young women, you do so many different things now," Uncle Rudy said. "Are you in the army, young man?"

I wondered why my family thought that any man I was with would be in the army. "No, I work in the defense industry," Mark said. "I'm enjoying the beautiful scenery in Michigan. It's much greener than Arizona."

We went inside to see if mom needed any help. She suggested that we go to the store and buy some more soda pop because she had made lemonade but Susie's boys didn't like it. I was reluctant to make the trip just to please Susie's kids, but Mark wanted to, so we walked to the convenience store.

"I like your family," Mark said as we walked toward the store. "I especially like your dad. He seems to be your favorite, too. Seeing the auto body shop was interesting. You can tell how enthusiastic he is about his work. He makes fixing dents sound like creating a work of art. Will more of your relatives come?"

"More people will drop by later. Some of my cousins will come, and the adults will start drinking. The event will go on through the evening. People will order takeout pizza or get fried chicken for dinner. I can take it for only a few hours, and then I get annoyed about their questions. I don't have to justify my life choices to my relatives. These events are always the same. I'd rather run or go over to LuAnn's."

"I like your relatives. I'd like to stay longer and meet more of your extended family."

"Okay, but if we get pizza, I'd like to scavenge it out of garbage in back of pizza places," I said. "Maybe we can find some anchovy with pineapple or something disgusting like that."

"You have a warped sense of humor, Pam." We brought the soda back to the party, and Mark began playing catch with Susie's boys, who began calling him 'Uncle Mark,' much to the amusement of my relatives.

"I like your boyfriend," several people told me.

I sang the army song again, "Hi, hi, hey, the army's on its way. Shout out your numbers loud and strong." I joined my dad in the garage for a few slugs of rotgut out of his flask and a little car talk.

"I like your new fellow," dad said. "Friendly type, talks to everybody. I saw him making the rounds of your mother's relatives. Are you serious about him?"

"I have a few reservations," I said. "He is lively tonight, but he is usually quiet. He doesn't have a good job, either. He works for a big defense contractor, but his job doesn't use his education, and he seems satisfied with that."

"I suppose he needs time to get used to being a civilian. Maybe he can get a better job later, when he gets more experience outside the military. You said he is quiet. Maybe that's good. You are often quiet, yourself, as though you liked being with your own thoughts more than being with other people. You stopped talking much when you went to college. Some relatives thought you were a snob because you went to college and they didn't. Sometimes I thought that you were being quiet because you didn't want to give your relatives something to talk about."

"I never cared for listening to people talk about the people who aren't here."

Dad said, "Anyway, come over to the shop some Saturday, and we'll have a fancy lunch out. Bring your boyfriend along, if you like. I'd like to get to know him. He's probably led an interesting life."

Uncle Matt joined us then, and the men talked about televised sports.

Mark and I made a trip out for pizza. He refused to fish pizzas from the garbage and paid for fresh ones.

I drank a beer with Susie. I could remember when I loved Susie and wanted to be with her. She was a cute baby. I would watch her while she slept. I looked at her knee where she had gotten stitches when she was a kid, and I could hardly see the scar any more. She had cried a lot when she cut her knee.

I got tipsy with the booze that dad, Uncle Matt, and I consumed in the garage, and sang, "Anchors Aweigh." Mark took me to the car as I kept singing, "And 'til we meet again, here's wishing you a happy voyage home."

We went to my apartment, where I fell into bed with my clothes on. The last thing that I was aware of was Mark pulling off my shoes.

I woke up the next morning, staggered out of bed, undressed, and got into the shower. I looked in the mirror. I looked awful. My eyes looked bruised.

We grabbed a quick breakfast. Mark said, "I meant to ask you last night, how come your father hangs out in the garage during family parties?"

"All the relatives are my mother's family. My dad's relatives live on the other side of the state. When my dad got out of the army, my mother's family didn't think he was good enough for her or something like that."

I paused. "There's more to it. My mother was pregnant with me when they got married."

"That's an issue after thirty years?"

"Well, her family didn't like it, so it's an issue for her. She tries to show off to her sisters by giving these parties, which is humorous because the house looks awful. So many repairs need to be done. The family money and energy is invested in the business." I suddenly thought that my mom identifies with Susie because she was pregnant without being married, too.

"So it sounds like there are just a lot of old conflicts that go way back," Mark said.

"The other problem is that my relatives repeat themselves and bore him. He would rather work. He's kind of a workaholic, and he likes the guys he works with better. He should like them, because he hired them."

"I've got to go home and change clothes," Mark said. "Are you sure you want to go to work instead of calling in sick?"

"Sense of duty, sir," I snapped.

"They must love you at work," he said, as he left.

CHAPTER 13

FAMILIES

I went to the office, showing my badge to security, and looking briefly at the camera monitoring the back door. I went into the security office next door to check out my work package, which was classified. After walking down the line of cubicles to my desk, I called dad at work and told him that I really wanted to visit Grandma. I asked if he had Jimmy's phone number because I wanted to coordinate a time when he was going to visit Uncle Ron and Grandma.

Dad said that he would arrange our trip, but I said that I would like to talk to Jimmy before we went. "Tired of your mother's relatives and want to talk to mine?" dad asked. "I have it, unless he and Amber moved recently. I haven't seen him for about two years." He looked up the phone number; it was for a Chicago suburb. I looked forward to calling Jimmy all day.

After six o'clock Chicago time, I called Jimmy from home, and he agreed to call my dad or me before he and his family went to see his parents. "We don't go to visit them often," he said. "Now that the kids are teenagers, they are involved in weekend sports and activities, and don't like going to Michigan much." We talked about our engineering careers for an hour, and I looked forward to seeing him again in western Michigan some day.

I called Mark and left a message. I thought of Mark asking me to show him some affection, and how rarely I remembered to kiss him or hug him. Perhaps he had gotten some affection from Cecily, having her curl up next to him.

When he returned my call, I thanked him for being so patient with my family and me the day before. "I liked your family," he said. "I didn't hear any of the quarreling that I had been warned about by you and your father. You and your sister Susie seemed to get along fine. Your family must have a fetish about kissing scars. I saw you kiss her knee, and I'm sure I saw Susie put her hand on the scar near your ankle."

"When we would fall down and get a bruise or something, we always wanted mom to kiss it and tell us it would be all right. Sometimes I substituted for mom. Susie was five years younger than me, and when she was learning to walk and falling down, I would often get a band-aid."

Mark said, "It's too bad the party was Sunday and not Saturday. It lasted so long because everyone had a good time. You kept singing the army song, and then danced with some of your cousins to songs on the radio." I had enjoyed dancing to the radio, although I couldn't remember what music we danced to. "I think you should go to bed and get a good night's sleep, and I should, too."

"My family is so sexist," I said. "Notice how they asked you about killing people in Iraq, and nobody asked me. I had to keep telling them that women carry guns, too. They think that women are just in the way and that men have to protect us all the time."

Mark said, "Pam, if you want to talk about killing people in Iraq, I think you should talk to other people who have been in the army. Your father might understand because he was in Vietnam, but I don't think that many of your relatives would. That's why I told your nephews that combat experiences should be kept in the army. You could talk to Pete or me about your army experiences. You have too many expectations for your family. I wish I had cousins nearby, and knew my aunts and uncles better. Some of my European relatives visited us when I was growing up, but I don't speak German well enough to participate much in a conversation."

"Were your relatives Vonns or your mother's side of the family?"

"They were from my mother's side of the family. There aren't any Vonns. I had my name legally changed a long time ago. Our surname is Stutzer—actually von Stutzer. My family was insulted by my changing my name, especially my brother. I don't think he ever forgave me for it."

"I'm surprised. Mark von Stutzer?"

"Mark Stutzer. My grandfather stopped using the 'von.'"

"When I think of von Stutzer, I think of von Braun."

"Of course," Mark said. "My grandfather was a rocket scientist and surrendered to American forces in the company of von Braun."

I was surprised. I hesitated before saying, "For some reason, I pictured your grandparents coming here because they were fleeing Nazis. I thought that they came here with people like Einstein and Fermi."

"But instead of fleeing Nazis, they were Nazis. Surprise!" Mark responded. "Most scientists aren't interested in politics.

Either side can use them. I suppose my grandfather went along with whatever he was told to do. Is developing military equipment a war crime? It depends on who uses it and for what, I suppose. The victors decide who the war criminals are. You're in the weapons business now, and so am I. Civilians, as well as the armed services, can have the blood of their country's enemies on their hands."

I may have pictured Mark's family as being victims because he seemed to lack self-confidence. I don't think a confident person educated in science would choose to work in security.

Mark continued, "The strange thing about our name was that when my grandfather died and we went to the funeral in Huntsville, my grandmother asked my father to help her change her name back to von Stutzer legally. She said that von Stutzer was the name she was married with, and her maiden name was von Herrmann, and she wanted to keep the old naming tradition. She wanted a classier name. At least that's what I understood. My German isn't good enough for subtleties."

"Did your grandmother stay in Huntsville?"

"Yes. My father offered to have her come live with us in to New Mexico, but she said that her English wasn't good enough to live anywhere else but Huntsville, and all her friends were in Alabama. Our name kept evolving and becoming more American- sounding," he continued.

"So your grandfather was a rocket engineer?"

"Yes. We don't look like the Germans in the movies, though."

"Are you in contact with your brother much?"

"No, since he lives in Nevada. I don't have nephews to play catch with like you do. My brother was very angry about my changing my name. He didn't come to my wedding but sent a present and card. He never even sent me a get-well card when

I was disabled from the accident and didn't come visit when I was in New Mexico recovering. We talked on the phone a little because he called my parents, and they insisted that we talk."

"It's too bad he took it personally," I said.

"Well, it's not the whole story. My parents were very strict and that made me rebellious. Roger wasn't like that. He was more straight laced, so he disapproved and thought our parents were too easy on me when I goofed off so much in high school."

"High school is a world of its own," I said. "Full of meaningless events only important to high schoolers. He would have been in college when you were in high school, and it's hard to relate to high school after you've finished it. I used to get excited about high school basketball games. Now I'd rather play sports than watch somebody else play. Pot parties are another thing. The kids get stoned and say the same things over and over, and think they're being funny."

"Sounds like you've been at a few," Mark said. "I picture you smoking a joint, not getting high, and talking about the fluid dynamics problems inherent in vehicle fuel tanks while other people get stoned."

"You're right," I said, and laughed. "I guess you have my number."

"You had another family as well as your birth family," I continued. "Tell me about your wife's family."

"Darlene and I lived together before we got married. Our parents knew about it, of course. As I look back at it, Darlene and I were two children playing house. We thought of having an apartment as a way of entertaining our friends and having fun with the people we had gone to college with. What we didn't know was that most of our college friends would move away after they graduated. Without our undergraduate social set, we were lost. When I decided to go into the army, maybe I was still a rebellious little kid who wanted to do things my parents wouldn't approve of. I spent my college days preparing for the future and my army days believing that I didn't have a future."

"Do you mean that you thought that you didn't have a future because you might be killed in the war?" I asked. "That's how I felt, sometimes. When I was in Iraq the second time, I didn't plan my life after the war."

Mark said, "I spent so little time in Iraq compared to most people. Sometimes being in the war didn't seem real to me. I kept hoping it was a dream, and I would wake up and be in California or Korea or New Mexico." He paused for a while. "It's getting late. See you soon."

I felt tired enough to go to bed. I wished I had Mark and Cecily with me. I thought about Cecily purring when she was petted. I should show Mark more appreciation when he held me on his lap and hugged me.

How strange, to change your last name, I thought. Then I remembered that I had nearly changed my last name to Michael's. I felt sad after our conversation. I thought about walking near the mall in Washington with Michael, and talking about the war and making plans for the future.

When I was with Michael, we were both so delighted with life. I pictured us together in Washington, excited about being back in the United States. We went running on streets near the National Mall. He was faster than I was and waited, marching in place, for me to catch up. He picked me up, laughing. "How about a snack?" he said. "You're so small, you weigh only as much as an artillery shell." We walked into a business district and saw a drugstore. Michael wanted to go inside, where he bought a birthday card for me.

"It isn't my birthday," I said.

"We should celebrate your birthday every day," he said. "What would I do if you hadn't been born?" We both laughed, and bought some soda and trail mix, and ate it walking down the street, looking in store windows and talking about the future. I never planned for the future after Michael died, and I went to Iraq again.

I lay down on my bed; I cried and fell asleep. I dreamed of being in Washington.

CHAPTER 14

ANN ARBOR

Mark was going to Ann Arbor Sunday morning to attend a Buddhist program and asked me to join him. I was hesitant about committing myself to sitting on the floor on a cushion for hours, but Mark told me that chairs would be available. We could walk around the University of Michigan campus afterward, and I could show Mark where I had gone to school.

I thought that Mark went to this event because he was looking for a group to belong to. Without the army, we both needed to make new friends.

Mark and I entered a storefront building and registered for the program. A woman who introduced herself as Katie immediately launched into a discourse on her widowhood, her personal problems, and the help she was receiving by listening to the speaker, Sogyal Rinpoche, and reading his books. I was put off because she sounded like she was trying to sell a product.

"Why does it cost so much?" I whispered to Mark after Katie left to greet someone else.

Mark answered, "He comes from California to make a Midwest tour every year or so, and his travel costs money. He's written several books." The hall was different from a Zen Center, decorated with bright colors and tapestries, each one a painting surrounded by a framework of pieces of brocade and attached to a fabric scroll. The speaker's podium held colorful floral arrangements, and behind the speaker were more tapestries and flowers. The colors vied for my attention.

Most people were sitting on cushions on the floor, but rows of chairs were behind the row of cushions. I headed for a chair, so Mark followed and sat next to me. Many of the people sitting on cushions were fingering strings of beads.

After a while, the speaker came in and took his seat. To my surprise, I had seen him come into the room before. Sogyal Rinpoche was a small Asian man who had arranged some items on a table near the podium and then lay face down in front of it. Now he wore a maroon robe with a yellow shawl over his shoulders.

In spite of his dress, his appearance was casual, even jolly. He began talking about the importance of interacting with our surroundings while maintaining a nonjudgmental attitude toward them and not labeling everything in terms of what we liked and disliked. I watched and listened, but I also watched the audience. Some of the women were looking at him with admiration, almost as though they were in love with him.

He talked as though he was addressing each of us individually. After an hour, there was a break, and then we meditated—I mean, I tried to meditate. Some people were using prayer beads. Then he lectured again and took questions. I dropped my skepticism and became absorbed in his speech. When the lecture was over, the speaker opened the floor to questions. I tried to phrase a question about the war, so that

I could judge his astuteness by what he said. I decided to ask him what he thought about our country participating in wars in foreign countries.

After he answered the questions of the people in the front of the room, he took my question, too. "War is another concept that we like, dislike, or don't care about," he said. "Conflicts and war happen in the world and in our minds. Perhaps we perceive a war coming and judge it in terms of whether it would benefit us, harm us, or leave us unchanged. Perhaps some people start a different war to avert that one. It is all the nature of the world, and the nature of our mind."

"I liked that," I said to Mark after he finished speaking.

"I think he's a good speaker," Mark said. "He is very easy to follow."

"And he has quite a following," I said.

"Well, it isn't his personal trip but the teachings of the Buddha."

"Some of his students take it so personally that they seem to be in love with him," I said.

"This audience has a lot of female energy," Mark said. "One common meditation in the Tibetan tradition features visualizing a woman radiating light. The people holding beads were probably doing that kind of meditation and repeating the name of the woman, Tara. You could learn that meditation, if you want to."

"I don't think I want to do that," I said. "Meditating the standard way is hard enough. How does a person become a Buddhist, anyway?"

"Usually, in a formal ceremony," Mark said. "I was at a Tibetan ceremony a couple of times. At one, a high lama, a Tibetan Buddhist teacher, spoke for a few minutes. The atmosphere was quiet and focused. People in the audience just watched him and remained silent. A group sat on the floor in front of him. He said, 'When I snap my fingers, you become one of the family of the Buddhas.' They chanted, 'I take refuge in the Buddha, I take refuge in the Dharma, I take refuge in the Sangha.' Whenever I watched a group taking refuge, I was so glad that I belonged to this religion that I loved being a Buddhist as much as I have ever loved anything."

"What is the Sangha?" I asked.

"The Buddhist community."

The teacher sat at a table outside the lecture hall with two women. He was handing wrapped candies to people who walked by. Mark stopped for some candy and pocketed it. As we left, a group of people from the lecture were going to a Mongolian barbecue a few buildings down the street, and we joined them.

"I'm Henriette. Have you been here before?" the woman sitting next to me asked.

"I haven't been to this center because it's far from Detroit," I answered. "I'm glad we came here to eat. I always liked Mongolian better than Chinese because the food is freshly fried and hasn't been sitting in grease."

"That's what I like, too," she said. "And since I'm a vegetarian, I have a better selection of food."

The conversation turned to Buddhist practice in other countries, and Mark began talking about studying Zen in Korea, Zen temples in Korea, and the trip he made to Japan to see Buddhist temples and their remarkable gardens.

"Did you go only to Korea and Japan or also China on your vacation?" someone asked.

"I was stationed in South Korea in the army," Mark said. "From there, I took a vacation in Japan."

"You were in the army?" someone asked.

"Yes, I spent several years in the army."

"Were you in the war?" someone else asked.

"Yes, a year or two after I was in Korea, I was sent to Iraq."

The group was quiet, as though struck speechless. Finally, somebody changed the subject to the schedule of programs at the center. I decided not to say that I had been in the army too, since the people seemed to want to avoid the subject.

"This group has a talk every Sunday, and it's normally free," Mark said to me as we began walking toward the campus. "First they meditate, then have a talk, and then meditate again. I might like to join them again on some Sunday. Most of the people here seem to be professional people. I wish Ann Arbor was closer to Detroit, so I could get to know the people better."

"Your saying you were in the army was a show-stopper," I said.

"Yes, sometimes it is. But, after all, I can't hide that I was in the army, nor would I want to."

"I have that experience, too," I said. "People don't expect me to have been in the army. Often when I mention the army, the people I am talking to act surprised. Unless they have been in the army themselves, they rarely ask about what I did in the army or where I was stationed or why I went into the army. Sometimes they ask if I was in the war, but if I start telling them about Iraq, they act like they don't really want to know."

"Yes, and sometimes they look at you as though their whole opinion of you needs revising," Mark said. "Or they say something that implies that your family must have been very poor, so that you couldn't go to college right away out of high school."

"I find that, too," I said. "They usually assume I went into the service after high school and went to college later. They're surprised that I started my army career in Officers' Candidate School."

"Many people have a stereotype of army officers. A lot of writing about the war is stereotypical, too. The story starts with a group of soldiers, one black, one Hispanic, the rest white, some troubled, one wealthy, one adventurer, and an officious officer. Then they all go this place or that, get shot at, return fire, somebody gets wounded, and somebody unexpectedly is a hero. The army has more variety than in most civilian workplaces, I think. That probably happens because a company has a narrower selection of tasks to be performed than the army."

"Army people live together and socialize together and work together, so you get to know how varied the people are. Most of the civilians don't seem to know much about the people they work with, at least where I work."

Mark said, "The people where I work don't gossip that much about each other, and that is good because it's more fair to people. But it's bad because you don't get to know them as well, so you can determine if you should trust them."

"Do you mistrust people at work?" I asked.

"Working in security, it's our job to mistrust people."

"Do you like the people here more than those at the Zen Center?" I asked.

"I like both groups of people, but they're very different. Some people who do Zen are quite fanatical. A man told me that he took up meditation because it was such good discipline. I suggested that he go into the army if he wanted to learn discipline." Mark laughed. "I would like to meet more of the people who came here."

"I liked this better than the Korean Zen Center," I said. "This group seems less rigid and formal, less like the army." I thought that Mark might have found some people to be friends with, if Ann Arbor was not so far from Detroit. Then I thought that if he came here a lot, he would meet a woman who shared his religion and stop seeing me.

"I want to hold hands," I said, as we began walking through town.

Mark switched positions behind me and held out his left hand. "Can you write with either hand?" I asked, and then regretted saying that because it seemed insensitive.

"A little," he said. "I practiced with my left hand enough to sign my name, but I usually type, and I use both hands on the keyboard."

We walked over to the campus. I said, "I didn't have much time to enjoy the variety of things that the university has to offer. Engineering school was very hard, and I had to study and do homework for hours every day." We walked toward the science and engineering buildings. Flowers were blooming. The campus was quiet because it was a weekend, but a few students sat on the lawns, reading or talking like I used to do.

"After all this time, I don't have a feeling that the campus is a special place," I said. "I used to walk down these paths to go to class, eat in the student union, and go to events here. I don't feel emotionally attached to it anymore. School wasn't as interesting to me as the army, where I traveled to different bases and worked on a big variety of equipment."

"Did you have a lot of boyfriends in college?" Mark asked.

"Not many. I remember one I really liked, but he wanted to be a minister, and I couldn't see myself as a minister's wife.

Another was from the same high school as I was but was a year ahead of me. I had thought he was neat when we were in high school, but in college, he was so condescending to me that I couldn't really like him any more."

I continued, "I dated various other college students, too. College boys aren't very interesting. Most university students live in a dream world of some kind because they are trying to plan their future but don't have the right kind of information."

"What did you like best about school?"

"The laboratory classes. Also, browsing through the libraries and seeing all the subjects people wrote books about. And I liked the swimming pools. When I lived in dormitories, so many of the girls I lived with just wanted to meet boys. Then they would have a date at some sushi bar and talk as though sushi was the most important thing in the world. A lot of conversations were about meeting boys, which wasn't hard for me, majoring in engineering."

"College wasn't what I expected," Mark said. "The best part of Berkeley, California, was how easily we could cross the bay bridge and go to San Francisco. My father wanted us to go to school in Berkeley, so we could see big city life while studying physics at a good school.

"I was in a fraternity, and we had a lot of social events. Darlene and I went to her sorority social events, also. We met our second year of school. I was very happy in that secluded world of classes, parties, and going to San Francisco with friends. I made a major mistake in my attitude to school. Both San Francisco and Berkeley had many inexpensive cultural events, and I could have gone to plays, museums, and concerts, to broaden my horizons more, but I didn't. I don't even keep in touch with any friends from college. I liked some of my fraternity brothers, but I lost track of them after I went into the army."

Mark's statement seemed to confirm Pete's assessment of Mark as a heavy drinker, at least when he was going to college. Mark's story didn't make sense to me. He loved college when he was there but didn't regard it highly later. He liked his fraternity but didn't keep in touch with any of his fraternity brothers.

Mark said, "I liked college well enough. I should have applied myself more. Many things about school seem silly and immature to me now, but they seemed important ten years ago. We grow up."

"Did you feel depressed in college, too?" I asked.

"No, that started in the army. Especially my last two years. Fort Huachuca and Sierra Vista are boring places to live. For entertainment, you can look at the jackrabbits or go to a bar and watch soldiers and defense contractors falling off the barstools. There isn't even a city worth going to nearby."

I said, "I didn't mind Fort Irwin, and it's in the desert, too."

"You probably weren't there very long," Mark said. "These remote bases are all right for a little while, but then the lack of variety gets to you. I had to drive to Tucson to meditate with a Buddhist group."

We walked around the campus for an hour, admiring the architecture, and then decided to go back home. We walked through town to the car, stopping to buy overpriced coffee and pastry at a coffee bar. "I used to think that downtown Ann Arbor was special. Maybe I had been so enthusiastic about it because I didn't have a car at school, and I only visited places I could walk to." I watched Mark eating his pastry slowly.

ANN ARBOR

"Did you have much social life in Sierra Vista?" I asked. "There must be something to do besides going to the bars and the Fort Huachuca Officers' Club."

"Sierra Vista is big enough to have restaurants and movies. I didn't date much. I used to date a Hispanic woman there, but she mainly wanted a ticket out of the border area and a meal ticket. You probably had a lot of social life at places you were stationed."

I didn't want to talk about the men I had been seeing after Michael. I thought of a black officer with the most beautiful male legs I had ever seen. I met him in the summer, and he was wearing shorts. I saw his legs under a table when a group of us was playing poker. Then I looked at the man. He wasn't handsome, just okay. We had some fun until he was sent to Afghanistan. Then there were some civilian guys. The officers I knew were usually married, and I don't date married men. "I didn't go out much after Michael, except to group events because most of the male officers were married, just like most of the men at the Friday happy hour," I said.

"Don't feel you need to recount your male friends to me, if you don't want to, Pam," Mark said. "We aren't young, and there are people in our past. I don't want to pry into your life. Since women are a small minority in many army settings, I'm sure that you had as much social life as you wanted."

"I don't think you are prying into my life," I said. "Sure, I've dated some men here and there. We didn't have much in common." I didn't want to tell him about picking men up at Tequila Tom's and similar places near various military bases. Perhaps I should get a test for AIDS.

We found our car and began the trip home.

"I'm glad you liked the program," Mark said. "I don't think Buddhism is for everyone, though meditation can be a complement to Christianity. Eastern Orthodox Christians are more involved in meditation than Western European churches are. Christianity has one of the most powerful stories possible. Christianity says that we live in a cycle of sinning, repenting, and being redeemed, as we act a part in an emotionally powerful story. If a man pushes you away from certain death by a speeding car and saves your life, does that change you? Of course. Christianity says that you were saved from the consequences of sin, just as your life was saved from that speeding car because Christ died for you."

"I've never heard Christianity described that way," I said.

"The literary motif of one man dying in place of another has appeared in European literature many times because it is one of the most emotionally affecting stories possible. Maugham's *The Razor's Edge*, or Dickens's *A Tale of Two Cities*, for example."

"You've read more widely than I have," I said. "We engineering majors didn't read much that wasn't in our discipline. My education was math, statics, dynamics, hydraulics, and circuits. Tell me about the books you mentioned."

We went to Mark's place for the night because Cecily had been alone all day. She was pleased to see us and moved from one of us to another as I used Mark's computer to access my e-mail, and Mark sat on a cushion on the floor to meditate. Lily e-mailed me that she was going to take two weeks leave in Cleveland and asked if I would like to visit her there. She said that they had a lot of room since her sisters had left home and apologized for not answering most of my e-mails.

I e-mailed back that I didn't expect many replies because people are so busy when they are overseas. I hadn't kept up with my e-mail in Iraq, although I tried to answer my dad's e-mails within a couple of days, so that my family wouldn't worry about me. I accepted her invitation.

I looked forward to curling up with Mark and Cecily for the night. I remembered my previous resolve to be more affectionate to Mark and kissed him good night before we went to bed. "This life is the one I could have," I thought. "Mark, Cecily, and I could make a home for ourselves here."

CHAPTER 15

POWWOW

LuAnn found a powwow to attend on a weekend. I hadn't attended a powwow since I left Michigan for the army. I knew that Mark would be eager to go, especially since he liked LuAnn and Bob.

The ceremony was large enough to draw out-of-state dancers and vendors instead of only Midwest performers. The schedule was for one session Friday night, three on Saturday, and two on Sunday. LuAnn and I decided that we would go to the powwow Saturday morning and stay all day.

LuAnn had made some sweet rolls and urged them on us. Sandy came over and sat beside Mark. She put her hand on his forehead and asked, "Do you feel better, Uncle Mark? At our place, you were vomiting all over everything."

"You're so sweet," Mark said. "I was sick that day, but I feel fine now."

We all went to the management office to get Bob. He was apparently still asleep, so LuAnn beat on the door until he answered. He looked hung over. We all stepped into his apartment, which was littered with empty liquor bottles, newspapers, pizza boxes, and piles of garbage. After he shaved and dressed, we were ready to cram five people into my Jeep Liberty. Sandy obligingly went into the area behind the second row of seats and amused herself by riding facing the back.

The powwow was held indoors at a fairground because the weather forecast was for rain. We arrived in time for the opening ceremony, when veterans in uniform wearing Purple Heart ribbons bring flags into the dance site. Besides the Indian flag bearers, two of the veterans were Caucasians who probably came from the local Veterans of Foreign Wars or American Legion post.

"Just think, carrying the flag at a powwow is something you could use your Purple Heart for. A Purple Heart is required for a flag bearer," I said to Mark.

He said, "You mean people can use a Purple Heart for something? Most of these guys seem to be Vietnam-era vets. I wonder if you need to be old and wise, too."

"They revere the old in this culture," I said. "This is also a warrior culture. They don't believe that a good life is necessarily a long life. It's a life being who you are."

Mark said, "That's different from our culture, where people try to live as long as they can. Some military people share that Indian sense of values—live fully and die courageously. That's the attitude of some of the pilots, especially." Some of the Indians nearby gave us a dirty look for talking during the ceremony. Most Indians talked very little during ceremonies, and even the children were quiet and observant.

The first dance was performed in a circle around the center, and anyone could participate, whether or not they wore a costume. LuAnn and Sandy went to the dance floor, while the rest of us stayed in the stands. Sandy didn't know the dance steps and just skipped at first, then began trying to copy the dancers around her. LuAnn danced stiffly, the costumed dancers passing her up. After circling around the gym floor several times, she came back to sit with us. The drumming and costumed dancers were an absorbing spectacle, and the dance passed quickly. All dancers who registered as contestants wore large number tags, so the judges could evaluate them without knowing their names. I tried to figure out which dancers were the best to match my selections to the judges and understand the judging system.

"I like this," Mark whispered.

The next event began with announcements of how far dancers had come to participate. One group was from the Navajo Reservation and one from Connecticut. Canadian First Nation people had come from Ontario. The midwestern tribal groups were Sioux, Ho-Chuck, and Ojibwa. The Ojibwa were the most beautiful, I thought. LuAnn was a beautiful woman, with her long dark hair and heart-shaped face.

The first dance competition was the traditional dance for men. Men with elaborate costumes of deerskin, arrow pouches, and decorations of feathers, arrows, turtle shells, and other natural items performed a dance that consisted of examining the ground and looking up, as though they were tracking prey while hunting. The men wore bustles of feathers; a few wore headdresses of porcupine quills. Some had painted their faces in geometric designs.

The dancers fell into three categories: children, adults, and seniors, who are people over fifty. Fifty seemed young for senior citizens, but I remembered that Indians rarely have long lives. Most of the traditional dancers were seniors, but a variety of men and some young boys danced too. After a while LuAnn and Bob slipped away, leaving Sandy with Mark and me. I assumed that they had a flask and were going to take a few nips. Liquor wasn't allowed at a powwow, but some people would be drinking in the parking lot or in cars.

Next was the women's traditional dance; the dance primarily consisted of swaying to the drumbeats. About a dozen drum groups had set up at the edge of the gymnasium. The dancers wore long dresses with a tassel at the back that moved back and forth as they swayed.

After a brief break, the second type of dance began. The first dance was the grass dance for men, in which the dancers wore costumes decorated with colorful yarn to simulate grass. The long fringe on the bottom of the costumes was matched in color with the shorter fringe that decorated the chest and sleeves. The dancers moved in a step that caused the yarn fringes to sway like the grass moving with the wind in the Plains, where the dance originated. The costumes were in a variety of colors—shades of blue, red, and brown. I noticed that one dancer wore glasses and had devised a visor of strings of beads, which he wore on his forehead to cover his glasses while he was dancing. The visor seemed a clever way to match modern technology to his costume, which was beaded and fringed.

The most popular dance at any powwow was the jingle dance for women. The jingle dresses were made in two thicknesses, so that the outer dress, decorated with metal twists, slid loosely over the inner dress. The metal twists banged into each other, and the dresses "jingled" as the women danced. One of the dancing women, who was slightly younger than LuAnn and me, wore a two-tone pink dress. I kept looking at her because she looked like LuAnn had looked when she was in high school. I didn't remember LuAnn ever dancing competitively at a powwow. Maybe LuAnn never had time to sew a costume. She may not have had access to a sewing machine either. Suddenly I felt sad for LuAnn, without a mother to help her.

Although all ages danced in the men's grass dance, only one senior woman was a jingle dancer. The emcee asked other women to join her so that she wouldn't be dancing alone. The floor filled with jingle dancers in their colorful dresses. The dancer in pink joined the others.

Sandy told me that she would like to do jingle dancing, and I agreed that being a jingle dancer would be fun. I looked more carefully at the costumes to see how they were constructed. If I owned a sewing machine, perhaps I could make a jingle dress for Sandy. I asked Sandy if she knew where to buy the jingles, and she said that there were special mail-order catalogs for powwow supplies. She said that her uncle had many such catalogs because he made beaded cigarette cases and key rings, and sometimes sold them at fairs. I was surprised. I hadn't seen LuAnn's brother since he was a child, and I remembered him as a quiet little boy who always looked serious.

Mark said that the drumming and dancing fascinated him. "Do they perform the same dances in New Mexico?" I asked.

"I never went to one of these in New Mexico," he said. "Never occurred to me."

The fancy dancers performed last, and their costumes were the least traditional. Fancy dancing had no senior division. The young women wore colorful clothes, stepping high and kicking with their elaborately beaded boots. The men were athletes in gym clothes who had donned elaborately feathered bustles and multicolored headdresses for the dance. Some of the young men stepped so high that they seemed at risk of falling down. The little boys were gymnasts as well as dancers, some of them doing cartwheels.

At the noon break, LuAnn and Bob came back for Sandy. Bob carried the scent of cheap whiskey on his black T-shirt, which had an obvious liquor splash down the front. We all bought Navajo tacos from the food vendor. The fry bread was hot and delicious, but the meal was fattening, with cheese and sour cream over the fry bread, beans, hamburger, lettuce, and tomato.

"What is fry bread made of?" Mark asked.

"Just flour and water mixed and fried in lard," I said. "Fry bread isn't an original Indian food because they didn't have wheat and beef. It's often made from government surplus food."

"These taste like Mexican food, without hot sauce," Mark said.

Mark and I walked around to the vendors with LuAnn, Bob, and Sandy. We passed people selling jewelry, Indian blankets, honey, CDs and tapes, sewn jackets, and beaded souvenirs. Mark bought a few tapes of drum music, and a blue T-shirt with a dream-catcher motif on the front. He treated Sandy to a T-shirt, too. She chose a pink one with a dream-catcher like his. Mark talked with some of the vendors, asking about their reservations, as though he was planning to visit. Most of the Indians were urban Indians, though, and didn't live on Indian reservations. I pictured Mark and me taking a tour of Michigan Indian reservations, and seeing nothing particularly interesting.

Mark wanted to buy me something at one of the stands, but I hesitated. Almost everything I owned was utilitarian. I didn't have decorative items as Mark did.

"I'll think about it," I said.

Then I saw a stall with Indian art objects, some traditional, like little pots from the Southwest, but others more original and possibly made by local Indians. The Indian man tending the stall asked if he could help us, in an uninterested way. I saw that he was doing beadwork. The design was a turtle with four colors on its back, like the turtle in Bob's tattoo. "I'm admiring the turtle," I said.

"I do some beading when business is slow," the man replied.

"Is a turtle important to your tribe?" Mark asked.

"Some call North America Turtle Island," the man said. "Some tribes in the eastern United States say that the turtle dived to the primeval mud to help create the world."

"Could I buy it?" Mark asked.

"I usually don't sell the things I make myself," the man replied. "What do you want it for?"

"A present for Pam," Mark said, gesturing toward me. The man looked at me closely and nodded. "Turtles are for women. A turtle is for female power, fertility, and self-reliance."

I knew I wanted the turtle. "I was in the army," I said. "I'm very self-reliant." It seemed that I needed to qualify to own the turtle.

"Turtle gives long life and defiance of death," he continued. *I remembered picking up the rifle.* "Turtle is for inner knowledge." I thought, maybe I need inner knowledge. I had been to some army programs on war experiences and dealing with death, but they were about people in your own unit being killed.

"Come back after the evening session. I will finish it by then, and you can buy it," the man said.

"I'll be back," Mark replied.

We walked toward the next set of booths. "A turtle," I said. "They spend their life in a shell."

"They live by the water," Mark said. "You like the water. They know how to protect themselves. You are very good at protecting yourself."

When the afternoon session began, Sandy sat on the gym floor. I was amused to see her sitting beside a little boy. She was already like her mother, wanting to be with the men. The afternoon powwow program was similar to the morning program. Sandy stayed on the gym floor, in a state of absorption that continued even after the drumming stopped.

At the dinner break, we all had corn soup and hot dogs, which I personally detested. Bob wanted to treat us all to hot dogs, and I didn't want to insult him by refusing. I loaded the hot dog with pickle relish and mustard, so that I wouldn't taste the cheap, greasy meat. We went outside and watched the costumed Indians in the parking lot. The jingle dancer who wore pink was talking with a group of friends. I would have liked to ask her how to find a place to teach Sandy dancing, but I didn't go over to her. I would have been disappointed if she wasn't as friendly as LuAnn.

A Sioux traditional dancer approached Mark and me, and asked for gas money to get back to the reservation in South Dakota. "All the way from South Dakota," I said. I gave him a couple of dollars, and Mark gave him more. In return for the money, the Indian gave Mark a feather and bell from his costume. I was sure that Mark would keep them with the rest of the beads, bells, and pictures that he used to decorate the bookcase and dresser.

LuAnn said afterward that we should have refused the Sioux man money because he had probably been drinking and would spend it on liquor.

"I guess being panhandled is part of the experience," Mark said.

I was growing tired, but Mark was getting more enthusiastic and animated. I usually went to a powwow for only part of the day, but we needed to stay to pick up the turtle decoration that Mark had bought me. LuAnn began telling stories of her relatives on the reservation up north. She told Mark the story of their house burning down, which I had heard before. They used kerosene lamps, and one of their cats, which were bobcats, had knocked a lamp over. The lamp set the rug on fire and the house, a log cabin, quickly burned. Afterward they moved into a housing development on the reservation. Soon, her family moved to the Detroit area, so that her father could get a better-paying job.

The evening session began with a hoop dance by a single dancer. He moved the set of hoops around his body and down his arms in interlocking patterns. The rest of the session followed the standard pattern, with a smaller number of dancers. Each drumming group was introduced. The emcee pointed out that traditionally, only men performed drumming for the dances, but now the drumming groups were usually co-ed, and one of them was all women. LuAnn said that she had become interested in drumming, but when she had gone back to the reservation to inquire about it, she found that women traditionally don't perform drumming. She was pleased to see many women playing drums at this powwow. She spent part of the session outside with Bob, presumably drinking. Sandy, who was getting sleepy, came back up the bleachers and rejoined Mark and me.

As we were leaving, Mark said he wanted to come back on Sunday. I agreed. I had never seen him so happy. We bought the turtle from the vendor, who said that turtles should be respected for their strength and perseverance. Then we walked to the car.

"I grew up around Indian history and ruins, but I ignored the ceremonies of the present," Mark said. "The only time I saw dancing was for tourists at tours of pueblos."

"I've never seen a pueblo," I said. "But the Mound Builder Indian culture was centered just south of here, and we could go and see mounds if you want to. The area around Columbus, Ohio has some of the greatest Indian structures of the Americas."

Sandy and Bob slept in the car on the way home. LuAnn was quiet, but Mark was talkative. "Think of the Romans going up the Thames, with the local people signaling each other with drums," he said. "Think of people drumming at night on the Rhine. Our ancestors in Europe probably drummed and danced in ceremonies like this, maybe not so colorful."

We invited LuAnn and Bob to join us again the next day, but they thought that one day at a powwow was enough. They had spent so little time watching the dances that LuAnn might as well have said that an afternoon was enough. Bob probably went to the powwow just to please LuAnn and wasn't sincerely interested in the ceremony.

After saying goodbye to LuAnn, Sandy, and Bob, Mark and I went to Mark's place. Cecily was glad to see us. She meowed a lot and stamped her feet by her food dish, as though she wanted a late night snack. I picked her up to take her to bed with us. I liked the feeling of Cecily purring against my body.

"We should go to another powwow, maybe on a weekend next month," I said. "I've never seen you so happy."

"I would like to go to another powwow this summer," Mark said. "The program was so entertaining and so involving that I didn't think of anything else during it. I'm really looking forward to tomorrow."

"I was completely absorbed, too," I said. I needed a rest from the things I spent my week days working with, like vehicle armor, protection from IEDs, and rocket-propelled grenade damages. Perhaps Mark needed a break too. When he got very quiet, I often thought that he was thinking of war experiences that bothered him, but that he didn't want to tell me what they were.

Death and killing in a war are difficult to deal with. We all mourn, and we all die. As soldiers in a war, we kill. We know this theoretically until it becomes real. We grieve, we kill, and we die.

I fell asleep right away, but Mark slept so restlessly that he woke me up repeatedly during the night. Once I turned toward him, kissed his face, and smoothed his hair. He buried his face in the pillow.

CHAPTER 16

MARK'S STORY REVISED

We woke up late and would have to rush to get to the powwow. I put on my dirty clothes, but Mark lent me one of his T-shirts, which was blue with a Sterling Heights, Michigan, logo on the front. I couldn't understand why someone would want to advertise Sterling Heights, Michigan, where the main streets looked like a series of auto-parts factories and stamping mills.

On the way, Mark talked about how much he liked the powwow. "But a powwow isn't just an entertainment. It's a celebration of life," I said. "We usually forget to celebrate living. Every time I was in a convoy, I felt that just surviving was a reason for a celebration."

The morning session opened with the flag ceremony and then continued with the dances, as before. At the end of the traditional dance, the emcee suddenly announced that a person not qualified to touch an eagle feather had picked one up. Apparently, only a military veteran was allowed to pick up a fallen eagle feather. I whispered to Mark, "I told you this is a military culture."

"They take this pretty seriously, don't they?" Mark said.

A Sioux Indian walked up to the podium and handed the emcee a pack of cigarettes—tobacco was a respectful gift for an Indian elder. He was a big, fierce-looking man wearing a wolf-skin headdress. He said that he was the person who had picked up the eagle feather, that he had served in the army, and that he had faced his enemies directly in battle in Vietnam, so he was qualified to touch the eagle feather. The emcee yielded him the floor, and he continued talking, but no one apologized to him. Eventually the ceremony got under way again.

At the lunch break, Mark said, "I wouldn't have wanted to face that warrior wearing a wolf skin, in any battle."

"He was one of the most formidable-looking soldiers I've ever seen," I said. "I saw a woman with him, and she was tall and stately, too." We bought some Navajo tacos and ate on the lawn outside before going back in for the afternoon session and closing ceremony.

"I would like to find some more Indian-related things to do," Mark said after we got to my apartment.

I suggested that we go to see the mounds in Ohio—like a pilgrimage. "My family vacationed in Ohio a few times," I said. "We always took a week in the summer and rented a cabin in northern Michigan or southeastern Ohio. I'd like to have a bit of summer vacation, even just a long weekend. Could you get four days off in a row, including a weekend?"

Mark said he'd check into it, and since his coworkers probably wanted summer vacations too, perhaps they could swap some days with them. He then said he had made plans with Bob to help him clean up his apartment.

"He seems to have hit a triple in life," Mark said. "Alcoholic, parents are alcoholic, and his ex-wife and present girlfriend are heavy drinkers. Some people don't know how to live other than to drink whenever the opportunity arises. I know that living in a mess like Bob does gets depressing, too. Living in a mess is what Darlene and I used to do," Mark said.

I looked at him, shocked.

"I should have told you about this before," he continued. "The time never seemed right. Darlene and I drank excessively, and our bottle-to-mouth life caused us many problems. Our drinking wasn't pretty. Going to frat parties, bars, and nightclubs is fun when you are in college, but Darlene and I let alcohol absorb our lives.

"I started drinking heavily when I was a teenager. I would have done much better in school if I hadn't been drinking so much. I didn't continue in graduate school because the university didn't want teaching assistants who were lushes.

"Part of my attraction to you is that you don't seem to care whether you have liquor to drink. Darlene was getting tired of my drinking. She drank excessively herself, but I often went out to bars with my coworkers after work and came home drunk. I don't want to complain that my wife didn't understand me because Darlene knew that my first priority was the army, then came drinking, then the army, then drinking, and more drinking—she wasn't close to the top of the list."

"You weren't physically violent with each other, were you?" I asked.

"Not that I recall. Sometimes I couldn't recollect much of the previous evening. She might be very distant in the morning, and I would ask her if I had hurt her, and she always said no. Yet, sometimes she acted scared of me. She also used to tell me that she wished I were dead. That's a fine way to live, isn't it? Your spouse wants you dead.

"We had plenty to argue about. We were thrown out of base housing stateside because of our filthy living conditions. Our place looked as bad as Bob's. By the time we broke up, I would find liquor stashed in odd places because she liked a nip while she was doing housework and didn't want me to know. Sometimes she hid a particular bottle because she didn't want to share it with me.

"What started as enjoying frat parties and campus dives became a desire to drink after work and spend the evening drinking, sometimes with friends. And I mean drink a lot. Darlene and I were having serious conflicts before she left me. She said that either I was going to be home more, or we were going to get a divorce. I didn't make any effort to drink less. Our drinking sprees and bottle-to-mouth drinking got progressively sloppier and more private every year. In other words, we were both alcoholics.

"We were devastated by her miscarriage. She blamed me. I wonder if her miscarriage was connected with her drinking. I don't blame her now. When I drink, I think every screwed-up thing that I did is somebody else's fault—hers, my parents, the army's—when there is nobody to blame but me." Mark looked at me.

"The biggest difficulty with stopping heavy drinking is that all your friends drink, so to stop drinking you have to find new friends, as well as develop new habits for yourself. That's how AA can help. When you go to meetings, you're staying out of the bars and meeting people who don't want to drink," Mark said, and paused. "I wonder what you think of me now."

"I don't know what to make of this," I said. "I can't personally relate to alcoholism. I notice in your story that you and

Darlene had a social life that revolved around drinking with your friends, a pattern common in the army, too."

"The accident in Korea changed my life, and Darlene's way of looking at me. When I was in that jeep accident, the driver and I were both drinking. I had brought the liquor. He was a sergeant from my unit, and we were friends. My injuries were my fault. I might have been killed by my own behavior. Then my injuries were complicated by the fact that I was alcoholic and had to dry out when I was hospitalized.

"When I woke up, the pain in my arm was like an explosion. I couldn't talk because I had a tracheotomy tube in my throat. Although you seem to like scars, you didn't seem to notice the scar on my neck. I had convulsions, due either to my head injury or my alcohol problem. I could have died. I thought I would die. When I was in the hospital from the accident, detoxing from alcohol was hard, but I had so many pain drugs that I didn't miss alcohol as much as if I had been trying to stop drinking while I led a normal life with social events and bars around.

"I went right back to drinking as soon as I could. That was a stupid thing to do because the alcohol was out of my system. Later, I took some risks by drinking while using pain medication. I should have told you about my problem before. I kept thinking, now is the time, and then, no, it isn't the time, some other time would be better." He waited for my reaction.

"I think Darlene should have waited to get a divorce," I said. "Remember the old saying about not kicking a man when he's down. You couldn't drink for a while, and maybe the two of you could get along better when you had to stop drinking. You could have gotten a new start."

Mark replied, "Some men say that abandonment by their wife when they were injured was worse than the injury. For me, what was worst was my guilt."

MARK'S STORY REVISED

Mark was confessing to being alcoholic, as Pete had told me. "I don't understand why people find alcohol interesting," I said.

"Drinking gave me confidence. I thought I got hold of myself better when I had some liquor," Mark said. "I was deceiving myself. Also, life seemed nicer when I was drinking, and I was happier. The world I lived in was brighter, life was a party, my friends were the most clever and brilliant people in the world, and I laughed at the funniest jokes that I had ever heard."

"When you drink the world is magnificent and full of fun, and when you're sober you live in a drab world and feel sad?" I asked.

"Yes, that's right. When I drink, I feel more like myself. I can remember when I used to be happy, and I was happy when I was drinking. Drinking turns routine activities into a party. I've been afraid to tell you about this," he said. "It isn't a nice story. I messed up my career, my marriage, my health, and everything I had because of my drinking."

I had just heard Mark confess to alcoholism, drug abuse, and dereliction of duty. Just like Pete had told me.

"Remember the emotional-tone concept we talked about before," Mark said. "I felt best when I had something to drink—I was happier, and I felt like myself."

We were quiet for a while. Then I said, "Mark, you don't need to blame yourself for all of your problems. You didn't decide to be alcoholic. As your favorite book, the Bhagavad-Gita, says, we were born in a particular time and place and social status. Our society has easy access to alcohol, and some people are susceptible to consuming too much liquor. In my family, some people have drinking problems, too. My father uses alcohol to relieve tension that the family causes.

"Some people have an addictive liking for alcohol, and some people are indifferent to it," I continued. "I remember going canoeing with a group of people, and they said it would be more fun if we had brought rum and Coke in a thermos. I was surprised because I didn't want to blur my attention while I was canoeing."

Mark said, "When alcoholics see problems, they deny them, postpone dealing with them, or drink more. I knew that alcohol was more appealing to me than to most people and that drinking was getting me into trouble. When I realized that I drank compulsively, I should have stopped."

"If we had known ten years ago what we know now, we would be better off, wouldn't we?" I replied. "But that's true for everybody." I put my hand on Mark's shoulder. "Alcoholism isn't something you chose."

"Don't console me for being a drunk and a fool," he replied.

"Mark, it seems to me that what you are telling me is that you screwed up, and you ended up suffering badly for your mistakes. There isn't anything you can't recover from, unless you've damaged your health."

"I may have done that, too," he said.

I said, "I'm not going to beat up on you for drinking, because you don't do it around me. If you drink and get nasty with me, I'll deal with it then."

"Your father said you're not a good person to cross. I should have told you before that I'm an alcoholic, but I was afraid because I thought you'd be horrified by what I'm saying or that you wouldn't want to see me any more. If you want to drop me now, I'll understand."

I replied, "I have faults, too. Your former drinking problem doesn't make me feel differently about you—maybe a little warmer because I know you better now. I thought that you were hiding something, and now I know what and why." We sat in silence for a while.

"Does this mean that we shouldn't see LuAnn and Bob? We know they drink too much," I said.

"That's why I was so at home with them, and I ended up making a fool of myself," Mark replied.

"Maybe you could help Bob," I said. "He's gotten into trouble because of his drinking. You've heard him tell about the pool hall fight and his going to jail. LuAnn spent a couple of weeks in the county jail for some silly stuff she did while drinking, like smarting off to a police officer."

Mark asked, "Would you be able to do something for me? I would really like you to go to AA's companion program, Al-Anon, or at least to try it. I go to AA once or twice a week, and the Al-Anon program is for spouses or significant others. Could you go to some meetings for me? If you go two or three times, and you don't care for it, I'll understand." This sounded strange, but I told him that I was willing to do it. I would probably meet some other women. I hardly knew any local women, because I did a man's job and worked with men.

"I could go to some meetings," I said.

We lapsed into silence again. A rerun of "The Deadliest Catch" was on television. Mark sat on the floor and meditated to the sound of men on television yelling at each other about catching crabs. I tried to be warmer to Mark that night. I thought of the moonlight outside and of making love under the stars.

CHAPTER 17

DETROIT SUMMER

Mark and I went to an AA meeting one night that featured an Al-Anon meeting at the same time but in a different room. A group was socializing in a common area, and Mark began talking with two men he had known before. I struck up a conversation with a woman about my age; when it was time to split into two groups, she invited me to sit next to her. I was disappointed to find that she was headed to the AA meeting. She had a good sense of humor, and I thought that we could become friends if we were in the same meeting.

The people who went to the AA meeting greatly outnumbered the people in the Al-Anon meeting—just one man and seven women. Most of the women were older than I was, but I thought that I could make friends with some of them. As we introduced ourselves, I found out that I was the only one who wasn't married to an alcoholic. One woman suggested that staying single would be better than being married to an alcoholic. I listened to their stories of their husbands being unemployable or insisting on driving while drunk or cutting up their clothes, and I tried to picture Mark doing any of these things. I couldn't.

After the meeting, Mark introduced me to a man, Don, and an older couple, Robin and Bert. We all went to a restaurant for coffee and dessert, which they apparently did every week. Mark and Don had played chess some evenings and planned to play again. Mark had told them about me. Bert was interested in the work I did and asked me if there were opportunities in accounting or business administration at the company where I worked, since he didn't think that his job was secure. I suggested that he look on our Web site because I wasn't in a position to know.

I asked the group if they liked hiking because we could all go to the metropark some weekend and walk on some of the trails. No one seemed enthusiastic, even when I said that the trails came in many different lengths and were attractive. They all seemed nice, though. Maybe we could find something else that they would like to do.

I told Mark that I would like to go to more meetings because I might meet interesting women. I wasn't really too enthusiastic about meeting married women telling everyone else about how horrible their husbands were. I told Mark that the meeting was mostly women complaining about their husbands.

"That seems kind of depressing," he said. "I hope that I never give you anything to complain about to other people."

I said, "What bothers me in these meetings is that it's like going to the veterans associations. We concentrate on the thing that we put behind us."

"In AA, we try to encourage each other to not drink, and that's positive. Being in a meeting with people and interacting with them is more rewarding than watching television. You spend a lot of time watching television by yourself."

I said, "I don't even like watching television that much, but when I do my e-mail, or look things up on the Internet, I turn the television on. I often feel tired after work. We work nine hours a day, and I look forward to turning on the television and relaxing. I spend the day either doing math, like calculating loads on vehicle axles, or writing reports. It's interesting work, but when I get home I ask myself if I want to go someplace this evening or just curl up and do something mindless? Watching television wins out."

"If you socialized more, you might have more energy. We should be able to meet some other people. Maybe we could invite some of your neighbors over or even have a party."

As the summer went on, Mark and I saw each other more frequently. We spent most of each weekend together, and two or three weekday evenings. We enjoyed going to parks, museums, and Buddhist programs. We went to the Detroit Science Museum and the Cranbrook estate.

We often ran in the morning or evening. Some evenings we ran to a grocery store and brought food back to cook. Summer was beautiful, with trees budding out so quickly that a route to the grocery looked different each time we went. Lilac and honeysuckle had gone, and the summer flowers bloomed in the yards. Looking for closed stores became one of our routines when we ran, and we would detour into the strip malls to look for new closures. In some of the strip malls we passed, most of the storefronts were dark.

As the summer went on, we hiked less because of the heat and the mosquitoes. We had insect spray, but the buzzing sounds of insects and the smell of the spray were annoying.

We went to the happy hours to see our friends. Mark was much more skilled with people than I was. I became more aware of Mark's close relationship with Pete.

Mark decided to get an anniversary present for Pete and his wife Debra. Elizabeth from the Zen Center did calligraphy, and he decided to buy a calligraphy drawing from her and frame it for Pete and Debra.

I rarely went to Tequila Tom's anymore, and when I went, I ate a fish dinner and left soon afterward. I didn't accept the offers of men who wanted to buy me drinks, because I was with Mark now.

I liked having Cecily with me in the apartment sometimes, but the cat box, the hair, and her exploring annoyed me. But feeling her purr when I held her on my lap made up for the way she walked on the kitchen counters.

I looked on the Web sites for the National Guard. I wanted to know more about what being in the Guard would be like, what their rules were about age at joining, promotions, and what occupations generally available. I briefly talked to a recruiter on the telephone. I wouldn't join the Guard while we were still at war, but the wars might be over some day. Civilian life was boring compared to the army.

Since Mark and Bob had done some dumpster diving, I stopped ignoring dumpster divers and greeted the man who sometimes fished through the dumpster behind my apartment, extracting cans and bottles.

He told me that his name was Robert, and that God gave him a mission to pick up the cans and bottles in the street and the nearby park. He wore camouflage pants and told me that he used to be in the army. I told him that I had been in the army, too. I said I hoped that he wasn't homeless. He told me that he lived with his parents, which surprised me because he wasn't young. He said that he had a son who lived with his ex-wife. I asked him if he got help from the government. He said that he got help from Jesus, but he got some disability money because he had PTSD.

Robert thanked me for talking to him. He told me that Jesus had given him a job and that he had a mission, just like the prophets. I wished him well, and whenever I saw him after that, we talked.

Mark and I made another canoe trip. I was hoping that the canoe rental moved the canoes upstream, so that we only had to paddle downstream, but they didn't offer that service, and we had to paddle upstream against the current. The starting point was between a boatyard and a manufacturing plant that constantly burned a gas flare. The current was fairly strong because of recent rain. We struggled against the current, sweated, and got sunburned.

Mark reminded me that voyageurs paddled upstream for hundreds of miles, and had to portage around rapids. I pictured carrying a canoe around rapids in the summer heat with mosquitoes and flies in thick woods where the breeze was nonexistent. We passed a golf course a couple of miles upstream and went into a more heavily wooded area with a heavy population of insects, and then turned around. We resolved to drive farther next time and canoe on a nicer river.

The Society of Women Engineers met for a social dinner. Eight of us went to the meeting, which was held five miles from my home. Two had driven from the auto plants in the western suburbs and one was from the Volkswagen plant far to the northwest, but the rest of us worked nearby. Three were from the defense industry, four from the automobile industry, and one a civil engineer from the water department. We had a nice talk about engineering work and envied the civil engineer for being secure in her job in spite of the recession. I hadn't been in the company of a group of women, most about my own age, since I attended an army program for women. I decided to go to another dinner meeting even if it was farther from home.

Mark and I visited the Dharma Center at Ann Arbor twice. I took a class at the Zen Center, which Mark took a second time to be with me. I liked the way Elizabeth taught the class. I rarely meditated except before class and with Mark. I still couldn't quite catch on to meditating. I still had intrusive, repetitive thoughts about Iraq.

I admired Elizabeth's composure. I asked Mark if he thought she set a good example for people. Mark said that most of us live in a soap opera, but she learned to let go of her soap opera and live in the present. He added that the present is usually peaceful and serene, and that our memories of the past are often the source of our problems.

I said, "You mean, forget about the war." I pointed out that our soap opera comes from the story of our lives, which we can't forget, and our lives aren't always peaceful, especially when we are deployed in a war zone. "How could I forget mortars firing all night or convoys being fired on?" Mark said that if we dramatize our past less, we could look at it objectively, in the moment, and let go of our old thoughts about it. The thoughts and pictures that came with the fact that I picked up the soldier's rifle didn't go away. *I picked up the rifle. I picked up the rifle.*

I told Mark that I would like to be more objective about things that happened with my family and not get so mad. If I could go to visit my parents without being angry at my mother and sisters about things that happened a long time ago, I would go and see them more.

I hoped meditation might make me less nervous, so that I wouldn't bite my nails as much. People teased me sometimes about biting my nails. Mark started taking my hand out of my mouth and holding it, when I bit my nails.

I read some of Mark's books. I found myself concentrating better than I used to. I was less distracted by stray thoughts about being angry with my family and Iraq. I got a library card and took some books home. I hadn't read much while I was in the army. I asked Mark to recommend books. He liked reading Russian writers, and I found that I liked them too. Russian classics dealt with the big issues of life like war, peace, exile, adultery, crime, guilt, punishment, and love in a time of war.

Mark and I had Sunday dinner with Carolyn and Tim. I was surprised by their nice home, with its huge kitchen and recreation room with a fireplace. Apparently, Tim was very successful in the insurance business.

Carolyn held Bobby, and we talked while the men were watching sports on television. She said, "Having a baby is completely absorbing. I wonder how mom managed with the three of us, especially before you were in school."

"I've thought of that sometimes," I said. "Mostly, I remember doing a lot of housework when I got home from school. It seemed like a lot, anyway. I don't suppose a kindergarten girl really accomplishes much besides setting the table. The other things, I probably made as much a mess as I cleaned up."

"I'd like to see more of you," she said. "It would be nice for Tim, too. He doesn't get to watch sports with other men very often. His workplace is so small—only eight people, and he doesn't like being away from home or doing things like hitting the sports bars for company."

"They seem to get along," I said. "But I don't think Mark watches sports often. He doesn't own a television. He goes to religious services on Sunday, and then we usually walk in parks. When the weather gets cold, maybe he would like to watch sports. I know it's hard to meet people who share your interests. You and Tim must have friends from college nearby, though."

"We do," Carolyn said. "I can't imagine going so far from home like you did and not knowing anybody." We gossiped about Susie for a while.

"I don't know what helping Susie would consist of," I said. "If she wants to learn something that would bring her better work than being a waitress, I'm sure dad would pay for her training like he paid for our education. I think she mostly needs people to watch the children while she works and shops, but mom does that for her, I think."

"You might be able to find some time," Carolyn said. I could have said that I didn't want to help Susie, but I decided not to.

LuAnn and I talked on the phone a number of times, and I went to her apartment by myself twice. She was pleased with the powwow and gushed about Mark. She said that it was time

I got a boyfriend and that she was surprised I didn't get married in college or the army. I had never told her that I had been going to marry Michael while I was in the army.

When I didn't see Mark for a few days, I wondered if he was drinking.

Mark suggested that we host a party, since I wanted to get acquainted with more women. He said we should start very simply and invite some of my neighbors over for a Friday evening when we didn't have a happy hour.

"You must see your neighbors in the halls sometimes," he said.

"I rarely do," I said. "I think I leave for work too early. I hear the couple next door a lot. They argue very loudly."

"Maybe we should start with my neighbors," Mark said.

He invited eight people, figuring that four would come, and he was exactly right. An older woman, a couple, and a man came. Mark had bought some chips, dip, a vegetable plate, beer, a small bottle of some Asian liquor, and candy for the evening; he got two camping chairs so that six people could sit down. The man, Dick, had two children who picked up some snacks and went back home to watch a DVD while playing video games.

The older woman, Sue, was fascinated by Cecily and played with her. She agreed to take care of Cecily if we went somewhere for a weekend.

The couple, Tom and Barbara, was disappointed that Mark didn't have a television and invited us to watch football games with them when the fall came. They drank most of the liquor and some beer. Barbara also invited us to go to a casino with them because they usually went to a casino on Saturdays.

Sue invited us to go to Canada with her on a day trip. She said that she went to Canada a few times a year, to pick up Canadian tea, British toffee, and unusual cookies. "I never thought of that," I said. "Do you have to pay duty on Canadian groceries?"

"Theoretically you do, but they don't really care about collecting two dollars for some groceries. I buy only packaged groceries because there are issues about moving meat and produce across borders."

"How far do you go into Canada?" Mark asked.

"Just to the border city. Windsor is closer, but the traffic is bad, so I usually go up to Port Huron and cross to Sarnia, which is small but has grocery stores. I pick up Canadian money at the exchange station at the border."

"I should take the kids some day," Dick said. "A trip to Canada would give them something to write a theme about for school."

"Is there ethnic food?" Mark said, and Sue and I both suppressed laughter. "The same ethnic food as here," Sue said. "Chinese food, pizza places, and fried chicken stands. Canadian ethnic is probably beef stew with bread or the soup, sandwiches, and donuts at Tim Hortons, the Canadian sub shop popular in Michigan."

Everyone agreed that going on a day trip to Canada would be fun. Tom and Barbara wanted to go to a Canadian casino. I took down Sue's telephone number, and said that if Mark was going to work on a weekend, she and I would go by ourselves. "Don't go without me," Mark said. "I've never been to Ontario."

I was excited about the idea of going on the trip. Sue was older than I was, closer to the age of my mother, but I didn't need to find only friends my own age, to talk about men with like I had done in the army.

Everyone left after about three hours, and Mark and I talked about Canada the rest of the evening. We had sent the liquor and snacks home with our guests. "I'd rather go to Canada than a casino," I said.

"We could do both at once," Mark said. We agreed that the party had been a success, even though it hadn't looked promising at the beginning.

Mark picked up free magazines at health food stores that contained articles about health foods, advertisements for products, and lists of activities like yoga classes. "I've found an interesting program we could go to Saturday," Mark said. "It's about medicine wheels and peace pipes, and there is a sweat lodge. I'd like to learn more about Indian spirituality."

I had my doubts about anything advertised in a free magazine, but I agreed to go. "Is it taught by real Indians?" I asked. "What tribe?"

"I don't know. I suppose they'll tell us at the meeting. Does LuAnn go to Indian ceremonies?"

"No, she doesn't. Her family is Lutheran, but I don't think she attends church." Mark regarded Indians like LuAnn as people with special spiritual knowledge. I doubted that LuAnn performed any Indian ceremonies. She didn't identify much with her tribe, and rarely went to an Indian reservation.

"I think that we might as well go to the program Saturday," I said. "I select most of the things we do like going to parks and running."

"I'm willing to let you choose things because you're familiar with the area. You get excited about things you select, which makes then more fun," Mark replied.

I agreed to go to the Indian spirituality meeting. The meeting was held in the back room of a store that sold amulets, lucky stones, bells, and music. The bookshelves featured natural health, witchcraft, self-help, and miscellaneous superstitions. I called Mark's attention to a book on 'healing with crystal energy.' I said, "I feel sorry for people who believe in superstitions like this."

The speaker at the Indian meeting had a Sioux name, but didn't look Indian, even though some feathers were stuck in his headband. He kept referring to his Indian grandfather and quoted trite "words of wisdom" that sounded like phrases from a scouting handbook. The main point of his lecture was to sell a six-month series of lectures and seminars.

After his lecture, there was an intermission. "Do you like this?" I asked Mark.

"I don't have a good impression," Mark said. "New-age pseudo-Indians. The question is whether he has something positive to offer. I don't think any Indians are here."

"I see one," I said. "Look at the woman in back with the drums and rattles." We stayed for the drumming ceremony, led by the Indian woman, who introduced herself as a Dakota Sioux who taught literature in a junior college. We were supposed to make up a poem from our present experience and sing it while leading four other people in a circle, with the other people playing drums or shaking rattles. A song occurred to me, "Hi, hi, hee, I'm off to Picatinny, shout out your number loud and strong, and where ere you go, you will always know, the caissons go rolling along." Singing a take-off on an army song didn't seem quite appropriate for the occasion, so I tried to change it. "Over hill, over dale, we will hit the dusty trail"—no, that wouldn't work either. "The pond grows warm in sun, there the fishes swim." I kept saying it to myself until I had a chance to lead the circle.

I was the third person to lead the circle and singing while leading people around the room was energizing. I started out walking but then began to run. The people behind me couldn't keep up, and I had to slow down. Mark didn't participate at all. The Indian woman stopped in front of him, drumming and asking if anyone else wanted to lead the circle. Mark didn't accept the invitation. "I didn't feel positive about that ceremony," he said later.

"It was unique," I said. "Something I will probably never do again. I think the Indian woman was very sincere." If Mark wanted to come to this group more, I wasn't going to join him.

"I agree with you. If the Indian woman was teaching the whole seminar, it might be valuable," he said. "I couldn't connect with the people here. I like powwows better."

We drove home. "I didn't care much for that," Mark said. "It seemed to be derivative and not authentic. The drumming ceremony was all right, but much of the meeting seemed like a sales pitch. Mark was quiet the rest of the evening.

"I guess you're very disappointed," I said.

"I didn't expect much."

"I would rather go to more events at the Zen Center," I said.

I thought I should tell Mark that I wondered sometimes whether he had been drinking. I said, "I'd like to talk to you again about your drinking."

"Please don't start checking on whether I'm drinking. Can't you trust me if I say that I'm not?"

"When I first met you, it seemed as though you were concealing things like the nature of your job. When you tell me a story about your life, sometimes it contradicts a previous story you told."

"Pam, I hid my alcoholism because I was ashamed of it. I didn't talk about my job because it isn't a good job. You're saying that you don't trust me."

I thought about Darlene and said, "I don't mistrust what you told me. I just think that you don't tell the whole story."

"I guess I don't. Sometimes stories are in phases because they are part of an ongoing set of occurrences. You have to develop an understanding of what happened in the past in order to tell others about it. Your interpretation changes as you review the experience. I don't want to deliberately conceal things because I see what a problem that causes from the experience of my friend Jack," Mark replied. "He is an alcoholic and got some drunk driving charges, which he hid from his wife. Then his driver's license was suspended, and he drove anyway. He ended up getting arrested again and being sentenced to thirty days in jail, which he could do on weekends because he led a respectable life otherwise. He asked his wife if they could keep liquor out of their home, so that he wouldn't be tempted to drink.

"She said that she couldn't do that for him. I think she drank too much and didn't want to admit it. He didn't tell her not to drink at happy hours or avoid people who served liquor. He wanted to remove alcohol from their house, and she wouldn't go along with not having alcohol at home. So he felt he had to get a divorce in order to stop drinking permanently."

I said, "I don't see what that has to do with us, unless your driver's license is being revoked. It also sounds like my main attraction for you is the fact that I don't have liquor around."

"No, Pam. I just mean that some stories never finish cleanly because they're about things that happen and how you interpret them, which may change."

"There are things we don't have in common, too," I said. "Sometimes I think you look down on me."

"Pam, I don't look down on you. I don't have any right to look down on anybody because of the way I led my life. You think that because my parents had a little more money than yours, I had some extra advantages, which was true for our lives when we were young. However, you and I had the same status in the army. I didn't earn more than you did. Now I probably earn less than you do. What I hid from you was only my own problems and weaknesses. I was afraid that you wouldn't want me because of my drinking. I hoped that you would feel attached to me before I told you. I apologize if you think I misled you, Pam. You thought I was a nicer person than I am."

I laughed. "I guess I did. Nice and quiet, studious, and never any trouble but maybe not a very good soldier. I'm not a perfect person, myself. I think you know that by now."

"You're all right, Pam," he said. "In the army, we may lead a rough life. I'm not critical of other people's behavior, especially in war zones. We don't know how we are going to react to physical danger and enemy fire in war until it happens. You seem to spend your evenings either with me or watching television reality shows about people freezing in Alaska, Canada, or the Bering Sea. I don't think you have a secret life that you're not telling me about. What I don't know about you is the rifle you mumble about in your sleep, and what you did after you picked it up."

"You don't talk about Iraq, either," I said. "You haven't told me about your Purple Heart." I didn't want to tell him what I did in Iraq. I needed to understand what I did in Iraq and why, and tell it in a way that the listener wouldn't criticize me because of it.

CHAPTER 18

PETE AGAIN

Monday, I went to TACOM for our monthly progress meeting. First, I went to see Jerry. He told me stories indicating that civil service promotions in their department were unfair. I hoped that he didn't expect a promotion, since he kept reading magazines at work. He reminded me of the army sergeants who didn't seem happy unless they were griping about everything all the time.

Pete stopped me in the hall, and we went outside.

"I guess you're still seeing Mark," he said. "I don't like to see a nice woman waste her time with him. I'm sure you can do a lot better. You're young yet." People often thought I was younger than I am because I'm small.

"I'm thirty," I said. "I was engaged to a man who bought it in Iraq. West Point, career army, infantry."

"I'm sorry," Pete said.

"I'm not even sure how he died. We weren't allowed to see his body. His parents have the flag from Arlington National Cemetery."

"I'm so sorry, Pam. Tell me about him if you want to."

"Maybe I wouldn't have been a good army wife. I think of that." I paused. "How did you and Mark meet?"

"I'm surprised that he didn't tell you. We lived in the same town in New Mexico. I went to school with his brother, Roger. Roger and I used to camp and hike together, and sometimes we would take the younger kids along. My younger brother is a year older than Mark."

I asked, "Were your parents friends with Mark's parents, too?"

"They knew each other, but they weren't real friends. Did you ask Mark about his Purple Heart?" Pete asked.

"I asked Mark, and he told me he was shot but didn't elaborate."

Pete said, "Mark was involved in a messed-up operation, and he had some responsibility for the screw-up. Military intelligence is supposed to know the terrain and add the threats to the mapping, but they got lost and wandered into an ambush. Two soldiers were killed."

"And Mark got a Purple Heart," I said.

"Yes, he did. I always thought it was friendly fire."

"Friendlies shot him?"

"Somebody in his own unit is what it looked like to me. I went to visit him in the hospital. That wound was from behind him, so either he walked into the field of fire or somebody got mad and shot him. Unless he had his back to the enemy."

"He didn't tell me anything about this," I said. "I didn't notice that he had a bullet scar. When he told me that he had a combat injury, I thought of the scar on his arm. When he told me that scar was from a jeep accident, I was puzzled about how he got the Purple Heart."

"His scar is pretty small. The bullet grazed his scalp. The bullet must have come from behind, and his helmet must have been off when it happened. Of all the stupid things to do under fire, taking your helmet off is one of the most idiotic. He could have been killed.

"I visited him in the hospital. Somebody else replaced him at our morning briefing and told me that Mark had been hurt. Mark had dropped and lost his gun, too, apparently. How could you lose your gun? I can't imagine having somebody in my unit wanting to kill me, and others covering up for him."

I replied, "I can't either. I can hardly imagine Mark being in the army. He isn't the type. He doesn't have the attitude."

"That's right," Pete said.

I added, "But Mark is a civilian now. He adds to my life because he is better with people than I am. My family seems to like him more than they like me. Mark is one of the only people I have never gotten mad at."

"Never gotten mad at—that's a funny thing to say. I never noticed you getting mad, but I notice in meetings how nervous you are. You fidget. I have never seen adults bite their nails the way you do. Do you have PTSD? Many people have PTSD from Iraq or Afghanistan. How long were you in the war?"

"Three years," I said. "I've been back more than a year, though. I'm less nervous than when I just got back because I'm not sleep deprived. The mortar fire at night used to bother me. I don't know if I have post-traumatic stress. Nothing very bad happened to me in the war, if that's what you meant. I don't want to go back in the army during wartime, though. If it was peacetime, I'd probably go into the National Guard."

"Do you remember the war, with a fight-or-flight reaction? That's a symptom of PTSD."

"I never ran away, Pete," I said. "When I was in trouble, there was nowhere to run. I returned fire."

We walked slowly back to the office area. Pete had implied that Michael was a real man, but since he was dead, and I was getting old, perhaps I would have to settle for Mark. Maybe Pete was saying that Mark is inept, and I'm nuts, so we make a good couple after all.

Tuesday night, Mark called me. "Would you like to go to a barbecue Thursday evening at Pete and Deb's place? I know it's short notice, but he just asked me. They barbecue a couple of times a week, depending on the weather. Things will be very simple, just hamburgers, chips, lemonade, and the like. I'm going to bring some brownies and cookies."

"You baked some cookies?" I asked. "I didn't know that you liked them."

"No, my mother sent me some homemade goodies, like she did when I was overseas."

"I'd like to," I said. "Should I bring salad?"

"Well, you know kids," he said. "They probably don't want salad. Maybe some cut vegetables and dip would be nice for us adults. The meal isn't a big deal—just an easy way to cook that entertains their kids. Pete's parents used to barbecue often in New Mexico, too. Pete and Deb's place is kind of my second home. When I got out of the army, I came to visit them, found a job, and stayed here."

Thursday, Mark drove to a large apartment complex, and walked to the back of a building, where Pete and his wife were sitting in lawn chairs on the grass; a barbecue grill and small table were on a concrete patio. "Put your stuff on the table and sit down," Debbie said, and got up to look at the dessert package. "The kids are walking around the complex, and I'll put the dessert inside so that they don't see it before dinner. They won't want to spoil their appetites with dinner when all this dessert is waiting."

We sat down, and Pete began a discourse on the quality of the schools. "The kids here don't have good Christian values. They listen to horrible music and are disrespectful to their elders. Schools near army bases teach children to have manners and serve the country."

"I suppose they get exposed to all kinds of behavior because we're near Detroit," I ventured.

"Mostly bad behavior." Pete began talking about Jesus.

Debbie had returned from the kitchen and invited me to see their apartment. When we entered the living room, she said, "Our church encourages us to convert other people. Pete has been lecturing Mark for years. I don't try to convert anyone. God has his own timetable."

"Did you all grow up together?"

"No, I met Pete at church when we were at the University of New Mexico." She showed me the three-bedroom apartment, room by room. I noticed that they didn't have a television. She pointed out the calligraphy that Mark had given them, with the poetry lines "I could not love thee, dear, so much, loved I not honor more."

"Honor," I said. "It sounds like Pete."

"It's Pete's favorite poem. Duty, honor, and country, like Pete's favorite army phrase. I heard that you met Mark at the happy hour when Pete brought him." She paused. "We've known Mark a long time. Mark has quite a history."

"So do I," I said. "I spent eight years in the army and did a lot of living."

"I just wanted to make sure you knew he's divorced, if you're serious about him. But God never gives us more than we can handle. God brings us the things that we need."

We walked back down the hall from the master bedroom to the living room and patio. "This is a nice area to live in," I said. "Your apartment is almost like having a house with a lawn."

"I like not having to mow," she said. "I mean, Pete is here now, but he could go overseas again, and it's hard for me to take care of a house and yard. Life is sweet now, but it can be hard. Especially for the kids, when they have to change schools, make new friends, and go to different doctors and dentists."

The two children, a boy and girl, had returned and were fixing hamburger patties to put on the grill. "Our cooks came back from their walk," Pete said and introduced Cody, eleven, and Gail, nine. He called me "Miss Swenson."

"My friends' children call me 'Aunt Pam,'" I said. "Maybe that's a midwestern custom. "Miss Swenson sounds strange to me, since no one has called me that for so long."

"SWENSON!" Mark barked, and then laughed.

"Pam was in the army, too," Pete said to his children.

"Did you know daddy in the army?" Cody asked.

"No, I met him at his work in the Tank Command. I'm originally from this area, and I work for a defense contractor. Have you guys been to the local attractions like the parks and the zoo?"

We all talked about the local museums and parks. "I often wish our family could spend some time in Albuquerque, so that I could show the children the things I enjoyed at their age," Debbie said. "I'd like them to spend more time with their grandparents, too."

Pete said, "When I retire, we can live in Albuquerque. However, six or eight years from now, the kids will be in high school and not want to go anywhere with their parents. Next time I deploy overseas, Debbie, go to Albuquerque if you prefer it. You don't have to move back to Fort Benning."

"If you move anywhere, I'll help you pack," Mark volunteered.

Debbie said, "Pam, it's nice that you can live where your parents do and find a good job. When you have children, they will have grandparents and aunts and uncles and cousins nearby."

"I have local relatives on my mother's side of the family," I replied. "My father's relatives, like my surviving grandmother, live in a rural area in western Michigan."

"My dad owns an auto body shop in Southfield," I said to Pete and Debbie. "It's a good business. Good enough that my parents own a house and cars, and paid our college expenses, without my mother needing to work. Any work she did, like filing shop records sometimes, was just to free up some of my dad's time so that the family could go together to fairs and movies."

"Did your dad's business spark your interest in vehicles?" Pete asked. "It's rare to see a female tank engineer."

"I suppose it did. Sometimes I worked in the shop to get some spending money. I liked painting cars. Being with my dad and the guys in the shop was fun, too. Working in the shop helped me as an engineer, because I got used to working with men, using tools, and male jokes and humor."

We ate, chatting with the kids about school. Then we all visited the children's worm farm, a large container like an aquarium only more narrow, and saw the worms making burrows through the soil. Back outside, Mark began tossing a Frisbee with the children.

"Mark likes children," Debbie said. I noticed that Mark threw the Frisbee low so that the children could catch it.

"Mark likes various things. He especially likes liquid refreshments," Pete said.

"How long were you in the war?" Debbie asked, turning to me.

"Three years in Iraq. I came here from Maryland, though."

We settled into silence, a sort of watchful waiting, in which we all looked at the Frisbee game happening on the lawn. I watched Debbie as she watched Mark. I was amused, feeling the tension.

Debbie turned toward me again. "Do you miss the army? I miss being close to the facilities on a base. The guard base is nearby, but it's small."

"I don't miss the war or being afraid," I said. "I miss playing team sports and the social life of the army."

Debbie said, "Mark changed a lot since he left the army. He's quieter. Sometimes he used to visit us at Fort Benning or Lewis or wherever we were, and he always had a lot of stories to tell."

"He was glad to leave the army, though," Pete said. "Maybe he doesn't find enough drama in civilian life to talk about. Workers at the Tank Command sit at desks and analyze documentation. Sometimes there is an argument. Something weighs eight pounds instead of seven. The technical people find it exciting. You should hear their jokes. When you cross an elephant and a blackbird, what do you get? Elephant, blackbird, sine theta."

I was surprised by his needling. I said, "No drama. Sometimes people try to dramatize something, but it's never that mortar fire lasted half the night, so I didn't get enough sleep."

Pete continued, "Not only that—the people draw things. Ask them a question, and they try to draw the answer. If they can't measure it, it doesn't exist."

I laughed. "We even draw on cocktail napkins."

"Mark liked cocktail napkins, too. Spend the evening with Mark, and you have a whole stack of cocktail napkins," Pete said.

Debbie looked uncomfortable.

"I don't drink much," I said. "It muddies my thinking."

"Engineers seem to love their own thought processes," Pete said. "Their thinking is like 'I just figured out that if you hit the keyboard on the tank computer three times with the flat of your hand, the main computer may reboot. Wow. Try it sometime. It's a lot of fun, almost like playing computer games.' Right, Pam?"

I nodded, laughing.

"Do you like working at the Tank Command?" Debbie asked me.

"I like it," I said. "I like the civilian work better than the work I did in the army, because I work on new equipment. I wish there was an Officer's Club, though."

"Lots of cocktail napkins at the O Club," Pete said. "Gives you a lot of space for engineering conversations. Can't talk about anything abstract. Can't talk about how to lead your life. Can't talk about God because you can't see God. Can't talk about how your feel because numbers don't describe how you feel. Talk about the tires on your car. Draw the tread on your tires. Everybody loves the tires on their car." I was surprised by how belligerent Pete was getting.

"So, how do you like civilian life?" Debbie hurriedly asked. I began rambling about the trees, the parks, canoeing. Debbie kept asking, did I like this park and that one, as though she wanted to fill empty space with forced conversation.

Pete interrupted, "Mark's brother Roger and I introduced our younger brothers to booze when we used to go camping.

I ask God to forgive me for giving the kids beer and whiskey. They were hardly older than my two are now. I would be infuriated if somebody gave liquor to my kids behind my back."

I said, "Liquor is always around. Everyone tries some alcohol eventually." Debbie changed the conversation back to local parks, and what the children did in boy scouts and girl scouts.

Daylight diminished, and the number of insects increased until sitting outside was unpleasant. Debbie invited us inside, but Mark declined the invitation.

"Come over again," Debbie said. "We cook out a lot. We don't go out much except to events like school sports or scouts that involve the children."

"So, what did you think?" Mark asked me after we got in the car.

"They're very good friends of yours," I said. "Almost like having a second family. But Pete's religious talk gets annoying."

"I think he means some of it that way."

"How long have Pete and Debbie been married?"

"Thirteen years. They just had their anniversary, and I gave them a framed calligraphy. Did you see it?"

"Yes, and it's nice."

"Would you come with me here in the future, or was Pete too much to take?" Mark asked. "I don't know many other people to visit."

"I don't mind Pete," I said. "I was amused by his portrayal of engineers, and how literal we are."

"Pete is more perceptive than he seems at first," Mark said. "Did he do any imitations for you?"

"No, he didn't. I think he could do a great imitation of an engineer. Debbie is in love with you, isn't she?"

"Yes and no. Her fantasy about me would start with me becoming a born-again Christian. We were both married when we met, so we were off-limits to each other, making me a safe object for daydreams. We all know it, and we all ignore it. She can't read movie magazines or watch sexy guys on TV because of their religion, so her fantasies are about men she knows. If she could have me, she wouldn't want me."

So, Debbie is infatuated with Mark, and they all ignore it because nothing will happen. "Did they get married right after college?"

"Debbie finished before Pete, actually. They got married before he graduated. I think that he got a little behind schedule in school because he was in the National Guard and worked, while he was in school. Debbie is a little older than Pete, too."

So Debbie probably supported them until he finished school. Interesting. She must have found meeting staunch Christians difficult at work. But she met a fanatically religious army man, at church. We all make compromises. "I like Debbie," I said. "She is a very nice person."

Mark dropped me off at my place and went to his own apartment for the night.

PETE AGAIN

CHAPTER 19

OCTAGON

Mark had agreed to take a trip to Ohio. He arranged for Sue to feed Cecily, and we left on Thursday morning at five o'clock. We were on our way to visit the Octagon Earthworks in Newark, Ohio. Since Mark wasn't familiar with Indian mounds, I thought that he would form a favorable impression early by first seeing a geometric structure and observatory constructed by the Mound Builder Indians.

Driving to Newark took five hours; we quickly found the great octagon. I remembered the first time I saw it, as a child, and it still impressed me. The earthen walls surrounding the octagon were ten or more feet high, so that a person couldn't see over them. We climbed into a tower to have a view of the entire octagon area, which also held a golf course. This horrified Mark. "A golf course doesn't belong here," he said. "This is a sacred place."

"The country club that runs the golf course takes care of the mound site," I said. "I really think it should be a national historic site like a battlefield park." Mark was surprised that the inside area of the octagon was as big as several city blocks, perhaps fifty acres in size. I pointed out to Mark that a walled corridor led to a large circle, similar in height to the great octagon. I said, "We can walk around the outside of the octagon, corridor, and circle to see the structure from the ground."

We observed that the walls were doubled at some places, overlapping, to form narrow corridors for entrances to the octagon. A person outside the octagon couldn't see inside, and the entrance could be easily guarded, just like a theater line. "Maybe guards at the doorways screened people as they went inside," I suggested. "Maybe only a certain group was allowed in the sacred area. I wonder what types of ceremonies were performed inside the octagon? Perhaps some kind of initiations."

"Perhaps the octagon is so big because many people came to ceremonies," Mark said. "I wonder how many people lived around here?"

"Quite a few people must have lived nearby to build and maintain this complex. They must have needed to grow their food near here, too."

"In Chaco, one of the big sites in New Mexico, they think that people who came for ceremonies must have brought their own food," Mark said. "I can picture living near this setting and looking at this sacred edifice all of my life. That would be like living near the enormous Buddha statue that the Zen Center is raising funds for."

"The octagon and circle are just part of a bigger area, miles square, that includes more mounds and another circle," I explained. "We'll go to the other circle, too."

"This is more impressive than I ever expected," Mark said. "I pictured heaps of dirt. The Indians had to be good architects to make these geometric figures so symmetrical."

"Not only is the architecture is impressive, but this is also an astronomy observatory for the moon. Notice how straight the passageway between the octagon and circle is. If you stand on top of a certain mound, which they call Observatory Mound, at the right time of year and look across the circle through the passageway leading into the octagon, you can see the northernmost point of moonrise through an opening in the wall."

"Well, now I'm really impressed," Mark said. "I thought that all of the Native American astronomy features were in the Southwest."

"Since the Indians didn't have artificial light other than fire, I guess they watched the stars and moon, took note of the rising and setting of the moon and sun for years, and then plotted the opening in the wall."

Mark said, "In the Southwest, you can see the stars well at night, and the moon can seem enormous. With the cloud cover here, tracking the stars would be harder. I'll bet plotting sun and moon positions took centuries."

"This structure existed for more than a thousand years, so they had plenty of time to watch the moon. Do you miss the Southwest?"

"No," Mark said. "But I used to enjoy watching the stars and moon in Sierra Vista. In Michigan, with the city lights and the humidity, the view of the night sky seems diminished. But when a person goes outside into a star-covered vault every night, it's a different story. I wonder what these Indians thought the moon represented."

"I don't think that anyone knows," I said. "The Indians living in the area were long gone by the time the Europeans arrived. When I see the mounds, I think that a multitude of people came here for more than a thousand years and saw the same things as I see now. There are few places in the country where you can see man-made structures that have been around for a thousand years—maybe closer to two thousand years."

Mark said, "You sound like you want to join a crowd of other people sometimes, too. You thought that my desire to join a crowd was peculiar, but here we are admiring something that other people have admired for ages. Think of moving dirt in baskets to make this, like your parents and grandparents did, and knowing that your children will haul dirt, too. Think of Iraq, where people live in the land of their forefathers, and every step could be on the grave of an ancestor. In this country, we have to relate to LuAnn's ancestors to feel continuity with the inhabitants of a thousand years ago."

We slowly walked around the outer wall of the octagon-circle complex, which was about half a mile in length. If we ignored the golf course, we could picture the circle and octagon filled with a society of ancient people.

I remembered my resolve to be more affectionate with Mark. I said, "You must be stiff from all that driving," I said. "Let's sit on the lawn for a moment." When he sat down, I began rubbing his shoulders. "Does your right shoulder bother you?" I asked. "Should I treat it differently than the left?"

"No, it's okay," he said. "Thank you. That feels good. My left shoulder muscles are a little tight, though, because I drive left-handed." He continued, "I wonder if this area was forest, fields, or habitation when they were using this observatory."

"The housing rotted away long ago, of course," I replied. "Some museums have paintings and dioramas that picture the housing. The homes were pretty small and cramped. They apparently did their cooking outside. Reconstructions usually show the houses as being very close to each other, but I'm not sure if the ancient building sites can be dated well enough to duplicate a village.

"Once, you talked about how you wanted to work in an observatory. This is an observatory, too. If we lived in Ohio, near one of the large mound sites, you could probably volunteer at a park and have a connection with an ancient observatory."

"That's a novel idea," Mark said. "I don't know how much work there is around central Ohio, though."

"We could look on the Internet and find out."

Later, we drove a few miles to take a look at the bigger circle, with its high walls enclosing about thirty acres. We entered the circle and tried to locate the center, which I suggested may have represented the center of the world.

"Do you think their lives were simpler or more complicated?" I said. "Farming, building these mounds, and living a life without entertainment or books—was that easier than our life or harder?"

"One way it was easier is that they didn't go overseas to fight in wars," Mark said. "I'm sure they must have waged some wars, though. Being wounded must have been horrible in a time without antibiotics. But maybe living was easier when you spent your life in one place."

"Would you go in the army again?" I asked. "Knowing what you do now?"

"No" Mark said. "Looking back at my adult life, I regret all of it. The army, my drinking, my marriage—all my decisions."

We walked in silence around the circle, then headed back toward the car. No wonder Mark was depressed. He had spent eight years in the army, five years with Darlene, and he regretted the past and the way he led his life.

I said, "I'd join the army again. I had to be in the army to be who I am."

On our drive to Chillicothe to visit the Hopewell Culture National Historical Park, Mark was unusually loquacious, speculating about the life of the people who inhabited the mound area. "Think how they must have had the same concerns as we do," he said. "Food, shelter, war, religion, birth cermonies, death and burial cermonies."

"Seeing these sites gives me a sense of continuity with the past. I'm glad you're enjoying the trip." I felt pleased to show Mark something that he obviously enjoyed.

The Hopewell Cultural Park Visitor Center included a museum, where we were the only visitors. We saw a film that discussed the cultural artifacts of the Mound Builder Indians. Then we walked outside to the mounds, which were about the size of rooms in a house, and not very tall. The group of mounds near the museum was within a relatively small area and surrounded by a low earthen wall.

"Could I have a little kiss in the field of mounds?" Mark asked, pulling me toward him.

"You know it's a graveyard. Perhaps this is bad luck," I said before I kissed him.

"That's okay," Mark said. "Our whole land is a graveyard for American Indians."

A path led down to a nearby river. Mark put his arm around me as we walked down to the river.

"My family used to go to parks with mounds, perhaps because the parks were usually free and not crowded. When we went to mounds, I used to pick up brochures for LuAnn and her brother because Michigan has only low mounds and no geometric mounds." We went back inside to look at the artifacts again and to check out the bookstore. Archaeologists had excavated artifacts from the mounds, and most of the figures in the museum were animal effigies; some in the form of statues, some rendered as pipes, and some made from hammered copper. One item looked surprisingly like a parrot.

We ate dinner at a Chinese restaurant near our motel. Our TV had many more channels than the cable network I subscribed to, but finding a good reality show was difficult. I finally found a program about surviving in the Canadian north.

"I wouldn't like to live in the cold like that," Mark said. "I may have gone into the army to punish myself, but you have to be a real masochist to live in a frigid climate."

"Do you still like punishing yourself?" I asked. "I can assure you that it gets very cold in the winter here. I think that you have been stationed mostly in warm places. The army is a better place to be a masochist than in the defense industry, anyway. In the army, you have to take a lot of crap from people. You go on morning runs no matter how bad the weather is. You have to be in parades, and stand in formation."

"Don't remind me," Mark said. "I've had enough of standing in formation. Do you want a snack or a soda? We can sit in bed and watch television." Mark bought us some snacks from the vending machines.

"Shall we go to bed early?" he asked. "Let's shower and lie down, and I'll rub your feet."

"I suppose," I said.

"Pam, I try to be romantic. I get you to sit on my lap, and you don't think anything of it when I hold you and kiss you. We get amorous, but you're not sexually responsive. I'd like to do something that will warm you up, but I don't know what to do. So tell me."

I was at a loss. What he said was true. I hadn't been very romantic. "Why don't you rub my feet? I think I would like that. I wish I was warmer to you, and it isn't because of you—it's because of me. Somehow I need to get a fresh start because I like you," I said. "There's nobody I like more."

"You mean that there is nobody alive that you like more."

"How do I get beyond that? Michael is dead. Nothing holds me back from you except me." I reached down his slacks, and he removed my hand.

"That's so mechanical," he said. "I don't care about how some other men get warmed up. Let's find a way to be romantic."

"We can start where we are. Rub my feet," I said. "I might like it. Then pretend I'm a virgin and seduce me. We could pretend that we are stars in a romantic movie. Let's forget about showering. I'm used to sweat and dirt. I'll run some water over my feet to wash them off, and we can play some games—sweat and all." I smoothed his hair and then kissed his face and neck, and pulled his T-shirt off. I began kissing his spinal column, going down his back.

I put on a nightgown and climbed into bed. I lay down crosswise on the bed and put my feet on his lap. Lying that way was awkward, but his hands on my feet were relaxing. I fell asleep but woke up later. I tried to be warmer to him as we had sex. I pictured a bombing raid at night, the sky dark except for stars, then exploding with the light of tracers, followed by flashes of light from the explosions.

CHAPTER 20

SERPENT

Mark and I were sunburned on our faces and arms from the previous day. He complained that it was too early to get up, although it was seven o'clock. "We can stay in bed longer if you like," I said. "It's only about sixty miles to the serpent, but a couple of mound sites are on the road to the serpent, if we want to see them. Do you want to make love this morning?" I asked.

"No, I don't think so." He got out of bed. "I have a headache."

"We have such a big bed, we could have breakfast in bed," I suggested. "Maybe you have a headache from the sun and from not eating enough yesterday. I can go and get us something, and we can have breakfast in bed." I walked to the restaurant and brought back scrambled eggs, sausage, and pancakes.

"This is a luxury, Pam. I haven't had breakfast in bed in a motel in my whole life." Mark said. I didn't know if he was kidding me. The motel wasn't very classy, and the restaurant was a truck stop. I had eaten breakfast in bed with men in seedy motels near Fort Irwin, the tank testing grounds in the California desert. "If you don't feel well enough to go to another mound site, we could stay here."

He wanted to continue our trip, so I drove to the Seip mound, which was in a field beyond a roadside rest area and park. The mound was much larger than I expected, about forty feet high, a formidable flat-topped mountain of earth covered by brush and weeds.

We read about the mound on a bulletin board and began walking toward it along a path bordered by a field of knee-high grass and weeds. Wildflowers bloomed around us.

Soon Mark said that he would rather sit beneath a tree and admire the mound than walk closer, but that I should walk in the park as much as I liked. After he sat down, I walked alone to the mound, which stood by itself in the field. The sites of former Indian homes were marked with posts beside the trail. The mound seemed to grow taller as I approached. I turned back to look for Mark when I reached a point near its base, and waved when I saw him sitting in the grass.

I felt adventurous in the field of flowers near the towering mound. I tried to picture the ancient people living here. I wondered whether they took the mound for granted, regarded it with sacred awe, or felt proud that it embodied a big task, done well. Perhaps they were relieved when it was finished. I walked around the mound, which was oval in shape and covered with brush and weeds. Then I walked back through the grass, picking up stickers on my shoes and socks.

I sat in the shade with Mark for a few minutes. "We're seeing the mound's broader side," I said. "The shape surprised me because mounds are usually circular or rectangular if they are tall."

"It's much taller than I thought it would be," Mark said. "Think of all the work involved in hauling dirt up the side of that mound to make it that high."

"Building it may have taken centuries," I said. "Maybe people tired of the obligation of adding to it and grew to resent having to work on it. Or maybe they were always proud. Nothing I ever worked on will last a thousand years."

"The metal you design with will still be on earth someplace, in one form or another," Mark said. "We can't imagine what the vehicles will be recycled into in a hundred years, much less a thousand."

"I'm glad you said that," I said. "It broadens my perspective. But I'm sorry you don't feel better. Should we stop somewhere and buy a couple of caps? We should try to keep the sun off." I stroked his hair, then put my arms around him from behind and put my hand on his forehead, which was hot.

"I'm all right," he said. "I just need to minimize my time in the sun and not exert myself too much today."

We skipped seeing Fort Hill, an enclosed site, to save Mark's energy for the serpent mound. At a drugstore, we bought sunburn cream and some souvenir caps and bought a snack of nuts and fruit juice—Mark's choice.

At Serpent Mound, we climbed a tower first to get a bird's-eye view of the mound. Mark climbed the stairs slowly, as though each step jarred him. I admired him for not complaining more. I tried not to complain when I was sick, too. "This is supposed to be the largest effigy mound in the United States," I said. "Most of the effigy mounds are further west. Iowa has an effigy national park, and Wisconsin is supposed to have many effigy mounds. Would you like to see the other mounds in the Midwest?"

"I'd have to think about it," Mark said.

I continued, "My family only went to nearby places. We three kids would argue in the car, and our parents would get frustrated when we drove anywhere. My father didn't want

SERPENT

to be away from his business long, anyway. We never even went to Chicago." We began walking down the stairs of the tower.

Mark said, "The mound is much larger than I expected. Head to tail seems to be about the length of a city block, and the snake is coiled up near the tail. It has its mouth open and seems to be trying to swallow an egg, if I am interpreting it correctly."

We went into the museum and read about the construction of the mound, the geology, and Indian cultures of the area. Another exhibit showed that archaeologists have discovered that the head of the serpent is aligned to the sunset on the summer solstice, and the coils of its tail may point to the sunrise on the equinoxes and winter solstice. "This mound must have been an astronomical observatory too," I said.

"That's amazing, isn't it? Even the coils in the tail have significance. Planning and diagramming it out must have been difficult since it had to be in line with astronomical events that occurred infrequently."

"Now you sound like an engineer," I said. "Let's walk around it." We began walking around the serpent, which was about three feet high. We sat in the grass near its tail for a while.

"I feel better than I did this morning," Mark said. "The sunburn cream seems to help. I was skeptical about coming to Ohio on vacation, but I'm enjoying this trip. I didn't know that all these mounds existed, and I could never have guessed that walking around in the parks would be as much fun as exploring Indian ruins in New Mexico."

"For me, part of the mystery is that nobody knows how long the Indians lived in this part of the United States." I said. "People may have lived here for thousands of years before they built the mounds. A lot of organization is needed to build something like this."

Mark added, "The society has to form, and the people have to get sufficient food and shelter before they have any extra energy to build a mound."

"I wonder if the villages competed with each other on the size of their mounds? Our mound is bigger than yours. No, ours is more unique," I said and laughed. "The serpent is probably the most unusual mound in the country."

I asked Mark if he minded if I ran for a while because I hadn't gone for a run recently. He settled in the grass near the head of the serpent. I ran around the serpent twice, possibly annoying the half dozen other people walking around the mound, and then ran into the parking lot, and down the access road. I was exhilarated. After running for half an hour, I came back and sat by Mark.

"I wonder how the local Indians regarded snakes," Mark said. "Are any of the snakes here poisonous?"

"I don't think so," I said. "I used to pick up garden snakes if I could catch them. They always slither away when they see you."

"I asked because in the Indian ruins of New Mexico, poisonous snakes make dens in the rocks. I would like to take you to the western states on a vacation sometime." I was excited to think that Mark was planning a trip for us. He rarely talked about the future.

"I'd like to see New Mexico," I said.

I had so much energy that I decided to run around the serpent once more. Only three other people were walking around it. Mark waited in the grass, and as I got close to him, I interrupted my running by skipping and twirling in circles. I could be as silly as I liked because no one but Mark was watching. I put my arms around Mark and kissed him. "Did you just take a happiness pill?" he asked.

"If I had happiness pills, I'd share them with you," I said.

"I like the way you move. Maybe we could go dancing some time," Mark said. "Do you like dancing? I used to like it, but I haven't taken a woman dancing for a long time." I had a mental picture of Mark dancing with women in bars in Sierra Vista and felt jealous.

After we had enjoyed the mound a while longer, we headed out toward Cincinnati to visit Fort Ancient the next day. "You'll love the fort," I said. "The site is huge and there is a nice museum."

Mark said, "I wonder what the ruins of our own culture will be, and if they would last for a thousand years."

We drove in silence for a while, until I said, "I just had an idea. Once, you talked about joining a camera club. Would you like to join an astronomy club? You like these ancient observatories, and you could tell people in an astronomy club about them."

"That sounds like a great idea," Mark said. "I could join astronomy clubs instead of photography clubs. I was only interested in photographing the sky, anyway."

"Maybe we should go to all the local planetariums when we get back. At Cranbrook, we only went to the gardens, but the science museum there has a planetarium, with shows every day and special shows on some Friday nights. The science museum in Detroit has a planetarium and so does Wayne State University near downtown Detroit. Sometime we could even make a tour of the other planetariums and observatories in Michigan."

"I never thought of volunteering at museums with planetariums," Mark said. "Michigan is so flat that somehow I didn't think it had many astronomy facilities. The big observatory in northern California is on a mountaintop and in Huntsville, the observatory is on a large hill."

"I guess the clouds don't obscure starlight if you have the right equipment," I said. "I would like to visit observatories and planetariums, and learn more about astronomy. I enjoy looking at the pictures in your astronomy books and magazines."

We stopped for an early dinner. Mark seemed to have a good appetite. "Do you feel better?" I asked. "We could find a roadhouse and go dancing." Then I felt angry with myself for suggesting a roadhouse, because places with music and dancing served liquor, and he didn't want to drink any more.

"I think we should pass on the roadhouse and watch some television," he said. "Maybe there's a rerun of some show about seal catchers, polar bears or former Army officers practicing survival skills in Alaska. That's what you like to watch, isn't it?" Mark sounded sarcastic.

"Maybe we could talk instead," I said. "Could I ask what you did for your Purple Heart? You've never told me."

"I don't tell the story because I don't think I deserved a Purple Heart. I was in some action where my unit lost two men, but I didn't do anything to brag about," he began. "When I think of Iraq, I usually think of mundane things like the heat and the powdery sand. I remember the fear, which had degrees of intensity. Fear has different flavors—fear from nearby firing, from distant firing, and from explosions. Sometimes an anxious quiet descended onto a location, and the silence was more ominous than the sound of gunfire. I remember the hills in the distance and how beautiful they were, the sunrise, and the sound of birds. Iraq has some magnificent vistas."

"Where were you?" I asked. "I mostly remember garbage-filled streets with open sewage drains and blowing sand."

"I was in the countryside and in Baghdad. Sometimes we had missions to check certain sensors and implant others. Once we got lost, which was incredibly stupid because we were responsible for some of the maps. Possibly sand had blown over the unmarked turnoff to the road we wanted. Insurgents hiding in a livestock shed attacked us.

"Two men were killed. Wilson, a sergeant who was right next to me, was hit in the face, and his blood splashed on my clothing. I had never seen a man die up close before." Mark's voice quavered, and his hands shook.

"I replay the scene again and again. A bullet hit my helmet, and it felt like somebody hit my head with a hammer. I got down on the ground to try to help the sergeant and cut my hand on a piece of metal. I must have cut an artery because my hand spurted blood. I listened to Wilson's last breath, and my hand was on his neck as his pulse stopped.

"I was confused. I took my helmet off, dropped it, and was grazed by another bullet. I felt dizzy and vomited. I was disoriented and terrified. My head wound bled into my hair and eyes and down my neck. I was soaked in blood—both Wilson's and mine. I may have gone into shock—I think I drifted in and out of consciousness and then passed out. I remember lying on the sand, and people putting me into the vehicle. I'm not quite sure what happened at the conclusion of the confrontation. I think the insurgents ran away as my unit began firing back.

"Seeing Wilson dying was much worse than the bullet hitting my helmet or bleeding from the second bullet. I had never been so close when someone was killed. I was frantic because I thought I had lost my gun. The master sergeant had taken my gun for safekeeping when I passed out, but I thought that I had dropped my Beretta and lost it. I kept feeling for the gun and being alarmed that I didn't have it.

"I wasn't hurt badly. A medic put grease on my cuts to stop the bleeding. I eventually got two stitches in my scalp and one in my hand. I don't talk about the Purple Heart because I feel embarrassed.

"The first bullet that hit my helmet was from enemy fire, but I think that the one that hit me was friendly fire. I don't know if somebody accidentally fired too low or blamed me for the ambush and decided to kill me. I have heard stories from Vietnam of soldiers getting so mad at the officers that they shot them.

"I don't have a heroic story about getting the Purple Heart. I feel stupid because I didn't have my helmet on, which makes me look inept. In addition, the injury was caused by fire from behind me, as though I was running away. I wasn't a very good officer. Sergeant Wilson was one of the best soldiers I ever met. He knew what to do in any situation.

"Pete got worried about me when one of my coworkers talked to him the next morning, and he came to visit me in the hospital. I thought I would have some stitches and go home, but the medical facility was very busy. I was embarrassed when Pete came to see me, since I wasn't sure what to tell him about the incident. I couldn't tell Pete that I felt disturbed because a dying man bled on me. Pete always thought I was a coward, and that would confirm his opinion. If he had been wounded as I was, he would have pulled himself together and led the troops. I could have picked up Wilson's rifle and returned fire."

Mark's hands were still shaking. I reached for his left hand and held it steady. He continued, "I think Pete was always disappointed in me and regretted that he had brought me into the army."

SERPENT

"Could I see your scar?" I asked.

"I knew you would ask. Just fish through my hair around here," he said, putting his hand at the top of his head. "I can't seem to find it."

I ruffled his hair and finally saw the tiny scar. "The scar would have shown a little when your hair was army short, but your hair covers it now."

He pointed out a barely perceptible scar between his thumb and forefinger. "I knew you would want to see this one, too," he said, laughing.

"This is a cute one. I'll kiss it," I said and began laughing too. I lay back on the big bed. "Do you think of the incident very often? Does it bother you now?"

"I get panicky when I hear sounds that remind me of incoming fire. The worst part was seeing someone die, though. I was a desk jockey and didn't see much action. Maybe I could have gotten more used to combat, but I doubt it. Were you in situations where you were fired on? You must have been."

"I was in situations where people were firing at the convoy," I said. "I remember once when there was a big exchange of fire between our security contractors and some people in a building, but nobody was firing at me. Once an IED hit a troop transport in front of the vehicle I was riding in." I paused. "I think that you were lucky about Iraq. You were sent to Korea first and didn't get deployed to Iraq until later."

"I agree. I was very fortunate to spend so little time in Iraq. Because I was sent to Korea and was injured, my deployment to Iraq was delayed. Sometimes I think my accident was a blessing because it kept me out of Iraq."

"I spent three years in Iraq," I said. "The first year would have been enough, but after two years stateside, I was sent back. Then I extended so that I wouldn't have my life disrupted again before I got out." I paused. "I'm glad you're safe, and here with me."

"I'm glad that you survived three years in Iraq," Mark said and hugged me. "I would like to distract myself for a while. Let's do something different tonight—find a place to dance like you suggested before. We have never gone dancing."

"I hardly know how to dance," I said. "Remember that we are in the countryside, and there might not be a choice of places."

We asked at the motel desk, and the desk clerk said that there weren't any fancy nightclubs around, unless we were willing to drive about twenty miles. She said that since it was a weekend, there would be live music at a bar nearby.

The door of the bar said that motorcycle regalia and chains were not permitted. The bar was about forty feet square, with a bandstand on one side and two pool tables on the other. We sat at a table, ordered ginger ale, and ate the popcorn brought by the waitress while listening to the performers. The star performer was a not-so-young woman in a green-fringed cocktail dress who sang Rolling Stones songs.

"I wonder if they get paid for this," I whispered to Mark.

"I think they have to be members of the musicians union to perform for money," he said.

"That doesn't really answer my question," I said and laughed.

"I feel like drinking something heavier," Mark said. The next time the waitress came by, he asked for bourbon with water, so I got a rum and Coke.

"Will this make listening to this music seem entertaining?" I asked. "We should have been here on an evening when they play the juke box instead."

SERPENT

Mark sipped his drink. "I'm sorry I bought this. I had an anniversary coming up at AA—three months without a drink."

"In AA, you keep track of anniversaries of not drinking?" I asked.

"Sure," Mark said. "Especially yearly ones. I've never gone a year without drinking—yet."

"I hope that someday you celebrate your fiftieth, if that's what you want," I said. "Fifty years from tomorrow." Mark looked glumly into his drink.

The bar was filling up, mostly with older people. The waitress asked if we wanted some food because they could warm up frozen pizza.

"We aren't spending enough," I suggested to Mark when she left.

"You guys from around here?" a man at the next table asked us.

"Just passing through," Mark said.

"That's my cousin, playing the drum," the man said. "Sally, the singer, works at the insurance company downtown."

"She has a nice voice," Mark said politely. "You guys get some good entertainment."

"I want to leave," Mark whispered to me. "I don't even want to finish my drink, it's just cheap bar bourbon anyway and doesn't even taste good. If I keep drinking it, though, pretty soon I'll just want another. Let's go back to the motel and watch a film about seals or something."

"This was fun, but I don't really want to listen to this music longer," I said. We left our unfinished drinks on the table and went back to the motel. Mark turned on the television, and I found a program about people going to a remote area of Alaska, living there for a season, and walking out. "It's strange to watch

LOYAL TO OUR DEAD

television without my laptop," I said. "But a vacation is a time to do things differently. I'm glad we went out for the evening because I so rarely do it."

Mark lay down on the bed and fell asleep immediately. Later he woke up and said, "Maybe I am coming down with something, and I don't want to give germs to you. I think we should keep more space between us so that I don't sneeze on you if I turn out to be getting a cold or flu."

"Let's just sleep in a reverse from the usual way—you on your side facing away from me, and I'll put my arm over you. Do you miss Cecily purring at night? I do. Maybe I can purr a little."

"I'm willing to try that," he said. "But if you kick me too much, I'll need to retreat." He laughed.

He lay down on his left side, and I put my hand on his back. Later in the night, he was shivering and his T-shirt was soaked with sweat.

CHAPTER 21

FORT ANCIENT

Mark was feeling good in the morning. "If I was shivering, I must have been dreaming. Maybe I was thinking of the Alaskan survival stories on television," he said, teasing.

"Do you remember your dreams?" I asked. "Mine are often about being in the desert. Then I wake up and find that I am in bed, and it's cool."

"I don't dream about Sierra Vista," he said. "I dream about other places." I noticed that he used Sierra Vista as an example of the desert, not Iraq. He probably didn't want to touch on the ambush again.

We packed quickly to leave for breakfast and Fort Ancient.

"I wonder how far back their warrior culture extends," I said. "What if we are just the latest in a line of soldiers who have visited the fort for two thousand years?"

"Then I would hope that we are the last in line," Mark said. "That nobody else goes to war."

I was surprised. "I thought that war is just a natural part of human society and many people's lives," I replied.

"If people in our culture have nothing better to do than engage in foreign wars, maybe we should adopt the ancient Indian custom of hauling dirt in baskets and building earthen mounds to use up extra labor, time, and energy," Mark said.

We drove to Fort Ancient, where we looked inside the museum first. We noted that an exhibit said that the fort might be an observatory. Mark took notes so that we could try to find the astronomy sites as we walked. "We need to look for the gateways, too," I said. "See how wide they were, and where they lead. Fort Ancient couldn't have been a defensive fort because there are too many openings to the outside that aren't defensible."

The park road led into the fort, an enclosed area on top of a bluff that was as large as several city blocks. We found a parking place inside the walls and began walking counterclockwise around its interior, near the outer walls. The first lobe of the dumbbell-shaped fort was grassy, with some trees and ditches. Spying a secluded area away from the road, I suggested to Mark that we make love there.

"Pam, sometimes I think that you have some missing marbles," Mark replied. "Why would we want to perform an intimate act in a public place? We aren't teenagers. Your suggestion makes me wonder what kind of peculiar things you have done, and who you've done them with. I can't picture you and Michael screwing like rabbits in a public place, either. West Point men are trained to be 'officers and gentlemen,' to have dignity, and to show the flag at special occasions—not to show their underwear in public places."

I felt chastised. "I thought you might like some outdoor loving. You're so uptight."

Mark finally said, "Okay, I am uptight. I don't want to screw on the ground while watching to see if anybody is looking at us and picking up their cell phone to call the park police. There were at least a dozen cars where we parked, and there might be other cars parked in this place. There's a road going farther inside."

We walked in silence near the wall and looked through the openings in the wall to the ravine below. As we peered through one gap, Mark said, "In the museum, the exhibits about astronomy indicated that some openings are related to the sun and moon setting and rising. This must be an astronomy opening because it doesn't lead anywhere." The wall hugged the precipice closely. The enclosure began narrowing until we were walking near the road. "I'm not mad at you, Pam," Mark said. "Let's run a little and forget about sex until tonight."

We ran through the narrow part of Fort Ancient, until the narrows opened into a field, and the walls became higher, increasing from chest level to about twenty feet. He continued, "It's getting hot, so let's just stroll around the rest of the wall and relax a while in the shade." Part of the area was wooded, and we stopped to rest under a tree.

I said, "During and after the war, I've had a feeling that life is short, and we die soon. So we can be outrageous today, and no one will care because everyone is absorbed with survival. Remember that old saying 'Live, love, laugh, and be merry, for tomorrow we die?'"

"I understand," Mark said. "But you are likely to live to be eighty. You should figure out how you want to spend the next half-century, when you won't be dodging bullets in Iraq."

I hesitated. "You're right. I stopped planning for the future when I was in the army. My life didn't turn out quite as I expected. I need to make some new plans. So do you. What do you really want?"

"I would like to avoid drinking without having to make such an effort, and learn to calm down. In the army, there were two times when I could have died, and I had constant tension that didn't stop when I came stateside. I would like to feel safe, and then I can make more decisions about my life. I've been out of the army less than a year, and I'm still getting used to being a civilian and choosing from an almost overwhelming number of possibilities. In the army, I just needed to make a few basic decisions because the army decided everything else for me."

"I used to expect that my life would be like my parents' life," I said. "I wanted that and thought I would have it. But after Michael died, I just needed to get through the day and then the next one. I didn't look ahead or think about what I would like to have. I don't want to work, go home, and watch television for the rest of my life, but I can't picture the future."

"You also get caught up in the past," Mark pointed out.

"If you mean Michael, he was the first man I was ever serious about. The others didn't count." We sat quietly in the grass for a few minutes.

"Let's walk more before it gets too hot," I suggested.

We continued our walk and investigated the stone circles, ramps, and ponds within the walled fort. I noticed some secluded places where we could have had sex together, but I didn't bring the subject up again.

In the early afternoon, we drove to Dayton to see the reconstruction of an Indian village at Sunwatch Village. The original village was built about seven hundred years ago, and like most ancient sites, it was next to a river. Villages were probably located near a river for ease of collecting water and fishing. The film at the museum stated that the typical life span of the Indians was only about thirty-five years.

"At our age, we'd be considered senior citizens," Mark whispered at the end of the film.

"And we would have children in their teens, probably," I said into his ear. "We might even be grandparents."

"We would never have wondered what we should do with our lives. Everyone led their lives in the same pattern, unless they become a tribal chief or medicine man," Mark said and reached for my hand as we left the film. We walked into a flower garden and stopped to admire the plants before approaching the huts and marker poles of the reconstructed village.

We walked through the formerly inhabited area, stepping into the wooden huts, which were about twenty feet by fifteen. Baskets hung from the rafters. I said, "Knowing that the grain in your baskets was all the grain that you would have for the winter must have been frightening. The rodents would have been trying to get at the food, if they weren't hibernating. I wonder what the people did in the winter besides sleep, make arrows and pots, and hunt deer."

"I'm sure that they told a lot of stories, too," Mark said. "We should tell some more war stories. I've never heard yours." We walked down to the river before leaving the park to find a motel.

The room had a king-size bed. After dinner, we sat on the huge bed to watch television, but Mark wanted to talk instead. "I'd like to ask you a question, Pam," Mark said. "You mumble in your sleep about a rifle, but you never say what you did with it."

I wasn't eager to talk about the rifle. "I fired it," I said. "You probably guessed that already. An IED struck the troop carrier in front of us in a convoy, and the vehicle was burning. I grabbed the rifle. After the explosion, the streets were quiet for a moment, and then people started coming out on the second story of buildings and on the roofs. We took some fire from windows, I think. I heard the sound of firing as though it was pebbles thrown into water. I was high on adrenalin, and I wasn't afraid at all. The last vehicle in the convoy may have been engaged in a firefight, or they may have been laying down suppressive fire. I jumped out of the vehicle and took cover behind it. I fired into windows. The sound of the rifle firing was very loud against my face. I was just spraying fire, and not aiming. I didn't see any weapons, just groups of people on balconies. The people I was riding with began yelling at me.

"I was mad about the troop carrier. Some men had jumped out of it, but there was screaming and a hubbub going on around it. Soldiers had been injured or burned. Somebody from the troop carrier ran to our vehicle. I was so angry, and I wanted to kill Iraqis—I didn't care about anything else. The memory of firing the gun comes into my mind sometimes. I'll be working or running or driving, and suddenly I remember picking up the rifle and feel the adrenalin rush."

"Do you feel guilty about firing into a crowd?"

"Sometimes I feel guilty, but mostly I feel excited. I feel angry and afraid, but more excited than afraid. I dream about the scene. Sometimes I wish that the memory would go away because it pops up with a surge of adrenalin, and I have to calm down before I can concentrate again."

Mark said, "Being fired on makes everyone afraid, and at the time it's hard to know what to do. In retrospect, we look at what we did, without the fear, and interpret the action differently. You fired the rifle at the surroundings, but the fire also served to cover the troops. That's one way to think of it. An officer laying down covering fire for troops to move or retreat is a step beyond an officer's duty."

"You're saying I can make the story sound brave or noble, when in fact I fired to kill Iraqis. I didn't care if I was covering the troops, and I shot civilians. I thought of Michael being dead, and the coffin being closed at the funeral, so that I couldn't even see the body. Maybe he burned to death.

"When I took the rifle, the whole world narrowed to my firing, the flames in front of us, and my revenge and exhilaration. I have never felt so alive. I heard the shots, right next to my face as I was lying on the road, and the sound reverberated through my body. I didn't seem to be firing the rifle—it seemed as though the rifle and I were one. I shot off all the bullets I had and wished for more.

"Firing at the crowd was an expression of who I am. I think back and get an adrenalin rush, and I feel high and ecstatic. I was a different person than I'd been, and I was walking out in the new world. I felt intensely myself, as if I was more like myself when I was firing at the windows than I had ever been before. I repeat to myself sometimes that I picked up the rifle, and I get that feeling of readiness, adventure, and excitement— the excitement of being me. I don't know what else to say. I became thrilled about being myself."

Mark hesitated before speaking. "That is quite a story, Pam. Digesting your story takes some time. Some people feel that war brings out the best in them."

"I don't talk about this story often because I think other people will criticize me for it. In fact, I've never told anyone before. Liking to shoot people isn't something people talk about. You didn't like the war and regretted being in it, and that made it harder for me to tell you," I said.

"I can't make a value judgment of another person's experiences," Mark said. "I don't picture myself doing the same thing. My first thought was, I wondered where your own gun was, and if you were lying on it. I used to keep feeling for my gun."

"How and where did you use your own gun?" I asked. I had always thought that Mark shot someone close to him with his Beretta and had mixed feelings about the incident.

To my surprise, he said, "I didn't, except on firing ranges."

"I always thought that you had shot someone."

"I don't know what I said that led you to believe that," Mark said. "I didn't fire my gun at anyone."

I replied, "I didn't tell you about shooting the rifle before because I thought that you had killed somebody close up and personal."

I still wondered what he and Pete had done in Iraq. "Do you think much about Iraq now?" I asked. "Sometimes I remember the heat and the sound of mortar fire, and it is as real to me as anything happening in the present."

"You had a sense of invulnerability," Mark said. "We all have that for a while but lose it with time. Most people probably lose it in their early twenties, but lose it earlier in a war. I had a friend who was a pilot. He told me that when he was learning to fly in a simulator, if they made bad mistakes a message would appear saying 'you are dead now.' He said that he was twenty-one when he learned to fly, and he wasn't ready to hear that."

I replied, "I agree with you about the timing. Even when I went into the army, I didn't think about being killed. Being in the army didn't seem dangerous when I was on the firing ranges. It didn't seem dangerous until I heard mortars in Iraq and realized that the people firing them were trying to kill us."

"You and I were too old to go into the army," Mark said. "Teenagers aren't afraid."

"You must have felt more vulnerable in Iraq because you had been in that accident in Korea," I said. Mark had his arm around my shoulder, but I removed it and put my arm around him instead. "Let me hold you a little. Should I buy us something to eat? You're too thin. You need some cookies to fatten you up."

"No thank you," Mark said. "I have one mother, and I don't need a second one. It's nice of you to offer to cuddle me and give me cookies, but I'm a grownup now and don't even like cheap cookies."

I was glad that he laughed because I felt warm to him. "I was trying to be romantic," I said and laughed. "I guess I didn't get romantic correctly."

"Romance appeals to me more than comfort food. But I'll get you some cookies, if the vending machine has any and candy if it doesn't," Mark said, putting on his shoes and leaving the room.

"Did you ever hear the story of the appointment in Samarra?" Mark asked when he came back. "Sometimes I felt that my appointment must be in Baghdad."

"I remember it slightly," I said. "We used to joke about it in Baghdad and say that we planned to stay away from Samarra. Death brushes the man in Baghdad, so he runs off to Samarra for the night to avoid death. But death just jostled him in Baghdad, surprised to see him because they had an appointment that evening in Samarra."

FORT ANCIENT

"Death brushed both of us in Baghdad, but our appointments with death are someplace else, at some other time," Mark said. "Or else they were in Samarra, but we didn't keep them."

"I hope my appointment is in the United States, when I'm about eighty," I said. "I got jostled in Baghdad, though, in the convoy I told you about. Was your Purple Heart from Baghdad?"

"No," Mark said. "But I was in a convoy in Baghdad, where one vehicle got hit by a rocket grenade. So I may have gotten jostled. I don't have a story to tell about it."

"Let's just stay away from Samarra," I said. "I plan to. No more army, no more Iraq, and no Samarra."

I smoothed his hair and kissed him. "Let's enjoy our big bed," I said. "Tomorrow night we will be home."

I slept facing Mark's back, and he was shivering and sweating in the night again.

CHAPTER 22

AIR FORCE MUSEUM

In the morning, I had some trail mix and read brochures for a while. Mark slept until nearly eight. "You didn't seem to sleep very well last night," I said when he woke up. "You were shivering again."

"Yes, I woke up several times" he said. "Sometimes I don't sleep soundly in strange places. You should have awakened me earlier."

"Sunday is a good time to catch up on sleep," I said.

I started packing the car while he showered and dressed. We had breakfast at the truck stop and then got on the road.

"Miamisburg has one of the tallest mounds in the United States," I said. We approached the mound, driving on city streets through a populated area. Because of the buildings, the mound was invisible until we were close; it stood alone in a small city park. The mound was intimidating because of its height; walking to the top on the wooden steps that had no landings would be like climbing five flights of stairs in an office building. An information plaque said that archaeologists had excavated burials from the mound.

I counted the steps as we walked up the mound. From the top of the Miamisburg mound, we saw the town in one direction and a river valley hundreds of feet below in the opposite direction. "I feel like I'm standing on the top of the world," I said, and threw my arms around Mark. "Here in the Midwest, we don't have mountains, so these people built their own."

"I wonder if everybody could climb up the mound when it was built or whether only royalty could climb it," Mark said. "Maybe only funeral directors could come on top, since it was a burial mound."

"I laughed. "Funeral directors? It's true that we're standing on a graveyard," I said. "I wonder if the Indians who stood here thought of the burials within the mound, or if they just admired the view."

"Maybe they used the mound as a watchtower to see whether any enemies approached," Mark replied.

After leaving the mound, we drove to the U.S. Air Force Museum. We got a map and planned our tour of the aircraft, then went from one airplane to the next, sometimes standing under a wing or getting up close to feel the metal of the plane. I especially liked the engine exhibits, since some aircraft engines were very different from vehicle engines and had five, seven, or more cylinders. "Wait until we get to the space section," Mark said. "The engines of spacecraft are immense. In the Huntsville museum the engines are outside because of their size."

"Do you ever wish that you had gone into the air force instead of the army?" I asked. "I was interested in vehicles, so I didn't consider the air force or the navy."

"I didn't think of entering the air force," Mark said. "Since I had lived in Huntsville, near the Army Air and Space Command,

I thought only of the army. I knew Pete, and he was in the army. Now I wish I hadn't gone into the military at all."

"I wish you hadn't been in the army, since you didn't like it. Only we wouldn't have met if you hadn't been in the army."

We sat on a bench under the wing of a bomber. "I think that Pete and his family would like this museum," Mark said. "I liked the Huntsville army museum even when I was too young to appreciate most of the exhibits."

"Pete said that you knew each other in school. I've wondered why you didn't tell me that yourself."

"I thought I told you," Mark said. "I'm sure that I told you about going camping in the Indian ruins." He paused. "Do you see Pete often?"

Mark must wonder if Pete and I talked about him. "You told me about camping, but I didn't connect it to Pete until he mentioned it to me. I see him mostly at meetings. Pete seems to me like a religious fanatic."

"He was raised in a very religious family," Mark said. "Sometimes the religious atmosphere suffocated him. He liked getting away from home by going camping. He and my brother, Roger, would come back from college on holidays, and we would go hiking or camping. We even camped in the winter. I feel cold just thinking about it."

"I think that Pete finds life difficult," Mark continued. "He is a perfectionist and takes trivial things seriously. When we were young, everything was competitive with him. He's the kind of person who comes in second place in a track meet or works hard for an A and ends up with a B.

"Pete is a very smart person. His ability to deal with people makes him a good leader and successful officer. He reads books voraciously and knows a great deal about the history of war and stories from past wars. He took some shrapnel in the back of his thigh once, and he said that the hardest part of his injury was that he had to stand up or lie on his side to read a book, and reading helped to take his mind off the pain.

"You might ask Pete about the wrath of Achilles, in *The Iliad*, after his friend was killed, and Achilles' desire for revenge. Achilles even desecrated the dead bodies of the enemy. Becoming angry with the enemy, the way you were in Iraq, is a theme in ancient literature, as well our present military stories."

I felt more comfortable about Pete after Mark told me this. "I'd like to learn about the psychology of soldiers in war," I said. "Then I would understand my experience in Iraq better. I don't know if many other people shot into crowds like I did. I wonder what other people think, yet I don't want to ask them. I wonder if Pete has done anything like that or what he says to riflemen if they shoot into crowds. When people ask me about the war, I think of that scene, and I don't know what to tell them."

"Pete knows the actions riflemen take in various situations," Mark said. "If you talked to him, you might get a different perspective."

We were silent for a moment. I said, "Pete talked to me some about PTSD, but I wonder if he really knows anything about it. I'd like to know more about PTSD."

"You could probably find some books about it," Mark suggested.

"I can't concentrate on complicated subjects as well as I did in school," I said. "I read for a while but get distracted, and I can't get back into the mood of the book I was reading. Maybe that is related to PTSD."

We walked more and watched a film about a military pilot who flew a fighter plane that had enough thrust to fly straight up into the sky. "I'd like to do that," I said.

Mark answered, "I like to watch the air shows, but I never thought of flying a plane. You could learn to fly a plane if you wanted to. We can do a lot of things—it's a matter of picking out something we want and going for it."

We drove back to Mark's apartment building, dropped off our luggage, and went to Sue's apartment to pick up Cecily. Sue handed over Cecily, reluctantly. "I really liked having her," Sue said. "I'll miss her."

"I'll lend her to you again," Mark said.

Mark carried Cecily to his apartment, where we sat down and Cecily greeted us by climbing all over us.

"I hope you'll stay with me tonight," Mark said. "You can enjoy Cecily, and we can listen to the news. Unless you need a good night's sleep and haven't been able to get it with me."

"I'd like to stay here," I said. "I sleep all right here. Can you sleep soundly with me? You often said I kick you and talk in my sleep."

Mark replied, "I like company at night. I sleep better in a small space that I am familiar with. So maybe I won't keep you awake tonight."

"You never kept me awake long.," I said. "Do you dream about Iraq?"

"Sometimes I relive the time when I regained consciousness in the hospital after the jeep accident. Other times, I have dreams about Wilson dying beside me, and I think that I should be doing something, but I feel paralyzed by fear. I didn't pick up his rifle and return fire. Isn't that what I should have done? I chastise myself for not being good enough as a soldier. I'm not as good as Wilson was at thinking quickly, assessing a situation, and taking action. I'm not as good a soldier as you were.

"I know there are thrill seekers who perform daredevil stunts because they want to see how much fear they can take. I've already found out, and I think the answer is that I've had as much fear as I want. I'm not going to skydive or hunt sharks to see whether I can handle more fear than I've already experienced." Mark's voice was cracking.

I said, "I think that intense, emotional memories must be related to adrenalin. We feel an adrenalin surge, and then we feel an intense emotion like fear, and we relive other times when we felt that emotion. So the adrenalin surge from combat experiences intrudes into our lives later."

Mark said, "Feeling overwhelmed by fear causes us to recall other fearful incidents. Maybe I get frightened more easily than other people now. I don't talk about the Purple Heart because I am ashamed of my behavior. I acted dishonorably."

"I behaved incorrectly, too, if I killed any civilians," I said. "I feel an adrenalin rush when I think of it. Our military training should teach us to respond to situations automatically even when we are scared and not thinking clearly, but real situations aren't like being in training. Many riflemen don't fire their rifles in combat. We can't always predict our own behavior because we can't predict how strong emotion will affect our actions. People who seem frightened may be brave, and people who seem fearless may panic."

"Some people don't show fear," Mark said. "They seem calm even when obvious danger exists."

"You don't know what they feel, though. Maybe when they are fired on, they get angry and want to get even, and their anger is cold and directed," I said. "Other people are on edge all the time or cultivate adrenalin. You don't seem to get angry.

You are placid when things go awry." We were quiet for a while.

Mark replied, "If I could dream about Wilson's death or my accident without the sensation that they are happening in the present, I could sleep better. I used to get up and have a drink after having bad dreams. I often drank before I went to bed, too. Now I have found that when I don't drink, I have more energy." Mark had pulled me onto his lap, and I had one arm around his shoulders. I ran the other hand along his face and felt the stubble on his cheek.

I asked, "Could you get a medication that modifies adrenalin production? If you didn't relive frightening situations with such intensity in your sleep, I'm sure that you would sleep better. I'm certain that an adrenalin surge wakes you up."

Mark replied, "I think you are right about the adrenalin because I feel very alert when I wake up and start searching for the danger that woke me up. I read that some drug called a beta-blocker diminishes adrenalin somehow, and that it's been used for PTSD. It would be strange to take a pill that changes your emotions, even though we probably hang onto our emotional reactions too much."

"I think that civilian life will never have the complex issues that we dealt with in the army," I said. "I miss the army, though. I had so much more in the army."

Mark said, "You and I need to belong to more groups of people with similar interests, so we can make more friends. But we also need to know some people who were in the army, so we can discuss our lives with them."

He got up and added, "Let's go to bed early. I sleep more soundly at home, and I'm tired."

I lay down at Mark's back again, and expected to repeat the excitement of remembering the bombing runs in Iraq before

I fell asleep. Instead, I fell asleep right away, and I dreamed of Mark for the first time. We were walking along a creek together, and we came to a place where the path was flooded. Mark jumped over the flooded area and held out his hand to me. He was deeply tanned and his hair was cut short again. He looked strong, and he was laughing.

CHAPTER 23

LAYOFF

Rumors about cancellation of the Future Combat Systems project had circulated for a long time, and portions of the project had been cancelled over the past few years.

The company I worked for held a meeting for all of the people who worked on the project. An administrative assistant took attendance in the meeting, which was unusual, and I anticipated bad news. We were told that the government would cancel most of the ground vehicles that I had been working on and continue developing only one new vehicle for artillery. The vehicles in use and the new vehicles we were developing are vulnerable to roadside explosive devices. I thought that we could solve this problem with armor made of new materials—something strong but lighter than the armor currently in use. The Department of Defense decided to stop work on these vehicles and to develop a new chassis design that would more effectively deflect explosive devices.

I hoped to be transferred to a project on tanks or other vehicles. I would be glad to armor tanks, but I especially liked to work on troop carriers after seeing that troop carrier hit in Iraq. However, I got a layoff notice. I felt like crying in frustration that all the work I had done was wasted. Brian started crying. I was given only three more days at work, so I could arrange my data for an archive. I had worked on the new vehicle project for almost a year. Discarding my work on army modernization was like throwing a year of my life away.

I called Mark as soon as I got home from work. When I told him that I would soon be out of work, and I asked him if his job was secure. "I'm sorry that you got laid off," he said. "Nobody I know at work got laid off, at least not yet. I'm sure that we are affected by the project being cancelled. My department has vacancies, so I hope I am safe."

Mark came over to my apartment. I told him that one of the men I work with had started crying when we were being laid off.

"Only one?" Mark asked. "I suppose most people soldier it out when they are in a public place. Did you cry too?"

"No, not then. I have since I came home, though. Brian was probably crying because he was worried about losing his house."

"Go ahead and cry, if you want to."

"I think I've cried enough," I said. "Do you ever cry?"

"No, I guess I don't. Sometimes I feel like it when I get frustrated, but then I think crying would be childish."

"Crying is a good release of tension," I said. "Men should probably cry more—at home, anyway. I was a little embarrassed when Brian cried at being laid off."

"If he thinks he will lose his house, it's no wonder."

I said, "I'll pull myself together, and we can go out to eat. I will be going to work tomorrow and for the rest of the week. The office tomorrow will have a strange atmosphere since several of us got layoff notices. We will probably be looking for jobs on the Internet instead of doing any work. I don't think I have much chance of finding a job like the one I had."

While we had Mongolian barbecue, Mark said, "I know your job was important to you. You must feel terrible about losing it."

I replied, "I liked to think I was helping soldiers with my job. Armoring the vehicles is important, but now the program will be cancelled."

"You shouldn't define your existence as being an army officer or defense worker."

"I really don't. I wasn't as caught up in 'Duty, Loyalty, and Honor' as you were," I said. "Detroit isn't a good place to find work."

Mark said, "Can you take some time off from working, at least for a while? You can get unemployment compensation. You don't have to rush back to work, do you?"

I played with the stir-fry on my plate. "Maybe not working for a while is an opportunity I won't have again."

"We could get married," Mark continued. "One thing makes me hesitate, though. I hope you don't want to go back into the army or join the National Guard. I know how much you like the army, but I wouldn't want to deal with you being overseas if we got married."

"I liked the army very much, but I don't want to go back in because I am afraid of being in a war again."

"You talk about it so much, the army must have been the best time in your life. You still run, as though you want to keep in shape to go back."

"I miss the army. I thought that civilian life would be like being in the army, but without going to war. Instead, it seems like I have less in civilian life than I had in the army."

"If you would make more friends, you might not miss the army so much."

"You're probably right," I said. "Meeting people was easier in the army."

Mark said, "I'd like to get married. I'm concerned that I'm not good enough for you, though. We get along, but you need to be practical if you want a comfortable life."

I replied, "I chose an adventurous life. If I had married Michael, I would have been living on one base after another as he pursued his career, and many bases aren't comfortable. If I stayed in the army after we married, we might have gone overseas to work in different countries. I didn't expect an easy life. I knew your negative points before, and I accepted them already."

"I'd like to get married," I continued. "You're my best friend, and we seem to get along pretty well. We don't have arguments. You are willing to join me in doing things that I like. I join you to do things that you want to do like going to the Korean Zen Center, and I usually enjoy them. I have a bad temper and get angry a lot, but I never feel angry with you. You get along with my friends and family. You are considerate, and you respect me more than other people do. In addition, you don't care if I'm better at some things than you are, and most men are not secure enough to deal with women surpassing them."

"Are you are willing to promise that you won't rejoin the army?"

"I'll promise that I will stay away from the army, and the National Guard." I suggested that we walk home instead of running immediately after eating. The neighborhood was old, and the sidewalks were cracked, but strip malls lined the street, providing places to walk or run. We passed empty storefronts and a closed grocery store. "I feel lonely," Mark continued. "I never lived alone until now. I lived with my parents, with my wife, in a fraternity, in bachelor officers' quarters, or in shared apartments. I would rather not live alone. I'd like to be married again."

I wasn't used to being alone, but being alone didn't bother me. I didn't keep checking the door and windows like Mark did. I should have realized that Mark was lonely. He probably went to places I liked to have some company, even if the places we visited together didn't interest him. I had always thought of Mark as vulnerable, but now I saw him as lonely and sad.

Mark said, "Since I've been dating you, I haven't been drinking much, only a couple of times. Cecily helps keep me responsible about alcohol. I remind myself that if I drink by myself, pass out, and die, as some alcoholics do, Cecily would starve. Therefore, I avoid alcohol. I want a drink every day. Liquor makes me happy. You don't have liquor around, so I have an easier time staying away from liquor with you."

At the apartment, I looked through the television guide, but Mark said he would rather listen to the CDs he had brought over before. "We could listen to music more, and watch television less," I said. "I could use the computer while listening to music instead of watching outdoor reality shows."

"If you get a job in another city, I would be willing to live there," Mark said. "I could find some other job. I'm not concerned about my career. I'm willing to do whatever work I can get."

I answered, "I could go to some other city to work, whether you get an out-of-town job or I do. I've had enough time with my family. I would miss LuAnn, though. She is the best female friend that I ever had."

"Do you want to have children?" Mark asked. "I do. I mean, I think we should have children."

"When I went to college and when I went in the army, I always assumed that I would get married and have a baby or two," I answered. "But after Michael died, I didn't think of getting married. I think that you would be a good father."

"One thing bothers me, though," Mark said. "You are very forward, and I wonder about your conduct with men. My concern is that you may be seeing other men or want to if we got married. Since Darlene was chasing around, I don't want to marry somebody else who has a wandering eye."

"Since I've been seeing you regularly, I haven't dated other men," I said. "In the army, I wasn't seriously involved with army men after Michael because I was afraid that they might be killed in the war. We would enjoy the moment together, at the end of the world."

I hesitated a moment. "Are you worried about AIDS? You use condoms all the time even though I take birth control pills. I can get a blood test if you want me to." He said nothing. "I'll get a blood test," I volunteered.

"I'd like to meet your family," I continued. "I wonder if they will like me. In-laws can make a difference in your life, especially if they don't like you. Do you talk to your parents much?"

"I didn't tell my parents yet. We talk on the phone infrequently, but I will call them soon. You and I can go to New Mexico and meet my parents if you like. Since they live in New Mexico, I don't think that we will see them very often if we stay in Michigan."

"I would like to meet your parents before we get married. When could you take time off to go to see them?"

"I can trade some days with my coworkers again." Mark seemed very happy.

"I have always been curious about you and Pete working together in Iraq," I said. "Did you and Pete run into some trouble? I had the impression that you were in some action together there."

"We were never in physical danger together, but we were parties in a mistake," Mark said. "The mapping information provided by my section was incomplete, and Pete's unit attacked at the wrong coordinates. One or more of Pete's riflemen were killed because the area they went into was marked as friendly, but it held insurgents. The military is one place where people die from the mistakes other people make. When I became a military officer, I didn't realize at an emotional level that people could die because I gave them incorrect instructions, didn't lead them well enough, or didn't provide the right information.

"After you have been in country for a while, you lose perspective on human life, except the lives that you are responsible for. Pete felt guilty about the incident. He also got very angry and told me that whoever supplied the intelligence deserved to die. He blames me for that incident, but I don't feel responsible for our inaccurate information. Pete knew that insurgents might move into an area at any time, so he should have been more careful, even though intelligence indicated there was no imminent danger."

Mark continued, "I hope Pete isn't sent overseas again. He has been in Afghanistan and Iraq, and his luck may run out someday. I would hate to lose Pete."

I had expected another story of Mark being in a combat situation. "The army needs more responsible officers like Pete—but without the hyperbole," I said. "If civil servants make a mistake with the armor designs, soldiers can die. Everybody's job with the military is important for national defense, whether they're a soldier or a civilian."

Mark was very attentive to me that night. He made iced tea for me and held me on his lap while we watched television. I didn't feel like talking much and distracted myself by trying to imagine being in the settings of the television shows. But I was glad I was in Michigan and with Mark. Mark seemed happy that evening. He told me that he hadn't thought I would be willing to marry him. He said he always thought I was just playing around and would never be serious about him. He kept joking about the shows on television and cracked jokes about the people and the settings. I was glad that Mark was with me that night and had distracted me from the bad news I had received. I would have time in the future to think about getting another job.

CHAPTER 24

TIME OFF

The next three days at work passed quickly. When I performed a task, it occurred to me that I would never perform that task again after this week. In the army, I always knew that my next job assignment was waiting. Now I didn't know what came next. I thought that I would never have this desk again or be in this meeting room again. And the fact that many other people had lost their jobs didn't make me feel better about losing mine.

I spent the evenings at Mark's apartment, playing with Cecily and trying to read or meditate with Mark. Mark was effusive in his sympathy and seemed to have taken on the role of my caregiver. With Michael, I had always known that I was with a strong, capable man, and that he would be in charge of many of the decisions in the relationship. Mark had always seemed vulnerable and sad, but now he began to treat me as a parent might treat a child.

On Friday, we went to the happy hour and to the Chinese buffet afterward, where my former coworkers treated me to dinner. I was the only person present who had been laid off, but fewer people came than usual. People bought me drinks, and I got sloppy and tipsy, and enjoyed the evening very much. Mark tried to have a conversation with Charlie at the buffet and told me later that it was interesting to try to converse with someone so distracted that he can't always follow a conversation. "I guess he manages to do his job, though," I said. "People think that the way he mumbles about helicopters is a symptom of PTSD."

I took Pete aside and told him about the burning troop carrier and firing the rifle. Pete said, "Pam, throughout history soldiers have felt just like you did. You can get very angry with the other side in any conflict and feel like you want to hurt them. People can be mad at the opposition in team sports, too. If women played team sports more, they would understand anger against competitors, which becomes anger against an enemy."

"Let's look at it this way," he continued. "A troop carrier was burning, and the men had to flee. You laid down covering fire for them. Civilians were in the way. You're a soldier." Mark had said that Pete would give me a warrior's answer.

On Saturday, Mark worked and I went to the nature preserve alone even though the weather was rainy. I walked to the ponds and watched the ducks and geese. The trees cast reflections on the water, and turtles lay on the logs in the shallow water. Suddenly I felt nervous about being alone and exposed to imaginary enemies. Mark walked and ran in parks by himself, but I thought I would rather walk with him than alone.

Mark had decided that, to distract me, we should join Tom and Barbara, his neighbors, for their Saturday night trip to a casino. Tom drove to a casino near downtown Detroit, with both of them sympathizing with me about my job loss. Barbara had dressed up very nicely, while I was just wearing my work clothes. I was surprised by how crowded the casino was and clung to Mark, so that we wouldn't be separated. Mark and I tried some video poker, which I had never played before. After I lost ten dollars, I asked Mark how it was going for him. To my surprise, he was winning. A hostess offered us free drinks. Mark refused, so I did too. "I really would have liked to drink," he said.

I replied, "We could have gotten a soft drink. If they come by next time, I'll get some ginger ale."

Tom and Barbara came by to ask us if we wanted to have dinner, and we all stood in a long line to get food at the buffet, which they regarded as special because of its very large selection of everyday food. At dinner, they told us about the latest movies that were available for rent.

"Do you watch movies a lot?" I asked. I hadn't seen a movie in a year.

"Yes," Tom said. "Almost every night. We don't like network television, and cable is getting expensive."

"We would really like to go places more—like eating out and the movies, and other entertainment, but it costs too much," Barbara said. "Going to a movie in the theater and getting some popcorn, would cost us twenty dollars."

"We can't really afford to have a couple of drinks each in a bar," Tom said.

I played some slot machines; I was surprised by the variety—ones with birds or jewels or animals as tokens. Mark drifted off to join Tom in playing some card game. We stayed until midnight.

After we went home, Mark asked me how I had liked going to the casino. I said that it was interesting, but I didn't care if we did it again. "Maybe in the winter when we can't go many places because of the snow, we will be looking for indoor things to do. We could also drive to a casino on an Indian reservation, and see if they have an Indian-food buffet. I like American Indian food, like buffalo stew and wild rice soup."

I suggested that if we got together with Tom and Barbara again, it could be to watch a movie, but we should select the movie, after carefully reading movie reviews. Mark laughed at that. "I don't think they're very bright," I said. "When the weather gets bad, it might be nice to watch movies with them, though."

"They mean well," Mark said. "If they were smart, they would probably have better jobs than they do and live in a nicer place—unless they lose a lot of their money at the casinos."

After going to the Zen Center on Sunday, Mark and I went to the park by the river to see the ponds. We joked about my turtle relatives.

My first weekday with no work was Monday. I was used to being busy and didn't know how to fill the time. I cleaned house, did laundry, ran, and missed Mark. Daytime television wasn't interesting, so I left the TV off. But I cooked dinner, just like a homemaker.

Later in the week, I took Elizabeth to the zoo. She insisted on paying the admission herself, although I offered to treat. As we walked around the zoo, Elizabeth focused on sympathizing with the animals and their difficult life situation—being in cages or not having much companionship from the same species. "You mean they can't make friends?" I asked.

"They must be lonely," she said. "Also, picture leading your life in a shell like a turtle. They must feel very solitary. I also feel sorry for animals because they can't understand Buddhist teachings. They will have to lead good lives for a long time before becoming human and die difficult deaths many times."

She let me treat her to a film. It was a strange cartoon involving dinosaurs, which started in a frightening way, with the camera following a plane diving into the sea before it reached the island of dinosaurs. I had to close my eyes during the diving scene because I got dizzy. Some of the children asked to leave the theater, and they started the film over. Elizabeth was calm during the film and said afterward that it was very imaginative, but it didn't seem realistic!

We walked toward the polar bears. "Are Zen masters like Catholic priests who remain single?" I asked, as we watched the polar bears.

"No, most Zen teachers marry. In Japan, sometimes a Zen temple runs in the family, passed down from father to son," she said. "I notice how the seals and polar bears are separated by glass. The seals must be frightened as the bears approach them. How would they understand glass? What a difficult life for both of them."

Elizabeth was a very nice person, but I wouldn't feel comfortable confiding in her because she had a pat answer for every issue—meditate. I treated her to lunch at a restaurant just off the freeway, where I knew that she could get a vegetarian meal. I asked Elizabeth if she would like to go anywhere else, and she said that she would think about it. Perhaps Elizabeth, Mark, and I could go to a metropark sometime.

One day, I went to the auto body shop to talk to my dad. We went out back into the car lot so that his employees couldn't hear us. We stood near the old jeep so that dad could have a smoke without the possibility of damaging a customer's car.

"I'm going to marry Mark," I said.

"I'm glad you're getting married. He seems like a nice person," dad said. "I would describe him as kindhearted. You don't seem to be as happy with him as you were with the other fellow, though. When you came here with Michael, you acted like you were delighted with the world."

"Perhaps I'm not as crazy about him as I was about Michael, but I was younger then, too. Maybe I was more emotional."

"Maybe you were more boiled up about sex then," dad said. "After a while, sex becomes less of a novelty."

"Mark isn't as happy a person as Michael was. But Mark had a hard time in the war."

Dad said, "You were different after the war, too. In fact, you don't seem to be very happy since getting out of the army. At first, you were nervous and angered easily, and seemed dissatisfied with everything. You're a little more settled now. When I came back from Vietnam, I just wanted to get married, settle down, and lead a normal life. I was glad that your mother waited for me. She said she wouldn't marry me until I was out of the army."

He continued, "Has Mark been married before?"

"Yes, he has been divorced for about five years," I said.

"Do you know why? Sometimes the first wife wasn't wrong, and you would have the same problems with him that she did. Does he have children? He seemed to get along well with Susie's kids."

"No, they didn't have children."

"You should find out as much as you can about why they divorced. Divorced people often blame their former spouse and don't take responsibility themselves. Be careful," dad said.

"That's a good point. Mark and his ex-wife were about nineteen when they met. Their life together was immature, but then he grew up fast in the army, as we all do. Now he is religious and doesn't drink or even want to watch television. I guess that, like any other wife, I would hope he doesn't take up barhopping and cheating on me. I don't think that's likely."

My dad laughed. "He has to hope that you don't take up drinking, men, and booze too."

I said, "I wish that he was happier, and more fun-loving. He goes along with things I like to do, but he doesn't enjoy things much."

"Not being happy isn't a major fault. We all have to deal with our marriage partner's personality. Your mom and I agree on important things, so we don't quarrel much. You girls quarreled all the time and wanted us to settle your squabbles. Listening to you complain about each other was very annoying to us. But we were glad we had you, too. Raising you kids was the best part of our lives."

He continued, "I think you should meet his parents because they will be part of your lives together. See what Mark's dad is like, since Mark may be like that some day."

I understood his point. "His parents might not like me and that would be a problem. However, they live in New Mexico, and Mark rarely sees them."

Dad continued, "Check his parents out before committing yourself. Meet his siblings too, if you can. Faults you see in them may show up in him later. If he's too resistant to you meeting his family, maybe he is hiding something."

"He could have misrepresented his family," I said. "Also, they sound old-fashioned, so they might disapprove of my being in the army."

"That sort of thing is what you should find out." He paused for a moment. "We will pay for your wedding and reception, just like we did for Carolyn and Susie. Don't let him talk you into going to a justice of the peace just because he has been married before and doesn't want to go through a wedding again."

"I hadn't given much thought to a wedding, Dad. I didn't go to Carolyn's and Susie's weddings because I was too far away, and I didn't think about having a family wedding that is a party too. I have only a few friends who would come."

Dad replied, "Your wedding is for us as well as you. With a small wedding, we can plan a nicer dinner, with exotic food that all the guests will remember. Buy a beautiful white dress even though...well, even though you...I mean, Susie wore a white dress, and you should wear one too, because you haven't been married before."

I told Mark that I definitely wanted to visit New Mexico before we got married.

"We can go see the Indian ruins you talk about," I said. "You can show me around the city, too."

"In only four days, with all the flight and travel time, we can't see much anyway," Mark said.

"Don't you get any vacation yet?" I asked.

"When we get married, I'll use it on our honeymoon trip," he said. "I was in New Mexico and saw my parents when I got out of the army, so I don't feel a need to go back so soon. My parents worry about me, so they will be glad whenever I come,"

He continued, "My parents are intrusive because I stayed with them when I was ill, and they took care of me. I am too much a child when I am with my parents. They still want to protect me from life. Instead of having an adult relationship with them, I'm still their little kid. They mean well. They were afraid that I might die after I was in the accident, so they are overprotective."

I wished Mark had more enthusiasm about going to New Mexico. "I hope your parents and I get along," I said.

Mark and I joined Sue on one of her trips to Canada. She insisted on driving because her car was bigger. She drove northeast to Port Huron and we crossed the Blue Water Bridge to Sarnia. The drive to the bridge took a little over an hour, through attractive woodsy scenery, but then we sat in line for half an hour at the border crossing. To pass the time, Sue talked about her former husband, her divorce, and her job as a clerk in the office of an elementary school. I asked her what she did for recreation, and she said that she read many library books, and went to book clubs at the local libraries. I felt comfortable with Sue. I planned to read one of the books from the book club, so we could go to the book club together.

We bought groceries, window-shopped in a mall, ate at a Chinese restaurant, and drove back. The trip was fun, and Sue invited us to drop over any time for coffee, and to call her whenever I felt like chatting. I finally had a woman friend in civilian life.

Since I wasn't working, I began doing Mark's laundry as well as my own, cooking breakfast, packing Mark's lunch, and making dinner. Mark was concerned about putting on weight, even though he was thin.

We went running together sometimes, but usually I ran by myself in the mornings. I liked to run close to the stores in strip malls, so I could see how many had closed.

Dad called me and said that he had arranged for us to visit Grandma on Saturday. Jimmy and his wife would be there. "You better take Mark, too," dad said. "You would want Jimmy's approval of the man you plan to marry, wouldn't you?"

The three of us drove to Uncle Ron and Aunt Molly's place to see dad's brothers and Grandma. He said that Grandma was still sharp in certain ways but was getting a little forgetful in others.

As dad drove, he talked about growing up on the farm and milking the cows in the morning. He told about leaving home for the Detroit area when he was sixteen, and living with his aunt, uncle, and one of his cousins. He got a weekend job at a gas station to help out with the expenses. "Then I went into the army when I finished high school, to get it out of the way. I had taken classes in machining and one in small engines in high school. They assigned me to work on fixing army vehicles, which was all right. I had a better job in the army than I first did when I got out of the Army. In my first civilian job, I was just working in a gas station again. My next job was in a body shop. After a while, I thought I could run a body shop myself."

Jimmy and his wife were already at the house. Jimmy looked older now. His hair was a little thinner and had started to recede. He said that his teenagers were staying with friends because they had sports events on this weekend.

"You have an even longer drive than we did," dad said. "So it's good that you are staying overnight and don't have to drive back the same day."

"You remember my cousin, Pam," Jimmy said to his wife, Amber. "Pam, I haven't seen you for five or six years."

Grandma was sitting in the living room. "Pam," she said. "It's nice to see you again. How is the baby?" She had apparently mixed me up with Carolyn.

"Bobby is fine," I said, at a loss for words. "This is Mark." I thought I shouldn't introduce Mark as my fiancé because it would confuse her further if she thought I had a baby already.

Uncle Ron brought us snacks, and offered beer or soda. The men settled into a discussion of politics and current events, and asked Mark what he thought about Afghanistan. "I haven't thought much of the politics surrounding the wars," Mark said. "We aren't as tuned in to the details of politics when we are in the army. The attitude is that the civilians elect whoever they want to be our commander-in-chief."

"Well, you should follow the financial news anyway," Jimmy said. "This situation with the banks is a threat to all of us, and our way of life."

"Our whole way of life?" I asked. I pictured Jimmy sitting at his computer at work with a pair of headphones, listening to political talk shows.

Jimmy suggested that we collect some silver or gold coins, and hide them on our property, preferably in glass jars buried in the back yard. "That might be a good idea, but I live in an apartment," Mark said.

"You can rent a safe deposit box and keep them there," Jimmy suggested. He began talking about a conspiracy involving international banks. Amber looked bored. She had probably heard this many times.

Uncle Ron suggested that we go to visit the farm. The people who owned it were friends of his. We piled into his farm truck—Uncle Ron driving, with dad and Amber on the seat

TIME OFF

beside him, and Jimmy, Mark, and me sitting in the truck's bed, just like I had when I was a kid. We leaned against the truck cab to keep away from the breeze caused by the momentum of the truck. "Did you ever ride in a truck this way before?" I asked Mark. He shook his head.

Dad and Uncle Ron went to the house, and the rest of us went down to the creek, carefully walking along the edge of a planted field. When I was young, my uncles had dammed the creek, roughly, to make a swimming area. At the creek, I waded a little way in the shallows. Then I continued into the water and lay down, feeling the cold. "Come on in, the water is fine, just a little chilly," I said.

"You are getting your clothes all wet," Jimmy said.

To my surprise, Amber also waded into the creek next, with the men still standing at the side. "It's hot out. My clothes will dry," she said. Mark put his hand into the cool water, then pulled his shirt off, put it in the grass, and waded hesitantly into the water. Jimmy was the last to enter. "We will have to sit on the porch after this," he said. "We wouldn't want to sit on the living room furniture in wet clothes." Jimmy wasn't as adventurous as I remembered.

"That's fine," I said as I paddled on my back in the water. "Jimmy taught me to swim," I said.

"More or less," he answered. "I taught you to dog paddle a little. My own kids had swimming lessons." We all splashed in the water for a while, then got out, and sat in the sun to dry.

"This must have been fun when you were young," Mark said.

"I think it's fun now," I replied.

Amber said, "I always tried to keep my kids away from this part of the creek, so that they wouldn't get all muddy and track mud into the house. So I never swam here before."

"I used to get real muddy getting out of this pond," I said. "It was always fun, though."

Jimmy took me aside on the way back to the house. "I think it's time you got married," he said. "He seems nice. He's sort of shy and quiet for a military man."

"I think he doesn't like talking politics and national finances," I said. "Army people aren't all tough. All types of people go in the army. I spent as long in the army as he did."

"You're pretty tough," he said.

"Do you remember winning a teddy bear at a fair, and giving it to me?" I asked. He didn't. It had been my favorite toy, until it became Susie's.

The men were drinking beer on the porch when we came back. "Pam is going to drive home," dad said.

"No, Mark will," I suggested. "I always loved the farm, and I'm so glad we came here."

Amber invited us to visit them in Chicago. "I'd like to," I said. "Do you have a map of where the jars of coins are buried?" I asked her, when no one else could hear.

"There's a treasure map. If something happens to Jim, I may have to use a metal detector," she said and laughed. "I guess everyone has their personal idiosyncrasies. He earns good money, and I guess he can bury some of it if he wants. We can swim in Lake Michigan if you come. You seem to like cold water, and it's even colder than the creek."

Uncle Ron drove us back to his home in the truck, shivering from the cold. Both Mark and Jimmy abstained from drinking the beer that Uncle Ron offered when we got back.

Soon we said good-bye to Grandma, who had begun addressing me as Molly, who was her late sister.

"It's too bad about Grandma," I said to dad after we got in the car.

"She's well into her eighties," he said. "I hate to see it, too. She was so smart and had a lot of homespun wisdom. Her condition is the reason why I don't go there very often, although I like to see Ron. I hope I never get like that, although she might feel happy, for all I know."

"Your cousin Jimmy is very interesting," Mark said. "I was fascinated by his opinion of the financial system and the recession. I don't know enough about money to discuss those topics intelligently."

"He seems to be very opinionated," I said. "He wasn't that way when he was younger."

"Actually, he was," dad said. "I think you were too young to pick up on the opinions of politics, business, and finances that he had then and still has. After all, he's fifteen years or so older than you are, and you probably talked about parks and frogs and turtles, not government and banking."

"I enjoyed seeing him, though," I said. I was very sad about Grandma, and chatted with dad about the automobile industry and the auto body business, as we went home to Detroit.

Mark and I went to the Cranbrook science museum for our first planetarium visit. I insisted that we invite Sue. She accepted eagerly and was excited to go to Cranbrook, which she hadn't gone to for years. We walked around the exhibits in the science museum and went to the planetarium film about the sky in Michigan this time of year.

I registered us to see the bat program and tour of the bat house, which held many varieties of bats and a large sloth, almost invisible against the foliage in his cage. A mother bat hung upside down with her baby bat clinging to her fur. Sue was very enthusiastic about the bats and picked up information about doing volunteer work with the bats. Both Sue and Mark decided to join the Society for Bat Conservation. I was a little hesitant because the bat house was cramped and sort of smelly, and I liked outdoor things more. "Maybe you could volunteer for helping at the garden, and I'll volunteer for the planetarium, and Sue for the bats," Mark said.

"Let's see the other planetariums before we commit ourselves to this one," I said. I suggested that we wait until it rained or got cold, but Sue and Mark were eager to see the other planetariums soon.

After we dropped Sue off, Mark said, "You really like Sue, don't you? It surprises me because she must be fifteen years older than you are."

"That's all right," I said. "She is enthusiastic about things and reads a lot. Some army officers have a good education but are interested in only a few subjects—maybe poker, weight lifting, or target shooting. Many people, for recreation, just want to see a movie, eat out, and go to a bar. How many people go to Canada, go to Cranbrook, and decide that they like bats?"

Mark said, "Not many, just like few people go to Indian mounds. Don't knock army officers. Some have doctorate degrees."

Lily finally got her leave in Cleveland, and I drove down to see her for a few days. Lily looked a little different. For the first time, I noticed how high her cheekbones were, and the uneven coloring of her complexion. Maybe she wasn't wearing as much makeup as she used to. She used to have a bureau drawer half full of makeup. I asked her if she ran regularly, and she said, "Not when I'm on vacation."

I said, "After the drive, I wouldn't mind running."

"I'm taking you to the mall," she said. "We can walk all over it and get some exercise."

On the drive to the mall, she went on and on about a man she had met, who was from Colorado and wanted to go back there. Lily tended to get involved with one man after another. I asked, "Are you serious about each other? Moving to Colorado would be exciting."

"I'm not sure. He's married now, but he is going to get a divorce." I had heard Lily say that before.

I told her that I had a new boyfriend, and she asked what he was like. "He's complicated," I said. "He is very friendly with people and has a lot of interests—like music and photography. He's been in the army, but now he works in the defense business."

"Well, the defense business pays better than the army, so you probably go to some pretty nice places for entertainment."

"He's religious and doesn't drink."

"Oh, one of those good Christian types," she said. "At least he can take you to some nice restaurants. I like having shrimp cocktail as an appetizer before launching into a good piece of prime rib." I had a quick picture of Michael and me eating at an elaborate restaurant, with candles and wine glasses.

"He's sort of a connoisseur of Asian food," I said.

"Is he good looking?"

"He looks very army," I said. "Slender and strong. We go hiking and canoeing, and go to parks."

"I guess you like the outdoors," Lily said. "Can you tell him how you feel about things, as well as what you think? Most of the army men don't care what other people feel or think it isn't manly to have feelings."

"Exactly," I said. "They say that they feel they never made any mistakes because they don't know the difference between feeling and thinking. If they feel anything, they probably decide to soldier it out."

Lily took me to an enormous mall with multiple anchor stores, and we had lunch at a chain restaurant. Then she took me to one store after another, trying on clothes and shoes. We went into bookstores and gift stores, too. We probably went to half the stores in the mall, including expensive stores I had never visited.

She was right about shopping being a form of exercise, and I was tired when we got back to her home; we settled into companionable chatting about people we knew in the army. I had a tourist guide and suggested that we go to the science museum the next day, but Lily said that she had seen it many times. We had dinner with her parents and then went to a movie. I hadn't been to a movie in a theater since I got back to Detroit.

The next day we went to two more shopping centers. "I look forward to getting out of the army next year," Lily said. "I'd like to be able to wear nice clothes to work. Buying a new wardrobe will be a lot of fun. With six kids in our family, and me the youngest girl, I hardly ever had new clothes, just clothes my three older sisters had worn."

I said, "I was the oldest, and I never thought enough about how my sisters might feel at wearing clothes I had worn first. My middle sister has the same coloring I do, but my youngest sister has lighter hair and might not have liked the color of my clothes." Maybe Susie resented wearing my hand-me-downs. I bought some slacks for work. In the evening, we rented two videos and watched them in her family's recreation room that evening while drinking rum and Coke. I talked her into going to the botanical garden and greenhouse the next day.

Iraq was so different from anyplace in the United States that Lily and I didn't really know each other in Iraq. Lily used to talk about Cleveland and the interesting things she did there, but now she just wanted to go to shopping malls.

The next day we went to the botanical garden in the morning, and I drove back to Detroit and Mark and the lakes, parks, and hiking trails that I had come home for.

I thought about ways I could help Mark sleep more soundly. I said, "I would like to help you sleep better if I can. I am alarmed when you are shivering in the night."

"When you don't sleep facing my back, you don't seem to notice," Mark said.

I got Mark to lie with his head on a pillow in my lap while we watched television together before we went to bed.

"Mark, what makes you happy?" I asked. "Something you could do or something I should do? Were you happier some other place at some other time?"

"Drinking and partying with a group of friends is what always made me happy. I have to find other things now."

I went to LuAnn's place one afternoon. To my surprise, she said that Mark had come over to see Bob a few times and that they had gone to AA meetings together. She said that Bob was trying to cut down on his drinking. She baked a cake, and we talked about high school and our families, and the flower gardens in the city parks. We agreed to get together again on a Saturday, and find something to do that wouldn't involve drinking. Then we watched the police show on television and compared the characters to people we both knew.

Mark and I went to an AA meeting combined with an Al-Anon meeting once a week. We often had coffee with other people afterwards. I saw that Mark had found a way to get acquainted with people in an unfamiliar city.

"I don't plan to drink again, but I can't guarantee anything. I try to stay sober," Mark said to me. "In AA, we try to help each other."

"I've risked my life, and I can take other risks," I said. "I think that spending my life with you wouldn't be a big risk." I paused, and said, "I would like to socialize more with your friends from AA." I knew that would please him.

The next few weeks followed the pattern of the first one as I looked for a job and Mark tried to arrange for four days off in a row. Since his department needed to have personnel available at all times, he worked a varied schedule. I teased him, asking if he ever had to walk around and check that the lights were off. To my surprise, he said that sometimes he had needed to check whether the emergency lights would come on. I teased him, saying, "I think you are just afraid to go back to your home."

"You're probably right," he said.

I watched television quite a bit and started getting bored with the survival and Alaska stories. Since I was no longer reading army documentation most of the day, I had gotten some library books to read. I found many books on the Vietnam War but scarcely any about the wars in Iraq and Afghanistan.

At the end of the month, Mark would move into my apartment, to save money. Our first disagreements were about furniture and the arrangement of the apartment. I had never lived full time with a man before. "I need to have a place to meditate," Mark said. "I would like to meditate away from the television."

I wasn't happy about his implicit criticism of my television watching. "I think you could meditate in the bedroom," I said.

Deciding which furniture to discard was a conversation that lasted for days. My boxes of souvenirs and curios took up too much space. I asked Mark why he had so few remembrances of college and the army. He said that he had left many of his personal possessions with his parents, that his mother enjoyed having his high school yearbooks because she would sometimes meet the people he had gone to high school with.

CHAPTER 25

TO NEW MEXICO

Mark and I flew to Albuquerque to meet his mom and dad. Mark said, "Don't be nervous about meeting my parents. They'll like you and will want to please you because they are afraid that you will wise up and get away."

I glued myself to the window and watched the forest changing to plains, to the high mountains, and then to desert broken by high ridges. "I would enjoy driving across the country by car," I said. "Just to see the terrain close up, and see the plant cover change."

"Cross country is boring," Mark replied. "The terrain is the same for long stretches. Crossing the Rocky Mountains is the most interesting."

"I would like to do it anyway. And sometime I would like to visit the Rocky Mountains," I said. "I haven't seen the American West, except Fort Irwin in California and its surroundings in the desert."

"We could go to Colorado, but I would really like to go to northern Michigan and see lakes and waterfalls. Camping beside a lake and hiking in the woods would be a nice vacation.

I wanted to go north in Michigan even before I lived there," Mark said. "Maybe we can have a honeymoon in the north."

I replied, "Sometimes I am surprised that we have known each other less than a year, and we are getting married and talking about a honeymoon." I had expected to know a man for a year or two before we would get married. That plan hadn't worked out last time I was going to get married. I felt tears coming to my eyes.

We rented a car in Albuquerque and drove to the Indian Center near downtown. Mark wanted me to have a New Mexico-style Navajo taco, with green chile sauce. The restaurant in the Indian Center was bright and cheerful, and the Navajo taco surprised me: a plate-sized piece of fry bread piled with beans, hamburger, and salad, too much to eat in one sitting.

We went to the small museum, which contained a showcase for each pueblo, with examples of pottery and other craft items. Then we watched a film on making pottery and walked around the grounds. Some young Indian men in feathered costumes were practicing a dance. It seemed like Mark was trying to delay going to his parents' home.

"We'll go see some Indian sites tomorrow," Mark said as we began driving north. The land was open at first and then grew hillier, with plateaus in the distance.

I saw a sign pointing to Santa Fe. "Did we miss our turn?" I asked. "Your parents live north of Santa Fe, right?"

"We're going to Los Alamos," Mark said. "That's where they live."

Mark had never mentioned Los Alamos. I had thought that he was from a suburb of Santa Fe. This was just another example of his evasiveness and telling only part of any story, with the most significant parts coming later. I'd have to get more used to that.

Mark's mother greeted us at the house, a suburban ranch with Spanish-influenced architecture. I was a little surprised at how old she was, matronly and gray haired. She was probably over sixty, while my own mother was about ten years younger. She introduced herself as Dacie, and said "I'm glad to meet you, Pam. Mark told me that the two of you are going to get married. I'm so pleased that Mark is getting married again." She brought Mark and me lemonade as we sat down in the living room. The house had high ceilings and arched window-type openings in some of the walls. "Spanish style of cooling," Mark said. "Because hot air rises, the ceilings are high, and the interior windows ventilate the kitchen."

Dacie asked Mark about his health, remarked that he was too thin, inquired about his job, and asked if he liked Detroit. She spoke as though he had just gotten home after being away at summer camp. Mark's father came home from work early. He explained that he had started work at five in the morning in order to get home early and be able to spend more time with Mark.

"I'm glad you could come and visit us," he said to me. "Please call me Herman. Mark said that you are from the Detroit area, so you know people there already, and you and Mark have friends."

"Pam has friends and a big extended family," Mark said. "We went to a party at her parents' home, and I met her uncles, aunts, sisters, nephews, and cousins."

"My family liked Mark a lot," I said.

Dacie said, "Mark said that you were in the army too. I suppose both of you are relieved to be back from the army."

"Being out of the army takes a while to get used to," I said. "Working as a civilian is very different than being an army officer."

"I think it's easier," Mark said. "Nobody cares about your personal life, unless it gets in the way of your work. Nobody cares what you wear as long as it isn't outrageous. I feel much less restricted."

"How is your job going, Mark?" Herman asked. "I suppose it's very different from what you did in the army."

"It's all right," Mark said. "I like it so far."

As we snacked on lemonade and potato chips, Mark told his parents about our trip to see Indian mounds.

"We did that in Alabama, too," Dacie said. "You were young, and maybe you don't remember Moundsville."

"I remember some dioramas, now that you mention it. A river was nearby, and models of canoes in a building."

Herman said, "I'm sure there are lots of places to visit around Detroit. I never lived close to a large city but being able to go to professional theater and music performances would be very nice. Are you able to go to concerts and plays?"

"Yes, we could," Mark said. "The local colleges also have professional and semiprofessional events. Do you still play the violin?"

"Yes. Once in a while I get together with friends, and we play string quartets."

"What do you do for recreation around Detroit?" Dacie asked.

"We go hiking and canoeing," I said. "And we go to museums. We are planning to visit all the local planetariums."

"Sounds like both of you like the outdoors," Herman said.

"Pam is quite an outdoorswoman," Mark said. "We do other things, too. I play chess with friends, and we went to Canada recently. We go around to lectures and events at various places to get to know what things are available to do in the area."

"We want to go to all of the planetariums and observatories near us, since Mark likes astronomy," I added.

Mark's parents began telling stories about Mark's successes in high school. Besides garnering academic honors, he had won track meets and played the trumpet in the high school band. He had been mischievous, too. He and his friends had once climbed onto the roof of the high school and put up a witch figure for Halloween. At Christmas, they had rearranged the letters of the Merry Christmas and Happy New Year sign outside to read nonsense words. These pranks didn't sound like the quiet and self-effacing person I knew.

"You must have had a lot of fun in high school," I said to participate in the conversation. I had thought that Mark's parents would favor his older brother because Roger had become a professional physicist like his father. Now I thought that Mark might have been their favorite. He might have developed his reticence to hide his drinking from his parents.

Mark told his parents that we usually went running before dinner and that we were stiff from sitting on the plane and needed to run. We were already dressed casually, so we changed shoes and went outside. "You were very different in high school than you are now," I said as we walked down the driveway. "Did the army change you that much?"

"Well, we grow up sometime, don't we? High school antics seem so silly to me now. My parents talk about when I was in high school, maybe because it was a good time in their own lives. They had more free time, and could spend it on their own interests and doing things with their own friends."

"Do you still have friends from high school?" I asked.

"Pete."

I began running slowly so that we could talk as we ran.

"I feel smothered in New Mexico," Mark told me. "I need a little fresh air. I feel like I am a little kid being checked up on, in case I have done something without permission."

"You did. You went into the army," I said. "Your mother delights in you because she was afraid of losing you. Tell her some army stories. Let your parents know about your life in the army."

We ran on the sidewalks of the housing tract and into a business district with strip malls. After twenty minutes, we started back to his parents' home. I wouldn't have been able to tell their house from the houses surrounding it because they all looked so similar.

Dacie had prepared small snack sandwiches while we were gone. "We eat dinner late this time of year," she said. "Cooking heats up the house, so we eat outside on the patio."

We ate again. "The army never had such good food," I said, to break an uncomfortable silence.

"I am intrigued that you were an army officer, too," Mark's dad said.

"Pam is quite a soldier," Mark said. "One time she was in a convoy that took some enemy fire, and she grabbed a rifle and began returning fire. Most officers wouldn't have done that. The troops are supposed to protect the officers."

"Mark was a devoted soldier, too," I said. "He had been badly injured in South Korea, but stayed in the army so that he could be in combat in Iraq, where he got a Purple Heart." So what if he stayed for personal reasons and lost his helmet in combat? We can rewrite our past. Our past is a story that we rewrite in our thoughts every day.

"You never told us much about your injury in Iraq, Mark," his mother said.

"I didn't say anything at the time because you would want to go out to see me, and you couldn't come to Iraq. I had a couple of stitches. I was back at work in a day or two." He added, for my benefit, "My parents went to South Korea to see me after I was in the jeep accident."

"Of course we went to Korea," his mother said. "They called us and said that we should come because they hadn't determined the extent of your head injury." To me, she said, "He was in intensive care, and the whole right side of his face was so bruised and swollen that I could barely recognize him."

Mark added, "I was surprised to see my parents after I came to. I couldn't talk, and they could only visit for ten minutes at a time, so we didn't have a chance to communicate."

"His injuries must have terrified you," I said to Dacie.

Mark added, looking at his mother, "You weren't happy that I went into the army."

"We always worried about you," Dacie said. "Especially when you were in Iraq."

Herman said, "I was proud that you served your country. I always served this country, too. I could have worked in industry instead of civil service and made more money. Sometimes I considered jobs with defense contractors. Then I would think how my own father came here almost as a prisoner, frightened because he expected punishment, and thinking that he would spend the rest of his life in a prison camp. Instead, he had a good job, and eventually my parents had a nice place to live and everything they needed."

"I had everything I needed, too," Mark said. "I got a good education. I never felt envious of other kids when I was in school."

"I don't blame you for changing your name," his father continued. "There were probably war criminals with our name. The Nazi barbarians would have killed Einstein. They would have killed Fermi. Hitler's thugs would have killed your grandfather if they could have found him. They would probably have killed everyone who looked like my raven-haired beauty because they don't appear Aryan enough." He indicated Dacie. I was amused. "Your grandfather wouldn't use the *von* with our name because it was too German. I was satisfied with Stutzer, but why shouldn't you have a more American name?"

"I Americanized my German first name," Dacie said. "You know my name is pretty in German—Hogdace. My parents said they wouldn't have named me that if they had known how strange it sounded in English. Since I don't use my given name, why should I care if you wanted a different last name?"

The conversation drifted into pointless comments about the weather and recent events in Los Alamos, until Dacie served a large dinner of beef, potatoes, sauerkraut, and salad. Mark told his parents that they should feel free to have wine with their dinner and that he was getting used to avoiding alcohol.

"I don't care for wine," I said. "I'm used to drinking only water with dinner." I began talking about the army's restrictions on alcohol in Iraq and said that I rarely drank liquor because I wanted sharp senses and fast reaction times. Mark continued the topic by making a speech about AA and saying that he wasn't going to drink anymore and that being abstinent would be easy because I didn't drink.

After dinner, Dacie showed us the painting studio. I loved a painting of a tortoise eating a magenta cactus flower and imagined myself as a tortoise, eating a tasty floral treat. I told Dacie about my affinity for turtles. Dacie told me that we could have the picture as a wedding present if we got married.

Dacie showed me my room, which used to belong to Mark's brother. I overheard part of a conversation between Mark and his father out in the hall. His father said that since we weren't married yet, we couldn't spend the night together in their house because it would upset Dacie. "I didn't bring you up to take advantage of a woman," his father said. "If you want to have sex, get married. That's how you were brought up. You can get married tomorrow, if you like. But if you want to get together tonight, rent a hotel room instead of staying here."

"We can't marry immediately. You need blood tests to get married," Mark said. "Pam is like a widow. The man she intended to marry died in Iraq. They didn't want to marry until his tour was done." Tears came to my eyes.

"I'm sorry, but your mother wouldn't approve," his father reiterated and paused before adding, so softly that I had to strain to hear, "There are some extra blankets in a trunk in the garage that you could put in the car whenever you want to go see the Indian ruins." I heard them leave Mark's old bedroom and walk down the hall, presumably to find the trunk in the garage. I was amused. I thought that his father didn't really care what we did; he just wanted to keep correct appearances.

I was tired from the trip. I slept soundly even without Mark.

After breakfast the next day, Mark and I drove out to see the Indian ruins, as he had promised we would. I asked Mark if he had considered moving back to New Mexico. "Your parents are quite old," I said. "Your father will retire soon. Someday they'll need you more than they do now. If we live near your parents and have children ourselves, the children will have grandparents nearby."

"No, I don't want to move here." Mark said. "Do you think that this visit has gone well?"

"No. I think that if you spent more time together, the atmosphere would be more relaxed."

The ruins were collapsed stone buildings near a cliff. The number of building foundations implied that many people had lived there once. Mark showed me a place where water seeped from a crack into a cave in the cliff wall. "They even had running water," Mark said, laughing. He seemed to relax for the first time since he had been in New Mexico. "Los Alamos is an enclosed place, just like this cliff dwelling is," Mark continued. "I like to live in places more metropolitan, after growing up here and living in Sierra Vista." We walked silently on a trail that led beside a low cliff with Indian ruins inside alcoves.

"I spent eight years of my life in Los Alamos," Mark said. "Living in a small town has disadvantages, just like living on a small army base. You wouldn't like living here because you wouldn't like small-town life where everyone minds everyone else's business. There isn't enough to do here. My father mentioned plays and concerts. He would like to see Shakespeare's plays on the stage, and have season tickets for symphony music. He could attend professional performances if my parents lived in a bigger city." The trail went into a wooded area and began winding up toward the top of the cliff.

"Los Alamos is very small, but we could travel to the bigger cities," I said as we ascended the trail.

"Frankly, I never had a good impression of Santa Fe and Albuquerque either. All right for the tourists but too isolated to live in. From Detroit, we could drive in a long evening to Columbus or Chicago or Pittsburg, or go north to lakes, take boat trips, go to more mounds, or do a variety of activities. I never thought Los Alamos was worth talking about."

"Let's find a secluded place and relax," I said. I put my arms around him. "I like the idea of love among the ruins. No one else is here, so we don't need the blanket from the car." But I couldn't persuade Mark to try sex in the woods.

After our hike, we ate a picnic lunch that Dacie had prepared for us; it included sandwiches and chicken and fruit and cookies. Mark said, "The life my parents lead is very limited. In a small town, you find your place, and there are few opportunities to develop new interests or make new friends."

"You don't see the bad side of New Mexico," Mark continued. "This state is as crime ridden as Detroit. You and I are used to military bases, which are safe. The cities here are dangerous. In Albuquerque, parking-lot holdups occur in midday. Fast food places are robbed while full of customers. A woman should be careful when alone. When my mother sells her pictures, as she will tomorrow, my father will accompany her not just to handle her wares, but for her safety. If we consider moving, I will check the crime rate."

I was surprised into silence. "I didn't know that there is a lot of crime here," I said.

"Tourists usually don't see it—until they get mugged." Mark said. "I like my job. My father says that he could find me a job here, but civil service has rules about nepotism, and I might be ineligible to be hired. He has friends in the defense business here, but the base service contractors are insecure places to work. You know that from your own job loss. The government will get rid of one company, then hire another company that will hire many of the same people back, so employees often don't have steady work.

"Furthermore, you would be bored here. We would have to drive to Santa Fe for a Zen Center. Los Alamos is boring. I don't want to live here again." I wondered if Mark had started drinking because he was bored.

I said, "Mark, in the stories about high school, you sounded like a different person than the one I know. You were outgoing and adventurous. Could you be like that again?"

"I was careless and silly not adventurous," he said tersely. I think I'm more outgoing than you are. You don't seem to make friends on your own."

"That's been hard for me since I got out of the army," I said.

"You talk about the army so much," Mark said. "Can you let it go?"

"To really let it go, I have to find something to replace it. In the army, I had friends, recreation, and a job. Now I don't even have a job."

"For some people, the army becomes family and home. Now you will be getting a new family and home, and hopefully friends. I'm sure that you will get another job."

I pictured Michael, skipping on a trail by a creek and then tossing me a ball made of leaves he had just scooped up. He was laughing. I was happy with Michael, but maybe he didn't cause it. I just felt it with him. Now I would have to create happiness myself.

We walked again, and looked at petroglyphs on a group of rocks, and then drove to a more formal park where we followed trails and climbed on bluffs. We spent the entire day outdoors in beautiful weather.

The next day was Sunday, and we all went to Santa Fe, where Dacie was selling her paintings and art items at a fair. She had painted some scenes on fragments of rock, which she said were popular with tourists.

"The tourists like pictures of cliff dwellings and desert landscapes," Dacie said. "They buy them as souvenirs of their vacations," Herman said. "With Dacie's coloring, some people mistake her for an Indian and think that they are getting tribal art." Mark's parents were joking and laughing. Mark and I visited tourist sites in Santa Fe during the day and admired the famous square. I enjoyed the walk in the city, but began to see why Mark was bored. You would only walk around the square admiring the old buildings a few times.

That evening, Mark's parents suggested that I stay in Los Alamos with them for a few more days, so that Dacie could show me more of the area. Dacie said that she wanted to take some pictures of Indian ruins, for new views to use in her paintings, and needed to have someone with her while she took photographs. I said. "I would like to stay to see more because this is my first time in the West. I might be able to climb up someplace with a camera and get some pictures that Dacie couldn't take."

Mark agreed that I should do more sightseeing instead of rushing back to Detroit, and said, "Mother, could you take Pam to Bandelier? It might be Pam's best opportunity to see a national Indian ruin site." He added, to me, "I don't mind if you stay a few days, but I'll be lonesome with only Cecily to talk to. She never says anything interesting, and she repeats herself all the time—meow and meow." He laughed.

"Poor Cecily," I said. "She must worry when we are away. I hope that Sue is giving her some treats with her cat food. I'll ask your mother to show me how to cook some of the German food you like. "Dacie, you will show me some German cooking, won't you?"

She nodded. "I can give you a cookbook, too."

"Ask my parents about Huntsville sometime," Mark suggested. "They have some great stories about the German community in Huntsville."

"I could talk all day about Huntsville," Herman said, and Dacie laughed.

CHAPTER 26

IN LOS ALAMOS

On the way to the airport, Mark asked his parents if they had been to Huntsville lately. Herman said they had been to Alabama two years before and were considering retiring there because Huntsville had a large retirement community. Dacie said that she would like to go back to Huntsville because she still had relatives there, and it was a growing, vibrant area. I hadn't realized that they weren't planning to stay in New Mexico. "Later, please tell me about Huntsville," I said. "I was never stationed there, but Mark said nice things about it."

When Mark got on the plane, I began crying because I thought of Michael leaving for Iraq. I explained to Mark's parents that I had never seen Michael again because the casket had been closed when he was buried at Arlington National Cemetery.

On the way back from the airport, Mark's parents told me that they would pay for our honeymoon as a wedding present. They asked me if we would like to take a cruise for our honeymoon. I thanked them for their generous offer. I didn't think that I would like a cruise because I like to go outdoors on vacations and walk around. Then I realized that they wanted the four of us to take a cruise together. They said that the cruise boat would include swimming pools and a gym, as well as good food.

I said, "So far, we have three honeymoon or vacation, suggestions. Mark wants to go to northern Michigan, and I would like to go to the Rocky Mountains. The cruise might be something Mark would like. I'm not sure what he would think."

"If he knew that his father suggested it, he wouldn't want to do it," Dacie said.

I was surprised. "Upper Michigan is quite varied," I said. I wanted to please Dacie. "If we went there, we could all spend some time in a luxury hotel, and Mark and I could do some camping while you went to some tourist sites. We could take boat tours together on the Great Lakes. We could drive together and stop frequently to see the lakeshore and parks. I would plan the trip and arrange the accommodations. Upper Michigan isn't crowded in the fall, and it will be very colorful."

I added, "Mark is moving into my apartment, and we don't need to have privacy to get to know each other. Having more people around is just a chance for more fun, and for me to show Michigan to more people."

Wanting to join us on our trip was intrusive, yet Mark and I could spend time together without being on a trip. If they moved to Huntsville, Mark and I wouldn't be able to spend much time with them.

We stopped at Petroglyph Park in Albuquerque and walked the little trails near the parking lot. I loved the park and wanted to run through the canyons, but Herman said that I wouldn't be safe by myself.

Back in Los Alamos, I ran on the city sidewalks until I was tired.

At dinner, Dacie said, "I hope that Mark doesn't disappoint you." His parents began talking about Mark's faults. Mark didn't apply himself, he couldn't finish graduate school, he was undependable, his health might not be good, and he didn't have a career. They also wondered if he had been drinking a lot recently. Mark's parents had no confidence in him. Maybe they wanted to join us on a trip in order to keep an eye on him. No wonder he lacked confidence in himself.

After dinner, we sat outside again. Herman said, "Mark won't tell us about Iraq and the war. Do you know why?"

I said, "Sometimes military people find that talking to civilians about the war is difficult. Civilians often make insensitive statements about the war. When I go home, my relatives may tell me that women shouldn't carry weapons and can't shoot anyway. One of my nephews asked Mark if he had killed people—something that is obviously none of his business."

"Mark changed during the war," his father said. "My guess is that he had a hard time and doesn't know what to say about it."

"Mark doesn't like to talk about some of his experiences," I said. "A man standing near him was killed. Seeing a man die can be one of the worst things that happen to you in the army, especially if the person who was killed was your friend. Mark's job was primarily a desk job, so he was usually safe. Soldiers in combat zones usually don't get enough sleep and are nervous and edgy until they get used to the sounds of war."

I paused, then added, "Pete and Mark had a conflict about maps that Mark's section gave out. I didn't quite understand the issue, but Pete was very angry with Mark."

"Pete was the person who convinced Mark to go into the army," Herman said. "The army wasn't a good choice for Mark. Mark isn't like Pete at all."

I continued, "I think that the war affected Mark by making him feel unsafe at times when no threat exists. Sometimes I feel that way too." I hesitated. "I think that sometimes Mark is sorry that he went into the army, but that the army has been such a major part of his life that he can't picture what his life would be like if he hadn't been in the army."

Should I tell them my story? I had never told a civilian. I breathed deeply, and plunged in. "I was in a convoy that was fired on, and I took a soldier's rifle and fired back at the direction of enemy fire, even though I wasn't sure of the exact location of the people firing. I think about taking the rifle and even dream about it. I don't tell many people about it, though. Not many people could identify with taking someone else's rifle and firing it."

"I hope that your own children never fight in a war," Dacie said. "We worried so much."

"Mark and I wish that nobody would ever fight in a war again," I replied.

The next day, Dacie and I drove to Bandelier National Monument so that she could take photographs of the ruined buildings to use in her paintings. As Dacie set up her camera, I watched a lizard run across a rock. I was fascinated, but she said they were common. I saw more lizards and tried to pick them up, but they were too fast. I found a tortoise the size of the palm of my hand and picked it up to show to Dacie. I told her about the turtles I had found in Michigan. Being with Dacie was as much fun as going places with Mark.

Dacie did some sketches, as well as taking pictures. She said, "Sometimes I make a sketch and duplicate it, and then set up an easel and color it in with watercolors. People like to buy pictures to remind them of their trip."

I tried sketching, too. Dacie said that my sketches of the ruins were very good. She told me that she had a degree in art education. She had quit the University of Alabama to get married but finished school later. "I never had a chance to teach, though," she said.

Mark was like his mother not his father. "I wonder if Mark would have liked to teach," I said. "Maybe he should have gotten a teaching degree." Then I remembered that Mark's brother was a college professor, and I was sorry that I had said anything about Mark teaching. But I could picture Mark teaching high school math and physics. He would probably like it, and the students would like him, too.

"Mark could have been a doctor," Dacie said. "I think that he would have been a good doctor. He likes to help people."

"He understands people better than I do," I said. "I'm an engineer. I don't think the same way as most people, so I don't understand non-technical people sometimes."

"You mean that your reasoning process is different?" she asked.

"I think in pictures," I said. "Like television without the sound on."

"So do I," she said. "So does Herman. We both speak two languages, but sometimes we take out a piece of paper and draw for each other. You can express some ideas better by drawing, but you can't express what you feel about things."

"That's true," I said. "I don't talk about my feelings very much. We don't do that in the army. We get oriented toward evaluating what we do and ignoring how we feel when we do it. We were supposed to tough it out if we felt badly."

"I always wished that I had a girl, as well as two boys," Dacie said. "Helping a girl sew clothes and teaching her to draw would have been fun."

"Soon you will have a daughter-in-law," I replied. "My parents had three girls. Now they also have four grandchildren and take care of three of them while my sister works. So they have a daughter to spare."

"You have two older sisters?" Dacie asked.

"Younger sisters," I said. She must think that I am younger than my real age. "Mark and I are about the same age, and my sisters married young."

"Do you want children?" Dacie asked. "I hope you have children. Mark would be a good father, I think. He would be helpful with the children."

"Mark has a lot of patience with children," I said. "He played ball with my nephews and enjoyed it. He would probably be a better father than I would be a mother." I remembered Pete saying that people loved their children more than they loved their spouses. "I would like to have children."

Dacie's next set of stories, which she told as we enjoyed the picnic lunch she had packed, were about being ill, misunderstood, and unlucky. She sounded like Mark. We got back to Los Alamos as the afternoon was turning hot and unpleasant. Dacie gave me some photography books of the desert southwest to look at as she did some housework. I volunteered to help her, but she wanted me to look at the books.

When Herman got home from work, we sat on the porch and chatted. They each drank a beer, and I joined them. Mark and I would never be drinking together, at home. Herman asked what being in Iraq was really like.

I said, "It was like being numb, with occasional flashes of terror. Like boredom exploding into excitement. I liked Iraq more than Mark did."

"Mark seems happier than he used to be," Herman said. "I guess you get along."

"I think he's glad to be out of the army," I said. "Mark seems to do well in Detroit—I mean, Warren, the suburb where we live and work. He likes his job, and he has made friends with his neighbors and at Alcoholics Anonymous. He plays chess with a man he met at AA, for example. He likes going to museums and hiking in the northern suburbs."

"Enough about Mark," Dacie said. "Tell us about your life."

I told them about growing up in the suburbs, getting my mechanical engineering degree at the University of Michigan, and joining the army. Then I told them about the parks that Mark and I went to, and the new friends we were making.

Herman said, "I am glad that you and Mark have some common interests besides having been in the army. The army will fade in importance as you get older."

Dacie asked, "What do your parents do?"

I thought that Herman and Dacie might look down on my family. "My father owns an automobile body shop, in one of the western suburbs of Detroit," I said. "My mother is a homemaker." I wished that my mother had some hobbies like Dacie's painting. "It's a good business. They also fix some used cars and sell them."

"Did you work with Pete?" Herman asked.

"Yes, we worked on the same project but in different buildings. I was at a barbecue at his home once, with Mark," I said.

"I am curious about what you did in college," Dacie said. "Where did you live when you were in college?"

"I lived in dormitories," I said.

"That's good," Herman said. "You get to meet other students from all kinds of backgrounds when you live in dormitories. Roger lived in dormitories, too. I used to envy the fraternity members when I was in school, thinking I would have more friends if I lived in one. I encouraged the boys to belong to fraternities and make life-long friends. I don't think that Mark made any long-term friends from the one he joined. So maybe I was wrong."

I said, "What I am most curious about, from meeting you, is what Mark liked the most when he was young. What made him happy?"

"He liked school, sports, and going camping," Herman said.

Dacie added, "Don't forget music. Mark was not only a musician, but he knew a lot of classical music. He bought many orchestral recordings, and he could usually tell what a piece was from hearing it for only a minute."

"I didn't know that," I said. "I guess we haven't listened to much music."

"Are you getting tired?" Dacie asked. "You seem nervous."

"Not really," I said. "I'm just excited about being in a new place. I never traveled in the western part of the country before, except for a few army bases in California."

Dacie brought a plate of cookies from the kitchen. "Eat a little, you'll get more energy."

"I am so stuffed with food from dinner," I said. "How did Mark stay so slim eating all this good food?"

Herman replied, "Sports. He loved running and playing sports."

"We both run." I was excited about the things they had said about Alabama. Later that evening, I asked to use the Internet to see what kind of jobs existed in Huntsville. Maybe someday Mark would like to move back to Huntsville.

Dacie and I spent the next day visiting art galleries and a museum in Santa Fe. I liked being with Mark's parents better than I liked being with most of my relatives—almost as well as I liked being with my dad or Cousin Jimmy. I told them that I was eager to get married and begin calling them mom and dad.

CHAPTER 27

GOING NORTH

Mark met my flight, and I was glad to see him. I remembered to greet him affectionately, to please him. "I really like you," I said.

"I hope you like me, since you're marrying me," he replied. "How about saying, 'I love you, Mark?'"

I put my arms around Mark and kissed him. "You don't tell me that you love me, either," I said.

Mark protested, "I tell you, and you don't hear me when I say it."

"Saying 'I love you' is so easy for many people, but it seems to be hard for us," I replied.

"Maybe we don't think we deserve anything," Mark said. "But being loved isn't something anyone has to deserve."

"I missed you," I said. "There is no one else as important to me as you are." I told Mark about planning our honeymoon with his parents, and he was amused and halfway pleased. I added, "The only problem I have with your parents is that their opinion of you is from years ago and outdated."

"Their opinion is old," Mark said. "But it might still be right. I'm not as self-satisfied as you are. I need to improve myself, and you're fine as you are. You like being who you are."

When we got to my apartment, I took out my pictures of Michael and me, and showed them to Mark. "You look so happy in the pictures," Mark said. "I'd like to see you that happy again. Let me know what you need to be happy."

"Being outside, running, and going to parks. The things we do together," I said. "I enjoy them more when I am with you. Letting go of the past is hard. Believing that I will have a full life in the future is hard." I began putting the pictures into a box. "And what really makes you happy?" I asked. "After all this time, I don't know."

"I like being with people," Mark said. "I'm getting involved with new people and new activities now, which makes me happier than I used to be. I have a pet for company so that I'm not as lonely, I am making new friends, and now I am getting married. I will live with a person I love—a person who enjoys going new places and learning new things. My life gets better all the time.

"When I spend too much time by myself, I focus on the past too much and feel bad. My past experiences make me feel insecure. I think that we both have to keep our army experiences from dominating our lives and become oriented to the present and the future. I think that we both have a low level of post-traumatic stress disorder, and it diminishes our lives by directing our attention to past occurrences."

"This is one step in moving past the time I was in the army," I said, sorting the pictures of Michael from the ones of Michael and me together. "You and I could live any place we want. We can get different kinds of jobs. We can have children. We don't have to be involved with the army. We don't have to stay in Detroit. We can start over, just like we did when we left the army."

Mark said, "The army is part of our world, though, and we can't ignore it. I can give you a Buddhist prophesy of one of our future lives. We are soldiers. We are killed on the battlefield. Our side loses. It's about the repetitive nature of life."

"That's about futility," I said. "It's depressing."

"No, it's not about futility. It's about the nature of the world. Michael's life isn't depressing," Mark said. "He died doing what he loved to do and for a cause he believed in. A good life isn't necessarily a long life—it's a life in which you are able to be the person you want to be. Michael died manifesting who he was. A warrior's death is a good way to die."

"Christianity is more comforting than Buddhism," I continued. "You see the other person in heaven. Pete talked with me about expecting to meet his wife again in heaven, if he was killed. But heaven is difficult to believe in."

Mark said, "I know a Tibetan Buddhist ceremony for the dead. Take out a picture of Michael, and we can burn it in a candle flame in front of the bookcase. Then we can meditate in a particular way called Tonglen, sending out good wishes with our outgoing breath, and absorbing pain and confusion with our incoming breath. We can think of Michael, but we should focus on living soldiers or soldiers who died in the last forty days. Think of breathing in hot and breathing out cool. Take in unhappiness, uncertainty, fear, and pain, and send out calm and peace with your breath."

I said. "I'd like to do that for your friends and mine, and all the people in the army. We will never forget the army because it was our home when we were young." I chose one picture of Michael to burn and sealed the others in the box. "I want pictures of you. Let's take many pictures at our wedding and on our honeymoon trip."

We sat in front of the bookcase and burned the picture of Michael, and mediated for our war dead, and the soldiers in the army.

We were married in front of our families and LuAnn, Bob, Pete, Debbie, Sue, some of Mark's friends from AA, and a few of his neighbors. Jimmy and Amber came from Chicago. I wore Carolyn's wedding dress. I hadn't known that we are the same size because I always thought of my younger sisters as smaller than me. I told her that it was the nicest present that I could imagine and that I would give it back for the daughter she would have one day.

We had a fancy wedding dinner, with trays of exotic appetizers and little dessert cakes frosted in all the colors of the rainbow.

I met Roger, Mark's brother, who was a heavier version of Mark in glasses. Dacie, Herman, Mark, and I left for our honeymoon vacation on the west coast of Lake Huron. I had convinced Dacie and Herman that we really wanted them to come with us and see Michigan. We had rented a big vehicle to carry our luggage, picnic supplies, and some old camping equipment that Herman and Dacie brought. We would drive north, up the east coast of Michigan to the Upper Peninsula, and come back driving south on the Lake Michigan side of the state.

We stayed in a lakefront motel on Lake Huron the first night. Before dark, as the reflection of the sunset played in the sky, Mark and I went down to the rocky shore and admired the colors reflected in the icy water. I was delighted at being on the lake again. "I feel so happy," I said. "How do I share that with you?"

"I wish you could bottle it, and I'd have a drink," Mark replied and laughed. "It's probably addictive, though, and I wouldn't be able to stop drinking it."

"Happiness is addictive," I said. "Is sharing it possible?" I sat down on a rock and reached for Mark. He sat in the sand at my feet.

"Some things we think are impossible turn out to be possible," Mark said. "I remember the first time I stood up after my accident. I hadn't thought about standing up for so long that I couldn't understand what the nurse was telling me to do. She got a friend, and they shoved me onto my feet."

I said, "You just needed a push. Same with happiness—you were happy once, and you can be happy again. Reach out and shift your way of thinking, and you can remember how to be happy. Maybe I can give you a push." Mark and I took our shoes off and waded in the frigid water.

"I liked the wedding sermon," Mark said. "Being married as Christians not Buddhists was the right thing to do. Anyway, I think you're really a Christian at heart not a Buddhist. I picture you singing 'In-a-my-heart, Lord, I want to be a Christian, in-a my heart' and being delighted and joyful."

"I connect with meditating sometimes," I said. "Did you do the meditation you showed me for your friends killed in Iraq? It seems to be a way to be loyal to our dead and honor their memory."

"Yes, I did that meditation for Wilson," he said. "I did the meditation for forty days, after getting a group picture that he was included in and cutting his picture out to burn. I needed more ceremony. Losing a friend is incomplete without a ceremony like seeing him buried and throwing a clod of earth on the casket.

"Pam, I look for spiritual answers. I'm not saying that I know the answers. In Korea, my life was falling apart so badly I needed answers or at least to learn the right questions. I didn't want textbook answers, like in physics, but something I could feel." Mark continued, "Suppose, as a Christian, you reach out to God, and he would take your hand—or she. You can talk to God. She will understand.

"Look at the lakeshore, deep and wide, like the River Jordan you sang about in Sunday school. 'River Jordan is deep and wide, hallelujah. Starlit heaven on the other side, Hallelujah.'" Mark sang.

"Michael, row the boat ashore," I sang in response. "Hallelujah." Michael must be on that other shore, I thought, if it exists. I started to cry. I pictured Michael, tumbling down a grassy hill, standing on his head, cavorting in the grass, and laughing. Mark held me and seemed to have a tear forming in his eye. "You could cry if you like," I said. "We could cry together for all the people we knew who are gone."

"If I started crying, I would never stop," Mark said.

"Crying always stops," I replied. "Crying lasts a while, and then it stops. Just give in, and let it out."

"I feel like a little boy," Mark said. A tear ran down his cheek.

"That's fine," I said. "Let yourself be sad, and then you can let yourself be happy."

"Let's play like children do," Mark said. He splashed the icy water over his head, laughed, and kicked his feet into the moist beach sand. I joined him and took a handful of water, splashing him with it. We walked in the cold sand in our bare feet, and I started skipping. I was excited and held Mark's hand in mine, and we ran on the beach until we were tired.

I said, "I'd like to do the meditation again. I would like to do it with you for forty days or longer, and breathe out peace and calm to all the soldiers who were killed or hurt in the war. Could we meditate together? In a motel or a tent or by a campfire or home or wherever we are? Will it help me? I want to let go of Michael and Iraq and the rifle I took. I want to replace those thoughts with the place I am now, and the people in my life now. Let's go to our motel room and do the meditation, and let's breathe in sorrow and fear and guilt and terror, and breathe out joy and happiness for all of the soldiers in the United States Army."

"And the United States Navy, Air Force, and Coast Guard," Mark added. "And all our allies. And everybody. Peace and contentment for everyone in the world."